The Geste of Duke Jocelyn

Jeffery Farnol

My GILLIAN, thou child that budding woman art
For whom to-day and yesterday lie far apart
Already thou, my dear, dost longer dresses wear
And bobbest in most strange, new-fangled ways thy hair;
Thou lookest on the world with eyes grown serious
And rul'st thy father with a sway imperious
Particularly as regards his socks and ties
Insistent that each with the other harmonise.
Instead of simple fairy-tales that pleased of yore
Romantic verse thou read'st and novels by the score
And very oft I've known thee sigh and call them "stuff"
Vowing of love romantic they've not half enough.
Wherefore, like fond and doting parent, I
Will strive this want romantic to supply.
I'll write for thee a book of sighing lover
Crammed with ROMANCE from cover unto cover;
A book the like of which 't were hard to find
Filled with ROMANCE of every sort and kind.
I'll write it as the Gestours wrote of old,
In prose, blank-verse, and rhyme it shall be told.
And GILLIAN--
Some day perhaps, my dear, when you are grown
A portly dame with children of your own
You'll gather all your troop about your knee
And read to them this Geste I made for thee.

PRELUDE

Long, long ago when castles grim did frown,
When massy wall and gate did 'fend each town;
When mighty lords in armour bright were seen,
And stealthy outlaws lurked amid the green
And oft were hanged for poaching of the deer,
Or, gasping, died upon a hunting spear;
When barons bold did on their rights insist
And hanged or burned all rogues who dared resist;
When humble folk on life had no freehold
And were in open market bought and sold;
When grisly witches (lean and bony hags)
Cast spells most dire yet, meantime, starved in rags;
When kings did lightly a-crusading fare
And left their kingdoms to the devil's care —
At such a time there lived a noble knight
Who sweet could sing and doughtily could fight,
Whose lance thrust strong, whose long sword bit full deep
With darting point or mighty two-edged sweep.
A duke was he, rich, powerful — and yet
Fate had on him a heavy burden set,
For, while a youth, as he did hunt the boar,
The savage beast his goodly steed did gore,
And as the young duke thus defenceless lay,
With cruel tusk had reft his looks away,
Had marred his comely features and so mauled him
That, 'hind his back, "The ugly Duke" folk called him —

My daughter GILLIAN interposeth:

GILL: An ugly hero?

MYSELF: That is so.

GILL: An ugly hero, father? O, absurd! Whoever of an "ugly" hero heard?

MYSELF: I'll own, indeed, I've come across but few —

GILL: But a duke—and ugly! Father, this from you?

MYSELF: My duke is ugly, very, for good reason, As shall appear in due and proper season!

GILL: I'm sure no one will want to read him then, For "heroes" all should be most handsome men. So make him handsome, please, or he won't do.

MYSELF: By heaven, girl—no, plain heroes are too few!

GILL: Then ev'ry one will leave him on the shelf!

MYSELF: Why, then, I'll read the poor fellow myself.

GILL: I won't!

MYSELF: Then don't! Though, I might say, since you're set on it, child, My duke was not so ugly when he smiled—

GILL: Then make him smile as often as you can.

MYSELF: I might do that, 't is none so bad a plan.

GILL: And the lady—she must be a lady fair.

MYSELF: My dear, she's beautiful beyond compare.

GILL: Why, then—

MYSELF: My pen!
    So here and now I do begin
    The tale of young Duke Jocelyn,
    For critics, schools,
    And cramping rules,
    Heedless and caring not a pin.

    The title here behold
    On this fair page enrolled,
    In letters big and bold,
    As seemeth fit—
    To wit: —

The Geste of Duke Jocelyn

FYTTE I

Upon a day, but when it matters not,
Nor where, but mark! the sun was plaguy hot
Falling athwart a long and dusty road
In which same dust two dusty fellows strode.
One was a tall, broad-shouldered, goodly wight
In garb of motley like a jester dight,
Fool's cap on head with ass's ears a-swing,
While, with each stride, his bells did gaily ring;
But, 'neath his cock's-comb showed a face so marred
With cheek, with brow and lip so strangely scarred
As might scare tender maid or timid child
Unless, by chance, they saw him when he smiled,
For then his eyes, so deeply blue and bright,
Did hold in them such joyous, kindly light,
That sorrow was from heavy hearts beguiled—
This jester seemed less ugly when he smiled.

Here, O my Gill, right deftly, in a trice
I've made him smile and made him do it—twice.
That 't was the Duke of course you've guessed at once
Since you, I know, we nothing of a dunce.
But, what should bring a duke in cap and bells?
Read on and mark, while he the reason tells.

Now, 'spite of dust and heat, his lute he strummed,
And snatches of a merry song he hummed,
The while askance full merrily he eyed
The dusty knave who plodded at his side.
A bony fellow, this, and long of limb,

His habit poor, his aspect swart and grim;
His belt to bear a long broad-sword did serve,
His eye was bold, his nose did fiercely curve
Down which he snorted oft and (what is worse)
Beneath his breath gave vent to many a curse.
Whereat the Duke, sly laughing, plucked lutestring
And thus, in voice melodious did sing:

1

The Geste of Duke Jocelyn

"Sir Pertinax, why curse ye so?
Since thus in humble guise we go
We merry chances oft may know,
Sir Pertinax of Shene. "

"And chances woeful, lord, also! "
Quoth Pertinax of Shene.

"To every fool that passeth by
These foolish bells shall testify
That very fool, forsooth, am I,
Good Pertinax of Shene! "

"And, lord, methinks they'll tell no lie! "
Growled Pertinax of Shene.

Then spake the Knight in something of a pet,
"Par Dex, lord Duke—plague take it, how I sweat,
By Cock, messire, ye know I have small lust
Like hind or serf to tramp it i' the dust!
Per De, my lord, a parch-ed pea am I—
I'm all athirst! Athirst? I am so dry
My very bones do rattle to and fro
And jig about within me as I go!
Why tramp we thus, bereft of state and rank?
Why go ye, lord, like foolish mountebank?
And whither doth our madcap journey trend?
And wherefore? Why? And, prithee, to what end? "
Then quoth the Duke, "See yonder in the green
Doth run a cooling water-brook I ween,
Come, Pertinax, beneath yon shady trees,
And there whiles we do rest outstretched at ease
Thy 'wherefores' and thy 'whys' shall answered be,
And of our doings I will counsel thee. "

So turned they from the hot and dusty road
Where, 'mid green shade, a rill soft-bubbling flowed,
A brook that leapt and laughed in roguish wise,
Whereat Sir Pertinax with scowling eyes
Did frown upon the rippling water clear,
And sware sad oaths because it was not beer;
Sighful he knelt beside this murmurous rill,
Bent steel-clad head and bravely drank his fill.

2

Then sitting down, quoth he: "By Og and Gog,
I'll drink no more—nor horse am I nor dog
To gulp down water—pest, I hate the stuff! "

"Ah! " laughed the Duke, "'tis plain hast had enough,
And since well filled with water thou dost lie
To answer thee thy questions fain am I.
First then—thou art in lowly guise bedight,
For that thou art my trusty, most-loved knight,
Who at my side in many a bloody fray,
With thy good sword hath smit grim Death away—"
"Lord, " quoth the Knight, "what's done is past return,
'Tis of our future doings I would learn. "

"Aye, " said the Duke, "list, Pertinax, and know
'Tis on a pilgrimage of love we go:
Mayhap hast heard the beauty and the fame
Of fair Yolande, that young and peerless dame

"For whom so many noble lovers sigh
And with each other in the lists do vie?
Though much I've dreamed of sweet Yolanda's charms
My days have passed in wars and feats of arms,
For, Pertinax, this blemished face I bear,
Should fright, methinks, a lady young and fair.
And so it is that I have deemed it wiser
To hide it when I might 'neath casque and visor—"

Hereat Sir Pertinax smote hand to knee
And, frowning, shook his head. "Messire, " said he,
"Thou art a man, and young, of noble race,
And, being duke, what matter for thy face?
Rank, wealth, estate—these be the things I trow
Can make the fairest woman tender grow.
Ride unto her in thy rich armour dight,
With archer, man-at-arms, and many a knight
To swell thy train with pomp and majesty,
That she, and all, thy might and rank may see;
So shall all folk thy worthiness acclaim,
And her maid's heart, methinks, shall do the same.
Thy blemished face shall matter not one jot;

To mount thy throne she'll think a happy lot.
So woo her thus—"

"So will I woo her not! "
Quoth Jocelyn, "For than I'd win her so,
Alone and loveless all my days I'd go.
Ha, Pertinax, 'spite all thy noble parts,
'Tis sooth ye little know of women's hearts! "

"Women? " quoth Pertinax, and scratched his jaw,
"'Tis true of dogs and horses I know more,
And dogs do bite, and steeds betimes will balk,
And fairest women, so they say, will talk. "

"And so dost thou, my Pertinax, and yet,
'Spite all thy talk, my mind on this is set—
Thus, in all lowliness I'll e'en go to her
And 'neath this foolish motley I will woo her.
And if, despite this face, this humble guise,
I once may read love's message in her eyes,
Then Pertinax—by all the Saints, 'twill be
The hope of all poor lovers after me,
These foolish bells a deathless tale shall ring,
And of Love's triumph evermore shall sing.

"So, Pertinax, ne'er curse ye so
For that in lowly guise we go,
We many a merry chance may know,
Sir Pertinax of Shene. "
"And chances evil, lord, also! "
Quoth Pertinax of Shene.

Now on a sudden, from the thorny brake,
E'en as Sir Pertinax thus doleful spake,
Leapt lusty loons and ragged rascals four,
Rusty their mail, yet bright the swords they bore.

Up sprang Sir Pertinax with gleeful shout,
Plucked forth his blade and fiercely laid about.
"Ha, rogues! Ha, knaves! Most scurvy dogs! " he cried.
While point and edge right lustily he plied

And smote to earth the foremost of the crew,
Then, laughing, pell-mell leapt on other two.
The fourth rogue's thrust, Duke Joc'lyn blithely parried
Right featly with the quarter-staff he carried.
Then 'neath the fellow's guard did nimbly slip
And caught him in a cunning wrestler's grip.
Now did they reel and stagger to and fro,
And on the ling each other strove to throw;

Arm locked with arm they heaved, they strove and panted,
With mighty shoulders bowed and feet firm-planted.
So on the sward, with golden sunlight dappled,
In silence grim they tussled, fiercely grappled.
Thus then Duke Jocelyn wrestled joyously,
For this tall rogue a lusty man was he,
But, 'spite his tricks and all his cunning play,
He in the Duke had met his match this day,
As, with a sudden heave and mighty swing,
Duke Jocelyn hurled him backwards on the ling,
And there he breathless lay and sore amazed,
While on the Duke with wonderment he gazed:
"A Fool? " he cried. "Nay, certes fool, per De,
Ne'er saw I fool, a fool the like o' thee! "

But now, e'en as the Duke did breathless stand,
Up strode Sir Pertinax, long sword in hand:
"Messire, " he growled, "my rogues have run away,
So, since you've felled this fellow, him I'll slay. "

"Not so, " the Duke, short-breathing, made reply,
"Methinks this rogue is too much man to die. "

"How? " cried the Knight; "not slay a knave—a thief?
Such clemency is strange and past belief!
Mean ye to let the dog all scathless go? "

"Nay, " said the Duke, square chin on fist, "not so,
For since the rogue is plainly in the wrong
The rogue shall win his freedom with a song,
And since forsooth a rogue ingrain is he,
So shall he sing a song of roguery.
Rise, roguish rogue, get thee thy wind and sing,
Pipe me thy best lest on a tree ye swing! "

Up to his feet the lusty outlaw sprang,
And thus, in clear melodious voice, he sang:

"I'll sing a song not over long,
A song of roguery.
For I'm a rogue, and thou'rt a rogue,
And so, in faith, is he.
And we are rogues, and ye are rogues,
All rogues in verity.

"As die we must and turn to dust,
Since each is Adam's son,
A rogue was he, so rogues are we,
And rascals every one.

"The Abbot sleek with visage meek,
With candle, book and bell,
Our souls may curse, we're none the worse,
Since he's a rogue as well.

"My lord aloft doth hang full oft
Poor rogues the like o' me,
But all men know where e'er he go
A greater rogue is he.

"The king abroad with knight and lord
Doth ride in majesty,
But strip him bare and then and there
A shivering rogue ye'll see,

"Sirs, if ye will my life to spill,
Then hang me on a tree,
Since rogue am I, a rogue I'll die,
A roguish death for me.

"But i' the wind the leaves shall find
Small voices for my dole,

"And when I'm dead sigh o'er my head
Prayers for my poor rogue soul;
For I'm a rogue, and thou 'rt a rogue,
And so in faith is he,
As we are rogues, so ye are rogues,

All rogues in verity. "

The singing done, the Duke sat lost in thought,
What time Sir Pertinax did stamp and snort:
"Ha, by the Mass! Now, by the Holy Rood!
Ne'er heard I roguish rant so bold and lewd!
He should be whipped, hanged, quartered, flayed alive—"

"Then, " quoth the Duke, "pay him gold pieces five, "
"How—pay a rogue? " the Knight did fierce retort.
"A ribald's rant—give good, gold pieces for't?
A plague! A pest! The knave should surely die—"
But here he met Duke Joc'lyn's fierce blue eye,
And silent fell and in his poke did dive,
And slowly counted thence gold pieces five,
Though still he muttered fiercely 'neath his breath,
Such baleful words as: "'S blood! " and "'S bones! " and "'S death! "

Then laughed the Duke and from the greenwood strode;
But scarce was he upon the dusty road,
Than came the rogue who, louting to his knee:
"O Fool! Sir Fool! Most noble Fool! " said he.
"Either no fool, or fool forsooth thou art,
That dareth thus to take an outlaw's part.
Yet, since this day my rogue's life ye did spare,
So now by oak, by ash, by thorn I swear—

"And mark, Sir Fool, and to my saying heed—
Shouldst e'er lack friends to aid thee in thy need
Come by this stream where stands a mighty oak,
Its massy bole deep-cleft by lightning stroke,
Hid in this cleft a hunting-horn ye'll see,
Take then this horn and sound thereon notes three.
So shall ye find the greenwood shall repay
The roguish life ye spared a rogue this day. "

So spake he; then, uprising from his knees,
Strode blithe away and vanished 'mid the trees.
Whereat Sir Pertinax shook doleful head:
"There go our good gold pieces, lord! " he said.
"Would that yon rogue swung high upon a tree,
And in my poke our gold again might be.
Full much I marvel, lord, and fain would know

Wherefore and why unhanged didst let him go? "

Then answered the Duke singing on this wise:

"Good Pertinax, if on a tree
Yon rogue were swinging high
A deader rogue no man could see—
'He's but a rogue! ' says you to me,
'But a living rogue! ' says I.

"And since he now alive doth go
More honest he may die,
Yon rogue an honest man may grow,
If we but give him time, I trow,
Says I to you, says I. "

At this, Sir Pertinax growled in his beard—

My daughter GILLIAN interrupteth:

GILL: A beard? O father—beard will never do!
No proper knight a beard ever grew. '
No knight could really romantic be
Who wore a beard! So, father, to please me,
No beard; they are, I think, such scrubby things—

MYSELF: Yet they are worn, sometimes, by poets and kings.

GILL: But your knight—

MYSELF: Oh, all right,
My Gill, from your disparagement to save him,
I, like a barber, will proceed to shave him.

Sir Pertinax, then, stroked his smooth-shaved chin,
And thus to curse he softly did begin,
"Par Dex, my lord—"

My daughter GILLIAN interposeth:

GILL: Your knight, dear father, seems to love to curse.

MYSELF: He does. A difficult matter, child, in verse—

GILL: Of verse I feel a little tired—

MYSELF: Why, if you think a change desired,
A change we'll have, for, truth to tell,
This rhyming bothers me as well.
So here awhile we'll sink to prose.
Now, are you ready? Then here goes!

"Par Dex, my lord! " growled Sir Pertinax. "A malison on't, says I, saving thy lordly grace, yet a rogue is a rogue and, being rogue, should die right roguishly as is the custom and the law. For if, messire, if—per De and by Our Sweet Lady of Shene Chapel within the Wood, if, I say, in thy new and sudden-put-on attitude o' folly, thou wilt save alive all rogues soever, then by Saint Cuthbert his curse, by sweet Saint Benedict his blessed bones, by—"

"Hold now, Pertinax, " said the Duke, slipping his lute into leathern bag and slinging it behind wide shoulders, "list ye, Sir Knight of Shene, and mark this, to wit: If a rogue in roguery die then rogue is he forsooth; but, mark this again, if a rogue be spared his life he may perchance and peradventure forswear, that is, eschew or, vulgarly speaking, turn from his roguish ways, and die as honest as I, aye, or even—thou! "

Here Sir Pertinax snorted as they strode on together, yet in a little they turned aside from the hot and dusty road and journeyed on beneath the trees that grew thereby.

"By all the fiends, my lord, and speaking vulgarly in turn, this belly o' mine lacketh, these my bowels do yearn consumedly unto messes savoury and cates succulent—"

The Geste of Duke Jocelyn

Whereat the Duke, smiling merry-eyed, chanted roguishly:

"A haunch o' venison juicy from the spit now? "
"Aha! " groaned the Knight, "Lord, let us haste—"
"A larded capon to thee might seem fit now? "
"Saints! " sighed the Knight, "but for one little taste. "
"Or, Pertinax, a pasty plump and deep—"
"Ha—pasty, by the Mass! " the Knight did cry.
"Or pickled tongue of neat, Sir Knight, or sheep—"
"Oh, for a horse! For wings wherewith to fly—"
"Or breast of swan—"

"Stay! nay, my lord, ha' mercy! " groaned Sir Pertinax, wiping moist
brow. "Picture no more toothsome dainties to my soul lest for desire
I swoon and languish by the way. I pray thee, let us haste, sire, so
may we reach fair Canalise ere sunset—yet stay! Hearken, messire,
hear ye aught? Sure, afar the tocsin soundeth? "

Now hearkening thus, they both became aware
Of distant bells that throbbed upon the air,
A faint, insistent sound that rose and fell,
A clamour vague that ominous did swell.
As thus they stood, well hidden from the road,
Footsteps they heard of feet that briskly strode.
And, through the leaves, a small man they espied,
Who came apace, a great sword by his side.
Large bascinet upon his head he bore,
'Neath which his face a scowl portentous wore;
While after toiled a stout but reverend friar
Who, scant of breath, profusely did perspire
And, thus perspiring, panted sad complaints
Thus—on the heat, his comrade and the Saints.

"O Bax, O Bax! Saint Cuthbert aid me now!
O Bax, see how to sweat thou'st made me now!
Thy speed abate! O sweet Saint Dominic!
Why pliest thou thy puny shanks so quick;
O day! O Bax! O hot, sulphurous day,
My flesh betwixt ye melteth fast away.
Come, sit ye, Bax, in shade of yon sweet tree,
And, sitting soft, I'll sagely counsel thee. "

"Not so, in faith, " the small man, scowling, said,

"What use for counsel since the cause be fled?
And since she's fled—Saints succour us! " he cried;
As 'mid the leaves all suddenly he spied
Sir Pertinax in his unlovely trim,
His rusty mail, his aspect swart and grim—
"Ha! " gasped the little man, "we are beset! "
And starting back, off fell his bascinet.
Whereat he fiercely did but scowl the more,

And strove amain his ponderous sword to draw.
"Hence, dog! " he cried, "lest, with my swashing blow,
I make thee food for carrion kite and crow. "
But in swift hands Sir Pertinax fast caught him
And, bearing him on high, to Joc'lyn brought him,
Who, while the captive small strove vain aloft
Reproved him thus in accents sweet and soft:

"Right puissant and potential sir, we do beseech thee check thy
ferocity, quell now thy so great anger and swear not to give our flesh
for fowls to tear, so shalt thou come down to earth and stand again
upon thine own two legs. And thou, most reverend friar, invoke now
thy bloody-minded comrade that he swear to harm us not! "

The stout friar seated himself hard by beneath a tree, mopped moist
brow, fetched his wind and smiled.

"Sir Fool, " said he, "I am thy security that thou and thy brawny
gossip need quake and tremble nothing by reason of this Bax, our
valiant reeve—he shall harm ye no whit. " Here, meeting Jocelyn's
eye, Sir Pertinax set down the small Reeve, who having taken up and
put on his great bascinet, scowled, whereupon Duke Jocelyn
questioned him full meek:

"Good master Reeve, of your courtesy pray you tell us why yon bells
do ring so wild alarm. "

The small Reeve viewed him with disdainful eye;
Sniffed haughty nose and proudly made reply:
'Our bells we ring and clamour make, because

We've lost our lady fair of Tissingors.
Our Duchess Benedicta hath this day
From all her worthy guardians stole away.
Thus we for her do inquisition make,
Nor, 'till she's found, may hope our rest to take,
And thus we cause such outcry as we may,
Since we lose not our Duchess ev'ry day.
So then we'd have ye speak us—aye or no,
Saw ye our errant lady this way go?
And, that ye may her know for whom we seek,
Her just description fully I will speak:
Her hair night-black, her eyes the self-same hue,
Her habit brown, unless 't were red or blue,
And if not blue why then mayhap 'tis green,
Since she by turns of all such hues is seen—"

"Stay, sir, " quoth Jocelyn, "'tis plain to see
No maid but a chameleon is she,
For here we have her brown and green and blue,
And if not brown then rosy is her hue,
And, if not red, why then 'tis very plain
That brown she is or blue or green again.
Now fain, sir, would I ask and question whether
She e'er is seen these colours all together?

"O fain would I a lady spy,
By countryside or town,
Who may be seen all blue and green,
Unless she's red or brown. "

But now, while fierce the little man did scowl,
The rosy Friar, sly-smiling 'neath his cowl,
His visage meek, spake thus in dulcet tone:
"Sir Fool, our Reeve is something mixed, I'll own,
Though he by divers colours is bemused,
Learn ye this truth, so shall he stand excused:
Our Duchess Benedicta, be it known,
Hath this day from her several guardians flown.
Ten worthy men her several guardians be,
Of whom the chief and worthiest ye see,
As first—myself, a friar of some report,
Well-known, methinks, in country, town and court.
Who as all men can unto all men speak,

Well read beside in Latin and in Greek,
A humble soul albeit goodly preacher,
One apt to learn and therefore learned teacher,
One who can laugh betimes, betimes can pray,
Who'll colic cure or on the bagpipe play.
Who'll sing—"

"Stay! " cried the Reeve. "Friar, what o'me? "
"Patience, O Bax, too soon I'll come to thee!
Who'll sing ye then blithe as a bird on bough—"
"Friar! " growled the Reeve, "the time for me is now! "
"So be it, then, " the Friar did gently say,
"I'll speak of thee as truly as I may:
Here then behold our port-reeve, Greg'ry Bax,
Who, save for reason, naught in reason lacks,
Who, though he small and puny seems to shew,
In speech he is Goliath-like, I trow,
Chief Councillor of Tissingors is he,
And of the council second but—to me.
For with the townsfolk first of all come I—"

REEVE: Since thy fat finger is in every pie—
"Saving your reverend grace, " Duke Joc'lyn said,
"What of this maid that turneth green and red? "

REEVE: Fool, then learn this, ere that our lord duke died,
Ten guardians for his child he did provide,
The Friar and I, with men of lesser fame,
Co-guardians are of this right puissant dame.

JOCELYN: Beseech ye, sir, now tell us an' ye may,
Why hath thy youthful Duchess run away?

"Fair Fool, " quoth the Friar, fanning himself with a frond of bracken, "'tis a hot day, a day reminiscent of the ultimate fate of graceless sinners, and I am like the day and languish for breath, yet, to thy so pertinent question I will, straightly and in few words, pronounce and answer thee, as followeth: Our Lady Benedicta hath run away firstly, brethren, for that being formed woman after Nature's goodly plan she hath the wherewithal to walk, to leap, to skip or eke to run, as viz. : item and to wit—legs. Secondly, inquisitorial brethren, she ran for an excellent good reason—as observe—there was none to let or stay her. And thirdly, gentle and

13

eager hearers, she did flit or fly, leave, vacate, or depart our goodly town of Tissingors for that she had—mark me—no mind to stay, remain or abide therein. And this for the following express, rare and most curious reason as—mark now—in a word—"

"Hold—hold, Friar John! " exclaimed the Reeve; "here sit ye here a-sermonising, venting words a-many what time our vanished Duchess fleeth. Knew I not the contrary I should say thou didst countenance her flight and spent thyself in wordy-wind wherewith to aid her! "

Now here, chancing to meet Duke Jocelyn's shrewd gaze, Friar John slowly and ponderously winked one round, bright eye.

Quoth he:

"Hark to our valiant port-reeve Greg'ry Bax
Who, save for reason, nought of reason lacks! "
"Howbeit, " fumed the Reeve, stamping in the dust, "here sit ye at thy full-bodied ease, fanning flies and animadverting—"

"Animadverting! " nodded Friar John. "A good word, Reeve, a fair, sweet word; in verity a word full-bodied as I, wherefore it liketh me well. So sit I here animadverting whiles thou kicketh up a dust in fashion foolish and un-reeve-like. "

"A plague o' words! " cried the Reeve. "A pest o' wind! Enough—enough, contain thy prolixities and rodomontade and let me to the point explain—"

"Aha! " quoth the Friar. "Good sooth, here's a noble word! A word round i' the mouth, rolling upon the tongue. Ha, Reeve, I give thee joy of rodomontade! "

"Thus then, " continued the Reeve, "I will, with use of no verbiage circumlocutory, explain. "

"Ho-oho! " cried Friar John, rubbing plump hands ecstatic. "Good Bax, ne'er have I heard thee to so great advantage—verbiage circumlocutory—and thou—thou such small man to boot! O most excellent, puny Reeve! "

Here the little man turned his back upon the Friar and continued hastily thus:

"A lord there is, a lord of lofty pride,
Who for our lady oft hath sued and sighed—"

FRIAR JOHN: Whom she as oft hath scornfully denied!

THE REEVE: A mighty lord who seeketh her to wife—

FRIAR JOHN: Though he, 'tis said, doth lead most evil life!
THE REEVE: To which fair lord our wilful maid we'd wed—

FRIAR JOHN: Since this fair lord the council holds in dread!

THE REEVE: But she, defying us, this very day
Like wicked thief hath stole herself away.
Thus this poor lord such deeps of gloom is in
Vows he'll not wash, nor shave again his chin
Till found is she: He groaneth, sheddeth tears—

THE FRIAR: And swears her guardians ten shall lose their ears!

THE REEVE: Wherefore are we in mighty perturbation,
Amazed, distraught and filled with consternation.
Thus do our bells ring out their wild alarms,
Our civic bands do muster under arms;
Drums shall be drummed the countryside around,
Until our truant Duchess we have found,
And we have wed this most elusive dame
Unto Sir Agramore of Biename.

THE FRIAR: And yield her thus to woes and bitter shame!

THE REEVE: So speak me, fellows; as ye came this way
Saw ye aught of this wilful, errant may?

Answered JOCELYN: "Neither to-day nor any other day. "

"Why then, " fumed the Reeve, "here have we been at great expense o' breath and time and all to no purpose. Come, Friar, beseech thee, let us haste to begone. "

15

So Friar John got slowly to his feet
Complaining loud of hurry and of heat,
But paused behind the hasteful Reeve to linger,
And to plump nose he slyly laid plump finger.

Now stood Sir Pertinax thoughtful, chin on fist, insomuch that
Jocelyn, thrumming his lute, questioned him:

"Good Pertinax, how now
What pond'rest thou
With furrowed brow?
Thy care, Sir Knight, avow! "

Saith Pertinax: "I meditate the way wondrous of woman, the
frowardness of creatures feminine. For mark me, sir, here is one hath
guardians ten, yet despite them she is fled away and they ten! "

"Why truly, Pertinax, they are ten, so is she fled. "

"Aye, but if they be ten that ward her and she one that would flee,
how shall this one flee these ten? "

"For that they be ten. "

"Nay, lord, here be twenty eyes to watch one young maid and
twenty legs to pursue the same, yet doth she evade them one and all,
and here's the wonder on't—she's but one maid. "

"Nay, there's the reason on't, Pertinax—she is a maid. "

"The which is great matter for wonder, lord! "

"Spoke like a very Pertinax, my Pertinax, for here's no wonder at all.
For perceive, the lady is young, her wardens ten grave seniors,
worthy wights —solemn, sober and sedate, Pertinax, wise and
wearisome, grave yet garrulous, and therefore they suffice not. "

"Aye, prithee and wherefore not? "

"For their divers worthy attributes and because they be—ten. Now
had these ten been one and this one a very man—*the* man—here had
been no running away on part of the lady, I 'll warrant me? "

"Stay, my lord, " said Pertinax, in deep perplexity, "how judge ye so—and wherefore—why and by what manner o' reasoning? "

"Ha, Pertinax! " laughed the Duke, "my lovely, loveless numskull! " So saying, he kicked the good Knight full joyously and so they trudged on again.

Till presently, beyond the green of trees,
They saw afar the town of Canalise,
A city fair, couched on a gentle height,
With walls embattled and strong towers bedight.
Now seeing that the sun was getting low,
Our travellers at quicker pace did go.
Thus as in haste near to the gate they came,
Before them limped a bent and hag-like dame,
With long, sharp nose that downward curved as though
It beak-like wished to peck sharp chin below.
Humbly she crept in cloak all torn and rent,
And o'er a staff her tottering limbs were bent.
So came she to the gate, then cried in fear,
And started back from sudden-levelled spear;
For 'neath the gate lounged lusty fellows three
Who seldom spake yet spat right frequently.

"Kind sirs, good sirs, " the ancient dame did cry,
"In mercy's name I pray ye let me by—"
But, as she spoke, a black-jowled fellow laughed,
And, spitting, tripped her with out-thrust pike-shaft,

That down she fell and wailed most piteously,
Whereat the brawny fellows laughed all three.
"Ha, witch! " they cried, as thus she helpless lay,
"Shalt know the fire and roasted be one day! "
Now as the aged creature wailed and wept,
Forth to her side Duke Joc'lyn lightly stepped,
With quarter-staff a-twirl he blithely came.
Quoth he: "Messires, harm not this ancient dame,
Bethink ye how e'en old and weak as she,
Your wives and mothers all must one day be.
So here then lies your mother, and 't were meeter
As ye are sons that as sons ye entreat her.

The Geste of Duke Jocelyn

Come, let her by and, fool-like to requite ye,
With merry jape and quip I will delight ye,
Or with sweet song I 'll charm those ass's ears,
And melt, belike, those bullish hearts to tears—"

Now the chief warder, big and black of jowl,
Upon the Duke most scurvily did scowl.
"How now, " quoth he, "we want no fool's-heads here—"
"Sooth, " laughed the Duke, "you're fools enow 't is clear,
Yet there be fools and fools, ye must allow,
Gay fools as I and surly fools—as thou. "

"Ha, look 'ee, Fool, Black Lewin e'en am I,
And, by my head, an ill man to defy.
Now, motley rogue, wilt call me fool? " he roared,
And roaring fierce, clapped hairy fist on sword.

"Aye, that will I, " Duke Joc'lyn soft replied,
And black-avised, swart, knavish rogue beside. "

But now, while thus our ducal jester spoke,
Black Lewin sprang and fetched him such a stroke

That Jocelyn saw flash before his eyes,
More stars that e'er he'd noticed in the skies.
Whereat Sir Pertinax did gaping stare,
Then ground his teeth and mighty oaths did swear,
And in an instant bared his trusty blade,
But then the Duke his fiery onslaught stayed.

"Ha! " cried the Knight, "and wilt thou smitten be
By such base knave, such filthy rogue as he? "

"Nay, " smiled the Duke, "stand back and watch, good brother,
A Rogue and Fool at buffets with each other. "

And speaking thus, he leapt on Black Lewin,
And smote him twice full hard upon the chin,
Two goodly blows upon that big, black jowl,
Whereat Black Lewin lustily did howl
And falling back, his polished bascinet
With ringing clash the cold, hard flagstones met.

Whereat his fellows, shouting fierce alarms,
Incontinent betook them to their arms;
And thus it seemed a fight there must have been
But that a horseman sudden spurred between—
A blue-eyed youth with yellow, curling hair,
Of slender shape, of face and feature fair,
A dainty knight was he in very truth,
A blue-eyed, merry, laughter-loving youth.

"Ha, knaves, what do ye with the Fool? " lisped he,
"Wilt strike a motley, dogs—a Fool? Let be!
Though faith, 't would seem, Sir Fool, thou hast a fist
That surly Lewin to his dole hath kissed.
If it can strum thy lute but half as well,
Then gestours all methinks thou should'st excel—

Ye rogues, pass Folly in, no man shall say
That from our town we folly turned away.
Come, follow, Fool, into the market-square,
And give us earnest of thy foolish ware. "

Now it was market day, and within the goodly square were people
come from near and far, a notable concourse, country folk and folk of
the town, farmers and merchants, rustic maids, fair ladies, knights
and esquires on horseback or a-foot, but who, hearing the jingle of
the Duke's tinkling bells, seeing his flaunting cock's-comb, with one
accord gathered to him from every quarter:

For when this long-legged gestour they espied,
They, laughing, hemmed him in on every side,
And, "See, a Fool! A Fool! The Fool must sing, "
And "Fool! A Fool! " upon the air did ring,
Wherefore the Duke betook him to his lute,
And strummed until the chattering crowd was mute.
Then while all folk did hold their peace to hear,
In golden voice he sang, full rich and clear:

"'A fool! A fool! ' ye cry,
A fool forsooth am I.
But tell me, wise ones, if ye can,
Where shall ye find a happy man?

19

Lived there one since the world began?
Come, answer ye
To me!

"'What of the king? ' says you.
Says I to you—'Go to!
A king despite his crown and throne,
Hath divers troubles all his own.
Such woes, methinks, as are unknown   .
To such as ye,
Or me! '

"'Ha, then—the rich! ' ye cry,
'Not so in truth, ' says I.
'The rich man's gold is load of care,
That day and night he needs must bear;
Less care he'd know if poor he were,
As poor as ye,
Or me! '

"For, sirs, as I do guess
This thing called 'Happiness'
Man leaveth with his youth behind;
So keep ye all a youthful mind,
Thus happiness ye all shall find
If wit have ye,
Like me!

"O list ye, great and small,
Proud knight, free man and thrall,
True happiness, since life began,
The birthright is of every man;
Seize then your birthright if ye can,
Since men are ye—
Like me!

"Thus I forsooth, a Fool,
Do now ye wise ones school;
Since of my folly, full and free,
I wisely thus admonish ye,
Be wise—or eke fools learn to be
In verity—
Like me! "

Now when the song was ended some there were who laughed and some looked grave, some talked amain and some wagged solemn heads, while many a good coin rang heartily at Duke Jocelyn's feet; smiling, he bade Sir Pertinax take them up, joying to see the proud Knight stooping thus to pouch the money like any beggar. But now, when he would fain have gone his way into the town, the people would by no means suffer it and clamoured amain on all sides, insistent for more; wherefore, lifting his scarred face to the sunset sky, Duke Jocelyn sang as here followeth:

"When man is born he doth begin
With right good will, to daily sin,
And little careth.
But when his grave he thinketh near,
Then grave he groweth in his fear
And sin forsweareth.

"This life that man doth cherish so,
Is wondrous frail and quick to go,
Nor will it stay.
Yet where's the man that will not give
All that he hath so he might live
Another day.

"Fain would I know the reason why
All men so fearful are to die
And upward go?
Since Death all woes and ills doth end,
Sure Death, methinks, should be a friend,
Not hated foe.

"So when Death come, as come he must,
Grieve not that we this sorry dust
Do leave behind.
For when this fleeting life be run,

By Death we all of us—each one,
True life shall find. "

Now while he sang melodious and clear
Amid the throng that closer pressed to hear,
Duke Joc'lyn of a sudden did espy

21

The "wherefore" of his coming and the "why. "
Yolande herself he, singing, did behold,
Her eyes, red lips, her hair of ruddy gold;
And all her warm and glowing loveliness
Did sudden thus his raptured vision bless;
While she, in gracious ease, her horse did sit
That pawed round hoof and champed upon his bit,
Arching proud neck as if indeed he were
Proud of the lovely burden he did bear.
As Joc'lyn gazed upon her thus, she seemed
A thousand times more fair than he had dreamed.
Now while he sang, she viewed him, gentle-eyed,
And quite forgot the gallant by her side,
A tall, dark-featured, comely lord was he,
With chin full square and eyes of mastery,
Who, when the Duke made of his song an end
Did from his saddle o'er Yolanda bend.
With eyes on her warm beauty he stooped near
To touch white hand and whisper in her ear;
Whereat she laughed and frowned with cheek flushed red
Then, frowning still, she turned her horse's head,
And rode away with dame and squire and knight,
Till lost she was to Joc'lyn's ravished sight.

"Ha, lord! " quoth Sir Pertinax, as they came within a quiet thoroughfare, "this lady is grown more fair since last we saw her Queen of Beauty at Melloc joust, concerning whom Fame, in troth, doth breed a just report for once. But, messire, didst mark him beside her—with touch o' hand, lord, whispers i' the ear—didst mark this wolf, this Seneschal, this thrice accurst Sir Gui? "

"Aye, forsooth, " answered the Duke, "but thou'rt an hungered, methinks? "

"To touch her hand, lord—aha! To whisper in her ear, lord—oho! A right puissant lord, Seneschal of Raddemore, Lord of Thorn and Knight of Ells! A lord of puissance and power potential. "

"And thou, my Pertinax, art but a hungry Knight, that trampeth with a hungry Fool, wherefore let us forthwith—"

"Aye, but mark me, lord, if this puissant lord with pomp and high estate doth woo the lady—"

"So then, my Pertinax, will I woo this lady also. "

"How, in this thy foolish guise? "

"Aye, forsooth. "

"Why, then, thou art like to be whipped for froward Fool and I for ragged rogue, and this our adventure brought to ill and woeful end—so here now is folly, lord, indeed! "

"Aye, forsooth! " smiled the Duke,

> "Whereto these bells give heed.
> But come, amend thy speed,
> Methinks thy fasting-need
> These gloomy vapours breed.
> Thy inner man doth plead
> Good beef with ale or mead
> Wherein, thou Fool decreed,
> I am right well agreed
> 'T were goodly thing to feed,
> Nor will I thee impede,
> So follow Folly's lead
> And food-wards we'll proceed. "

FYTTE 2

How Pertinax mine host's large ears did wring,
And Jocelyn of these same ears did sing.

* * * * *

Now the town was full, and every inn a-throng with company—
lords, both great and small, knights and esquires and their several
followings, as archers, men-at-arms, and the like, all thither come
from far and near to joust at the great tournament soon to be, to
honour the birthday of Benedicta, Duchess of Tissingors,
Ambremont, and divers other fair cities, towns and villages. Thus
our travellers sought lodgment in vain, whereat Sir Pertinax cursed
beneath his breath, and Duke Jocelyn hummed, as was each his wont
and custom; and ever the grim Knight's anger grew.

Until, at last, an humble inn they saw—
A sorry place, with bush above the door.
This evil place they straightway entered in,
Where riot reigned, the wild, unlovely din
Of archers, men-at-arms, and rogues yet worse,
Who drank and sang, whiles some did fight and curse.
An evil place indeed, a lawless crew,
And landlord, like his inn, looked evil too:
Small was his nose, small were his pig-like eyes,
But ears had he of most prodigious size,
A brawny rogue, thick-jowled and beetle-browed,
Who, spying out our strangers 'mid the crowd,

Beholding them in humble, mean array,
With gestures fierce did order them away.
"Nay," quoth Sir Pertinax, "here will we bide,
Here will we eat and drink and sleep beside.
Go, bring us beef, dost hear? And therewith mead,
And, when we've ate, good beds and clean we'll need."
"Ho!" cried the host. "Naught unto ye I'll bring
Until yon Fool shall caper first and sing!"
Said Jocelyn: "I'll sing when I have fed!"
"And then," quoth Pertinax, "we will to bed!"
"And wilt thou so?" the surly host replied;
"No beds for likes o' ye do I provide.

An' ye will sleep, knave, to the stable go,
The straw is good enough for ye, I trow. "

"Ha! " roared Sir Pertinax. "A stable? Straw?
This to me, thou filthy clapper-claw,
Thou fly-blown cod's-head, thou pestiferous thing! "
And, roaring, on the brawny host did spring;

By his large ears Sir Pertinax did take him,
And to and fro, and up and down, did shake him;
He shook him quick and slow, from side to side,
While loud for aid the shaken landlord cried.
Whereat the vicious crowd, in sudden wrath,
Shouted and cursed and plucked their daggers forth.
But, ere to harm our bold Knight they were able,
Duke Joc'lyn lightly sprang on massy table;
Cock's-comb a-flaunt and silver bells a-ring,
He laughing stood and gaily plucked lute-string,
And cut an antic with such merry grace
That angry shouts to laughter loud gave place.

Thereafter he sang as followeth:

"Bold bawcocks, brave, bibulous, babbling boys,
Tall tosspots, come, temper this tumult and noise;
So shall I sing sweetly such songs as shall sure
Constrain carking care and contumacy cure.
Thus, therefore—"

But here the surly landlord raised much clamour and outcry, whiles
he touched and caressed his great ears with rare gentleness.

"Oho, my yeres! " roared he. "My yeres do be in woeful estate. Oho,
what o' yon fierce-fingered rogue, good fellows, what o' yon
knave—'a did twist my yeres plaguily and wring 'em roguishly, 'a
did! Shall 'a not be beaten and drubbed out into the kennel, ha?
What o' poor Nykins' yeres, says I—my yeres, oho! "

"Thine ears, unsavoury scullion, " laughed Jocelyn; "thine ears,
forsooth? Hark ye, of thy so great, so fair, so fine ears I'll incontinent
make a song. List ye, one and all, so shall all here now hear my song
of ears! " Forthwith Duke Jocelyn struck his lute and sang:

25

"Thine ears, in sooth, are long ears,
Stout ears, in truth, and strong ears,
Full ears, I trow, and fair ears,
Round ears also and rare ears.
So here's an ear that all eyes here
Shall see no beauty in, 'tis clear.
For these o' thine be such ears,
Large, loose, and over-much ears,
Ears that do make fingers itch,
Ears to twist and ears to twitch.

If thine ears had gone unseen,
Pulled forsooth they had not been;
Yet, since pulled indeed they were,
Thine ears plain the blame must bear.
So of thine ears no more complain,
Lest that thine ears be pulled again.
So hide thine ears as best ye may,
Of which same ears, to end, I say
Thine ears indeed be like my song,
Of none account, yet over long! "

Now hereupon was huge laughter and merriment, insomuch that the thick-jowled landlord betook himself otherwhere, and all men thronged upon our jester, vociferous for more.

"Aye, but, bold tosspots, " laughed Jocelyn, "how now, sit ye without wine in very truth? "

"Not so, good Fool, " they cried. "Here be wine a-plenty for us and for thee! "

"Go to, tall topers, " quoth the Duke, "ye are witless, in faith, for there is no man here but is without wine, as in song will I shew — mark now:

"'Tis plain that ye are wine without,
Since wine's within ye, topers stout.
Without your wine, ye whineful show,
Thus wine-full, wine without ye go.
Being then without your wine, 'tis true,
Wine-less, ye still are wine-full too.

But, mark! As thus ye wine-full sit,
Since wine's within, out goeth wit.
Thus, truth to tell, tall topers stout,
Both wine and wit ye go without! "

By such tricks of rhyme, jugglery of words, and the like, Duke
Jocelyn won this fierce company to great good humour and delight;
insomuch that divers of these roysterers pressed wine upon him and
money galore. But, the hour growing late, he contrived at last to steal
away with Sir Pertinax, which last, having fed copiously, now
yawned consumedly, eager for bed. Howbeit, despite the Knight's
fierce threats, they found no bed was to be had in all the inn, and so,
perforce, betook them at last to the stable.

There, while our Knight cursed softly, though full deep,
Soon in the straw our Duke fell fast asleep.

My daughter GILLIAN propoundeth:

GILL: O, father, dear, I greatly fear
You 'll never be a poet!
MYSELF: Don't be too hard upon the bard,
I know it, girl, I know it!
These last two lines, I quite agree,
Might easily much better be.
Though, on the whole, I think my verse,
When all is said, might be much worse.
GILL: Worse, father? Yes, perhaps you're right,
Upon the whole—perhaps, it might.
MYSELF: But hark now, miss! Attend to this!
Poetic flights I do not fly;
When I begin, like poor Lobkyn,
I merely rhyme and versify.
Since my shortcomings I avow,
The story now, you must allow,
Trips lightly and in happy vein?
GILL: O, yes, father, though it is rather
Like some parts of your "Beltane. "
MYSELF: How, child! Dare you accuse your sire
Of plagiary—that sin most dire?
And if I do, small blame there lies;
It is myself I plagiarise.

GILL: Why, yes, of course! And, as you know.
I always loved your "Beltane" so.

MYSELF: But don't you like the "geste" I'm writing?

GILL: Of course! It's getting most exciting,
In spite of all the rhymes and stuff—

MYSELF: Stuff?
Enough!
My daughter, you're so sweetly frank.
Henceforth my verses shall be blank.
No other rhyme I'll rhyme for you
Till you politely beg me to.
Now then, your blank-verse doom you know,
Hey, presto, and away we go!

FYTTE 3

Tell'th how Duke Jocelyn of love did sing,
And haughty knight in lily-pool did fling.

* * * * *

Upon a morn, when dewy flowers fresh-waked
Filled the glad air with perfume languorous,
And piping birds a pretty tumult made,
Thrilling the day with blended ecstasy;
When dew in grass did light a thousand fires,
And gemmed the green in flashing bravery —
Forth of her bower the fair Yolanda came,
Fresh as the morn and, like the morning, young,
Who, as she breathed the soft and fragrant air,
Felt her white flesh a-thrill with joyous life,
And heart that leapt responsive to the joy.
Vivid with life she trod the flowery ways,
Dreaming awhile of love and love and love;
Unknowing all of eyes that watched unseen,
Viewing her body's gracious loveliness:
Her scarlet mouth, her deep and dreamful eyes,
The glowing splendour of her sun-kissed hair,
Which in thick braids o'er rounded bosom fell
Past slender waist by jewelled girdle bound.

So stood Duke Jocelyn amid the leaves,
And marked how, as she walked, her silken gown
Did cling her round in soft embrace, as though
Itself had sense and wit enough to love her.
Entranced he stood, bound by her beauty's spell,
Whereby it seemed he did in her behold
The beauty of all fair and beauteous things.

Now leaned she o'er a pool where lilies pale
Oped their shy beauties to the gladsome day,
Yet in their beauty none of them so fair
As that fair face the swooning waters held.
And as, glad-eyed, she viewed her loveliness,

She fell to singing, soft and low and sweet,
Clear and full-throated as a piping merle,
And this the manner of her singing was:

"What is love? Ah, who shall say?
Flower to languish in a day,
Bird on wing that will away.
Love, I do defy thee!

"What is love? A toy so vain
'T is but found to lose again,
Painful sweet and sweetest pain;
Ah, love, come not nigh me.

"But, love, an thou com'st to me,
Wert thou as I'd have thee be,
Welcome sweet I'd make for thee,
And weary of thee never.

"If with thy heart thou could'st endure,
If thou wert strong and thou wert sure,
A master now, and now a wooer,
Thy slave I'd be for ever. "

Thus sang she sweet beside the lily-pool,
Unknowing any might her singing hear,
When rose another voice, so rich, so full
As thrilled her into rapt and pleasing wonder;
And as she hearkened to these deep-sung words,
She flushed anon and dimpled to a smile:

"What is love? 'Tis this, I say,
Flower that springeth in a day,
Bird of joy to sing alway,
Deep in the heart of me.

"What is love? A joyous pain
That I ne'er may lose again,
Since for ever I am fain
To think and dream of thee. "

Now hasted she to part the leafy screen,
And one in motley habit thus beheld.

But when 'neath flaunting cock's-comb she did mark
His blemished face, she backward from him drew
And caught her breath, and yet upon him gazed
'Neath wrinkled brow, the while Duke Jocelyn
Read the expected horror in her eyes:
Wherefore he bowed his head upon his breast
And plucked at belt with sudden, nervous hand
As, cold and proud and high, she questioned him:
"What thing art thou that 'neath thy hood doth show
A visage that might shame the gladsome day? "

Whereto he answered, low and humble-wise:
"A Fool! The very fool of fools am I—
A Fool that fain would pluck the sun from heaven. "

"Begone! " she sighed. "Thy look doth make me cold,
E'en as I stand thus i' the kindly sun.
Yet, an thou 'rt poor as thy mean habit speaks thee,
Take first this dole for tender Jesu's sake. "

Then answered Jocelyn on lowly knee:
"For thy sweet bounty I do thank thee well,
But, in good sooth, so great a fool am I,
'Stead of thy gold I rather would possess

Yon happy flower that in thy bosom bloometh.
Give me but this and richer fool am I
Than any knight-like fool that coucheth lance—
Greater I than any lord soever,
Aye—e'en Duke Jocelyn of Brocelaunde. "

Smiled now Yolande with rosy lip up-curving,
While in soft cheek a roguish dimple played.
Quoth she: "Duke Jocelyn, I've heard it said,
Is great and rich, a mighty man-at-arms,
And thou but sorry Fool in mean array,
Yet"—from white fingers she let fall the flower—
"Be thou, Fool, greater than this mighty Duke!
And now, since mighty Fool and rich I've made thee,
In quittance I would win of thee a song. "

Now sat Yolande, white chin on dimpled fist,
Viewing him o'er with cruel, maiden-eyes,

So swift to heed each outward mark and blemish
(Since maids be apt to sly disparagement,
And scorn of all that seems un-beautiful)
While he did lean him by the marble rim,
His wistful gaze down-bent upon the pool,
Feeling her look and knowing while she looked:
What time he touched his lute with fingers skilled,
And so fell singing, wonder-low and sweet:

"Though foul and harsh of face am I,
Lady fair—O lady!
Fair thoughts within my heart may lie,
As flowers that bloom unseen to die,
Lady fair—O lady!

"Though this my hateful face may fright thee,
Lady fair—O list!
My folly mayhap shall delight thee,
A song of fools I will recite thee,
Lady fair—O list! "

Herewith he sighed amain, but smiled anon,
And fell anon to blither, louder note:

"Sing hey, Folly—Folly ho,
And here's a song of Folly,
All 'neath the sun,
Will gladly run
Away from Melancholy.

"And Fool, forsooth, a Fool am I,
Well learned in foolish lore:
For I can sing ye, laugh or sigh:
Can any man do more?
Hey, Folly—Folly, ho!
'Gainst sadness bar the door.

"A Fool am I, yet by fair leave,
Poor Fools have hearts to feel.
Poor Fools, like other fools, may grieve
If they their woes conceal.
Hither, Folly—Folly, ho!
All Fools to Folly kneel.

"What though a Fool be melancholy,
Sick, sick at heart—heigho!
Pain must he hide 'neath laughing Folly,
What Fool should heed his woe!
Hither, Folly—Folly, ho!
Fool must unpitied go.

"E'en though a Fool should fondly woo,
E'en though his love be high,
Poor Folly's fool must wear the rue,
Proud love doth pass him by.
Heigho, Folly—Folly, ho!
Poor Fool may love—and die.

"Though Wisdom should in motley go,
And fools the wise man ape;
Who is there that shall Wisdom know
Beneath a 'scalloped cape?
Heigho, Folly—Folly, ho!
Life is but sorry jape.

"So, hey, Folly—Folly, ho!
And here's a song o' Folly,
All 'neath the sun
Do gladly run
Away from Melancholy."

The singing done, she viewed him kinder-eyed,
Till eyes met eyes—when she did pout and frown,
And chid him that his song was something sad,
And vowed so strange a Fool was never seen.
Then did she question him in idle wise
As, who he was and whence he came and why?
Whereto the Duke—

My daughter GILLIAN interposeth:

GILL:

Dear father, if you're in the vein,
I'd like a little rhyme again;

33

For blank verse is so hard to read,
And yours is very blank indeed!

MYSELF:

Girl, when blank verse I write for thee,
I write it blank as blank can be.
Stay, I'll declare (no poet franker)
No blank verse, Gill, was ever blanker.
But:
Since, with your sex's sweet inconstancy,
Rhymes now you wish, rhymes now I'll
rhyme for thee:
As thus, my dear—
Give ear:

Whereto the Duke did instant make reply:

"Sweet lady, since you question me,
Full blithely I will answer thee;
And, since you fain would merry be,
I'll sing and rhyme it merrily:

"Since Mirth's my trade and follies fond,
Methinks a fair name were Joconde;
And for thy sake
I travail make
Through briar and brake,
O'er fen and lake,
The Southward March beyond.

"For I an embassage do bear,
Now unto thee, Yolande the fair,
Which embassy,
Now unto thee,
Right soothfully,
And truthfully,
Most full, most free,
Explicit I 'll declare.

"Thus: videlicit and to wit,
Sith now thou art to wedlock fit—
Both day and night

The Geste of Duke Jocelyn

In dark, in light
A worthy knight,
A lord of might,
In his own right,
Duke Joc'lyn hight
To thine his heart would knit.

"But, since the Duke may not come to thee,
I, in his stead, will humbly sue thee;
His love each day
I will portray
As best I may;
I'll sue, I'll pray,
I'll sing, I'll play,
Now grave, now gay,
And in this way,
I for the Duke will woo thee. "

Now, fair Yolanda gazed with wide-oped eyes,
And checked sweet breath for wonder and surprise;
Then laughed full blithe and yet, anon, did frown,
And with slim fingers plucked at purfled gown:

"And is it thou—a sorry Fool, " she cried.
"Art sent to win this mighty Duke a bride? "

"E'en so! " quoth he. "Whereof I token bring;
Behold, fair maid, Duke Joc'lyn's signet ring. "
"Heaven's love! " she cried. "And can it truly be
The Duke doth send a mountebank like thee,
A Fool that hath nor likelihood nor grace
From worn-out shoon unto thy blemished face—
A face so scarred—so hateful that meseems
At night 't will haunt and fright me with ill dreams;
A slave so base—"

"E'en so! " Duke Joc'lyn sighed,
And his marred visage 'neath his hood did hide.
"But, though my motley hath thy pride distressed,
I am the Fool Duke Joc'lyn loveth best.
And—ah, my lady, thou shalt never see
In all this world a Fool the like of me! "

Thus spake the Duke, and then awhile stood mute,
And idly struck sweet chords upon his lute,
Watching Yolande's fair, frowning face the while,
With eyes that held a roguish, wistful smile.
She, meeting now these eyes of laughing blue,
Felt her cheeks burn, and sudden angry grew.

So up she rose in proud and stately fashion,
And stamped slim foot at him in sudden passion;
And vowed that of Duke Joc'lyn she cared naught;
That if he'd woo, by him she must be sought;
Vowed if he wooed his wooing should be vain,
And, as he came, he back should go again.
"For, since the Duke, " she cried, "dare send to me
A sorry wight, a very Fool like thee,
By thy Fool's mouth I bid thee to him say,
He ne'er shall win me, woo he as he may;
Say that I know him not—"

"Yet, " spake Duke Joc'lyn soft,
"E'er this, methinks, thou'st seen my lord full oft.
When at the joust thou wert fair Beauty's queen
Duke Joc'lyn by thy hand oft crowned hath been. "
"True, Fool, " she answered, 'twixt a smile and frown,
"I've seen him oft, but with his vizor down.
And verily he is a doughty knight,
But wherefore doth he hide his face from sight? "

"His face? " quoth Joc'lyn with a gloomy look,
"His face, alack! " And here his head he shook;
"His face, ah me! " And here Duke Joc'lyn sighed,
"His face—" "What of his face? " Yolanda cried.
"A mercy's name, speak—speak and do not fail. "
"Lady, " sighed Joc'lyn, "thereby hangs a tale,
The which, though strange it sound, is verity,
That here and now I will relate to thee—
'T is ditty dire of dismal doating dames,
A lay of love-lorn, loveless languishment,
And ardent, amorous, anxious anguishment,
Full-fed forsooth of fierce and fiery flames;
So hark,
And mark:
In Brocelaunde not long ago,

Was born Duke Jocelyn. I trow
Not all the world a babe could show,
A babe so near divine:
For, truth to tell,
He waxed so well,
So fair o' face,
So gay o' grace,
That people all,
Both great and small,
Where'er he went,
In wonderment
Would stare and stare
To see how fair
A lad was Jocelyn.

And when to man's estate he came,
Alack, fair lady, 't was the same!
And many a lovely, love-lorn dame
Would pitiful pant and pine.
These doleful dames
Felt forceful flames,
The old, the grey,
The young and gay,
Both dark and fair
Would rend their hair,
And sigh and weep
And seldom sleep;
And dames long wed
From spouses fled
For love of Jocelyn.

Therefore the Duke an oath did take
By one, by two, by three,
That for these love-lorn ladies' sake
No maid his face should see.
And thus it is, where'er he rideth
His love-begetting face he hideth. "

Now laughed Yolande, her scorn forgotten quite,
"Alas! " she cried. "Poor Duke! O woeful plight!
And yet, O Fool, good Fool, full fain am I,
This ducal, love-begetting face to spy—"
Quoth Joc'lyn: "Then, my lady, prithee, look! "

And from his bosom he a picture took.

"Since this poor face of mine doth so affright thee
Here's one of paint that mayhap shall delight thee.
Take it, Yolande, for thee the craftsmen wrought it,
For thee I from Duke Jocelyn have brought it.
If day and night thou 'lt wear it, fair Yolande, "
And speaking thus, he gave it to her hand.
Its golden frame full many a jewel bore,
But 't was the face, the face alone she saw.
And viewing it, Yolanda did behold
A manly face, yet of a god-like mould.
Breathless she sate, nor moved she for a space,
Held by the beauty of this painted face;
'Neath drooping lash she viewed it o'er and o'er,
And ever as she gazed new charms she saw.
Then, gazing yet, "Who—what is this? " she sighed.
"Paint, lady, paint! " Duke Joc'lyn straight replied,
"The painted visage of my lord it shows—
Item: one mouth, two eyes and eke a nose—"
"Nay, Fool, " she murmured, "here's a face, meseems,
I oft have seen ere now within my dreams;
These dove-soft eyes in dreams have looked on me! "

Quoth Joc'lyn: "Yet these eyes can nothing see! "

"These tender lips in accents sweet I've heard! "

Quoth Joc'lyn: "Yet—they ne'er have spoke a word!
But here's a face at last doth please thee well
Yet hath no power to speak, see, sigh or smell,
Since tongueless, sightless, breathless 't is—thus I
A sorry Fool its needs must e'en supply.
And whiles thou doatest on yon painted head
My tongue I'll lend to woo thee in its stead.
I'll woo with wit
As seemeth fit,
Whiles there thou sit
And gaze on it.
Whiles it ye see
Its voice I'll be
And plead with thee,
So hark to me:

Yolande, I love thee in true loving way;
That is, I'll learn to love thee more each day,
Until so great my growing love shall grow,
This puny world in time 't will overflow.
To-day I love, and yet my love is such
That I to-morrow shall have twice as much.
Thus lovingly to love thee I will learn
Till thou shalt learn Love's lesson in thy turn,
And find therein how sweet this world can be
When as I love, thou, love, shall so love me. "

"Hush, hush! " she sighed, and to her ruddy lip
She sudden pressed one rosy finger-tip.
And then, O happy picture! Swift from sight
She hid it in her fragrant bosom white.
"O Fool, " she cried, "get thee behind yon tree,
And thou a very Fool indeed shall see,
A knightly fool who sighs and groans in verse
And oft-times woos in song, the which is worse. "
For now they heard a voice that sung most harsh,
That shrilled and croaked like piping frog in marsh,
A voice that near and ever nearer drew
Until the lordly singer strode in view.
A noble singer he, both tall and slender,

With locks be-curled and clad in pompous splendour;
His mantle of rich velvet loose did flow,
As if his gorgeous habit he would show;
A jewelled bonnet on his curls he bore,
With nodding feather bravely decked before;
He was a lover very point de vice,
And all about him, save his voice, was nice.
Thus loudly sang, with lungs both sound and strong
This worthy knight, Sir Palamon of Tong.

"O must I groan
And make my moan
And live alone alway?
Yea, I must sigh
And droop and die,
If she reply, nay, nay!

"I groan for thee,

I moan for thee,
Alone for thee I pine.
All's ill for me
Until for me
She will for me be mine. "

But now, beholding Yolande amid her flowers, herself as sweet and fresh as they, he made an end of his singing and betook him, straightway, to amorous looks and deep-fetched sighs together with many supple bendings of the back, elegant posturings and motitions of slim legs, fannings and flauntings of be-feathered cap, and the like gallantries; and thereafter fell to his wooing on this fashion:

"Lady, O lady of lovely ladies most loved! Fair lady of hearts, sweet dame of tenderness, tender me thine ears, suffer one, hath sighed and suffered for sake of thee, to sightful sue. Lovely thou art and therefore to be loved, and day and night thou and Love the sum of my excogitations art, wherefore I, with loving art, am hither come to woo thee, since, lady, I do love thee. "

"Alack, Sir Palamon! " she sighed, "and is it so? "

"Alack! " he answered, "so it is. Yest're'en I did proclaim thee fairer than all fair ladies; to-day thou art yet fairer, thus this day thou art fairer than thyself; the which, though a paradox, is yet wittily true and truly witty, methinks. But as for me—for me, alas for me! I am forsooth the very slave of love, fettered fast by Dan Cupid, a slave grievous and woeful, yet, being thy slave, joying in my slavery and happy in my grievous woe.
Thus it is I groan and moan, lady; I pine, repine and pine again most consumedly. I sleep little and eat less, I am, in fine and in all ways, 'haviours, manners, customs, feints and fashions soever, thy lover manifest, confessed, subject, abject, in season and out of season, yearly, monthly, daily, hourly, and by the minute. Moreover—"

"Beseech thee! " she cried, "Oh, beseech thee, take thy breath. "

"Gramercy, 'tis done, lady, 'tis done, and now forthwith resolved am I to sing thee—"

"Nay, I pray you, sir, sing no more, but resolve me this mystery. What is love? "

"Love, lady? Verily that will I in truth! " And herewith Sir Palamon fell to an attitude of thought with eyes ecstatic, with knitted brows and sage nodding of the head. "Love, my lady—ha! Love, lady is—hum! Love, then, perceive me, is of its nature elemental, being of the elements, as 'twere, composed and composite, as water, air and fire. For, remark me, there is no love but begetteth first water, which is tears; air, which is sighings and groanings; and fire, which is heart-burnings and the like. Thus is love a passion elemental. But yet, and heed me, lady, love is also metaphysical, being a motion of the soul and e'en the spirit, and being of the spirit 'tis ghostly, and being ghostly 'tis—ha! Who comes hither to shatter the placid mirror of my thoughts? "

So saying, the noble knight of Tong turned to behold one who strode towards them in haste, a tall man this whose black brows scowled fierce upon the day, and who spurned the tender flowers with foot ungentle as he came.

A tall, broad-shouldered, haughty lord was he,
With chin full square and eyes of mastery,
At sight of whom, Yolanda's laughter failed,
And in her cheek the rosy colour paled.

Quoth he: "Sir Palamon, now of thy grace,
And of thy courteous friendship yield me place,
To this fair lady I a word would say.
Thus do I for thy courteous-absence pray,
I am thy friend, Sir Knight, as thou dost know,
But—"

"My lord, " quoth Sir Palamon, "I go—
Friendship methinks is a most holy bond,
A bond I hold all binding bonds beyond,
And thou 'rt a friend right potent, my lord Gui,
So to thy will I willingly comply.
Thus, since thy friendship I hold passing dear,
Thou need but ask—and lo! I am not here. "
Thus having said, low bowed this courtly knight,
Then turned about and hasted out of sight.

"And now, my lady, " quoth Sir Gui, frowning upon her loveliness, "and now having discharged yon gaudy wind-bag, what of this

letter I did receive but now—behold it! " and speaking, he snatched
a crumpled missive from his bosom. "Behold it, I say! "

"Indeed, my lord, I do, " she answered, proud and disdainful; "it is,
methinks, my answer to thy loathèd suit—"

"Loathèd! " he cried, and caught her slender wrist,
And held it so, crushed in his cruel fist;
But proud she faced him, shapely head raised high.
"Most loathèd, my lord! " she, scornful, made reply.
"For rather than I'd wed myself with thee,
The wife of poorest, humblest slave I'd be,
Or sorriest fool that tramps the dusty way—"
"Ha! Dare thou scorn me so? " Sir Gui did say,
"Then I by force—by force will sudden take thee,
And slave of love, my very slave I 'll make thee—"

Out from the leaves Duke Joc'lyn thrust his head,
"O fie! Thou naughty, knavish knight! " he said.
"O tush! O tush! O tush again—go to!
'T is windy, whining, wanton way to woo.
What tushful talk is this of 'force' and 'slaves',
Thou naughty, knavish, knightly knave of knaves?
Unhand the maid—loose thy offensive paw! "
Round sprang Sir Gui, and, all astonished, saw
A long-legged jester who behind him stood
With head out-thrust, grim-smiling 'neath his hood.

"Plague take thee, Fool! Out o' my sight! " growled he,
"Or cropped thine ugly nose and ears shall be.
Begone, base rogue! Haste, dog, and get thee hence,
Thy folly pleadeth this thy Fool's offence—

Yet go, or of thy motley shalt be stripped,
And from the town I 'll have thee shrewdly whipped,
For Lord of Ells and Raddemore am I,
Though folk, I've heard, do call me 'Red Sir Gui, '
Since blood is red and—I am Gui the Red. "
"Red Gui? " quoth Joc'lyn. "Art thou Gui the dread—
Red Gui—in faith? Of him Dame Rumour saith,
His ways be vile but viler still—his breath.
Now though a life vile lived is thing most ill,
Yet some do think a vile breath viler still. "

Swift, swift as lightning from a summer sky,
Out flashed the vengeful dagger of Sir Gui,
And darting with a deadly stroke and fierce,
Did Joc'lyn's motley habit rend and pierce,
Whereat with fearful cry up sprang Yolande,
But this strange jester did grim-smiling stand.
Quoth he: "Messire, a fool in very truth,
The fool of foolish fools he'd be, in sooth,
Who'd play a quip or so, my lord, with thee
Unless in triple armour dight were he;
And so it is this jester doth not fail
With such as thou to jest in shirt of mail.
Now since my heart thy foolish point hath missed
Thy dagger—thus I answer—with my fist! "
Then swift he leapt and, even as he spoke,
He fetched the knight so fierce and fell a stroke
That, reeling, on the greensward sank Sir Gui,
And stared, wide-eyed, unseeing, at the sky.
Right firmly then upon his knightly breast
Duke Joc'lyn's worn and dusty shoe did rest,
And while Yolande stood white and dumb with fear,
Thus sang the Duke full blithely and full clear:

"Dirt thou art since thou art dust,
And shalt to dust return;
Meanwhile Folly as he lust
Now thy base dust doth spurn.

"Yea, lord, though thy rank be high,
One day, since e'en lords must die,
Under all men's feet thou'lt lie. "

Now, fierce, Sir Gui did curse the Fool amain,
And, cursing, strove his dagger to regain.
But Joc'lyn stooped, in mighty arms he swung him,
And down into the lily-pool he flung him.

With splash resounding fell the noble knight,
Then gurgling rose in damp and sorry plight,
Whiles Joc'lyn, leaning o'er the marble rim,
With lifted finger thus admonished him:

"Red Gui,

Dread Gui,
Lest a dead Gui,
Gui, I make of thee,
Understand, Gui,
Fair Yolande, Gui,
Humbly wooed must be.

"So, Gui,
Know, Gui,
Ere thou go, Gui,
Gui they call the Red;
And thou'lt woo, Gui,
Humbly sue, Gui,
Lest Love strike thee dead.

"Now while thou flound'rest in yon pool,
Learn thou this wisdom of a Fool;
Cold water oft can passion cool
And fiery ardours slake;
Thus, sir, since water quencheth fire,
So let it soothe away thine ire.
Then—go seek thee garments drier
Lest a rheum thou take. "

Sir Gui did gasp, and gasping, strove to curse,
Whereat he, gasping, did but gasp the worse,
Till, finding he could gasp, but nothing say,
He shook clenched fist and, gasping, strode away.
Then Joc'lyn turned and thus beheld Yolande,
Who trembling all and pale of cheek did stand.

"O Fool! " she sighed. "Poor Fool, what hast
thou done? "

Quoth he: "Yolande, to woo thee I've begun,
I better might have wooed, it is most true,
If other wooers had not wooed thee too. "

"Nay, Fool! " she whispered. "O beware—beware!
Death—death for thee is in the very air.
From Canalise, in haste, I bid thee fly,
For 'vengeful lord and cruel is Sir Gui.
Take now this gold to aid thee on thy way,

And for thy life upon my knees I'll pray,
And with the holy angels intercede
To comfort thee and aid thee in thy need.
And so—farewell! "Thus, speaking, turned Yolande.
But Joc'lyn stayed her there with gentle hand,
Whereat she viewed him o'er in mute surprise,
To see the radiant gladness of his eyes.

Quoth he: "Yolande, since thou wilt pray for me,
Of thy sweet prayers fain would I worthy be.
This I do know—let Death come when he may,
The love I bear thee shall live on alway.

Nor will I strive to leave grim Death behind me,
Since when Death wills methinks he sure will find me;
As in the world Death roameth everywhere,
Who flees him here perchance shall meet him there.
Here, then, I'll bide—let what so will betide me,
Thy prayers like holy angels, watch beside me.
So all day long and in thy pretty sleeping
'Till next we meet the Saints have thee in keeping. "

My daughter GILLIAN animadverteth:

GILL: The last part seems to me much better.
I like Yolande, I hope he'll get her.

MYSELF: Patience, my dear, he's hardly met her.

GILL: I think it would be rather nice
To make him kiss her once or twice.

MYSELF: I'll make him kiss her well, my dear,
When he begins—but not just here.
I'll later see what I can do
In this matter to please you.

GILL: And then I hope, that by and by
He kills that frightful beast, Sir Gui.

MYSELF: Yes, I suppose, we ought to slay him,

For all his wickedness to pay him.

GILL: And Pertinax, I think—don't you?
Should have a lady fair to woo.
To see him in love would be perfectly clipping.
It's a corking idea, and quite awfully ripping—

MYSELF: If you use such vile slang, miss, I vow I will not—

GILL: O, Pax, father! I'm sorry; I almost forgot.

MYSELF: Very well, if my warning you'll bear well
in mind,
A fair damsel for Pertinax I'll try to find.

GILL: Then make her, father, make her quick,
I always knew you were a brick.

FYTTE 4

How Pertinax plied angle to his sport
And, catching him no fish, fish-like was caught.

* * * * *

By sleepy stream where bending willows swayed,
And, from the sun, a greeny twilight made,
Sir Pertinax, broad back against a tree,
Lolled at his ease and yawned right lustily.
In brawny fist he grasped a rod or angle,
With hook wherefrom sad worm did, writhing, dangle.
Full well he loved the piscatorial sport,
Though he as yet no single fish had caught.
Hard by, in easy reach upon the sward,
Lay rusty bascinet and good broadsword.
Thus patiently the good Knight sat and fished,
Yet in his heart most heartily he wished
That he, instead of fishing, snug had been
Seated within his goodly tower of Shene.
And thinking thus, he needs must cast his eye
On rusty mail, on battered shoon, and sigh,
And murmur fitful curses and lament
That in such base, unknightly garb he went—
A lord of might whose broad shield bravely bore
Of proud and noble quarterings a score.
"And 't was forsooth for foolish ducal whim
That he must plod abroad in such vile trim! "
Revolving thus, his anger sudden woke,
And, scowling, to the unseen fish he spoke:

"A Duke! A Fool! A fool-duke, by my head!
Who, clad like Fool, like Fool will fain be wed,

For ass and dolt and fool of fools is he
Who'll live in bondage to some talk-full she.
Yet, if he'll wed, why i' the foul fiend's name,
Must he in motley seek the haughty dame? "

But now, while he did on this problem dwell,
Two unexpected happenings befell:

A fish to nibble on the worm began,
And to him through the green a fair maid ran.
Fast, fast amid the tangled brake she fled,
Her cheeks all pale, her dark eyes wide with dread;
But Pertinax her beauty nothing heeded,
Since both his eyes to watch his fish were needed;
But started round with sudden, peevish snort
As in slim hands his brawny fist she caught;
"Ha, maid! " he cried, "Why must thou come this way
To spoil my sport and fright mine fish away? "
"O man—O man, if man thou art, " she gasped,
"Save me! " And here his hand she closer grasped,
But even now, as thus she breathless spake,
Forth of the wood three lusty fellows brake;
Goodly their dress and bright the mail they wore,
While on their breasts a falcon-badge they bore.
"Oho! " cried one. "Yon dirty knave she's met! "
Sir Pertinax here donned his bascinet.
"But one poor rogue shan't let us! " t' other roared.
Sir Pertinax here reached and drew his sword.
"Then, " cried the third, "let's at him now all three! "
Quoth Pertinax: "Maid, get thee 'hind yon tree,
For now, methinks, hast found me better sport
Than if, forsooth, yon plaguy fish I'd caught. "
So saying, up he rose and, eyes a-dance
He 'gainst the three did joyously advance,
With sword that flashed full bright, but brighter yet
The eyes beneath his rusty bascinet;

While aspect bold and carriage proud and high,
Did plainly give his mean array the lie.
Thus, as he gaily strode to meet the three,
In look and gesture all proud knight was he;
Beholding which, the maid forgot her dread,
And, 'stead of pale, her cheek glowed softly red.

Now at the three Sir Pertinax did spring,
And clashing steel on steel did loudly ring,
Yet Pertinax was one and they were three,
And once was, swearing, smitten to his knee,
Whereat the maid hid face in sudden fear,
And, kneeling so, fierce cries and shouts did hear,
The sounds of combat dire, and deadly riot

Lost all at once and hushed to sudden quiet,
And glancing up she saw to her amaze
Three rogues who fleetly ran three several ways,
Three beaten rogues who fled with one accord,
While Pertinax, despondent, sheathed his sword.
"Par Dex! " he growled, "'Tis shame that they should run
Ere that to fight the rogues had scarce begun! "
So back he came, his rod and line he took,
And gloomed to find no worm upon his hook.
But now the maiden viewed him gentle-eyed;
"Brave soldier, I do thank thee well! " she sighed,
"Thou, like true knight, hast fought for me today—"
"And the fish, " sighed he, "have stole my worm away,
Which is great pity, since my worms be few! "
And here the Knight's despond but deeper grew.
"Yon rogues, " he sighed, "no stomach had for fight,
Yet scared the fish that had a mind to bite! "
"But thou hast saved me, noble man! " said she.
"So must I use another worm! " sighed he.

And straightway with his fishing he proceeded
While sat the maid beside him all unheeded;
Whereat she frowned and, scornful, thus did speak
With angry colour flaming in her cheek:
"What man art thou that canst but fight and fish?
Hast thou no higher thought, no better wish? "
"Certes, " quoth he, "I would I had indeed
A goodly pot of foaming ale or mead. "
"O base, most base! " the maid did scornful cry,
And viewed him o'er with proud, disdainful eye.
"That I should owe my life to man like thee!
That one so base could fight and master three!
Who art thou, man, and what? Speak me thy name,
Whither ye go and why, and whence ye came,
Thy rank, thy state, thy worth to me impart,
If soldier, serf, or outlawed man thou art;
And why 'neath ragged habit thou dost wear
A chain of gold such as but knights do bear,
Why thou canst front three armed rogues unafraid,
Yet fear methinks to look upon a maid? "

But to these questions Pertinax sat dumb—
That is, he rubbed his chin and murmured, "Hum! "

Whereat she, frowning, set determined chin
And thus again to question did begin:

SHE: What manner of man art thou?

HE: A man.

SHE: A soldier?

HE: Thou sayest.

SHE: Art in service?

HE: Truly.

SHE: Whom serve ye?

HE: A greater than I.

SHE: Art thou wed?

HE: The Saints forfend!

SHE: Then art a poor soldier and solitary.

HE: I might be richer.

SHE: What dost thou fishing here?

HE: I fish.

SHE: And why didst fight three men for me—a maid unknown?

HE: For lack of better employ.

SHE: Rude soldier—whence comest thou?

HE: Fair maiden, from beyond.

SHE: Gross Knight, whither goest thou?

HE: Dainty damosel, back again.

SHE: Dost lack aught?

HE: Quiet!

SHE: How, would'st have me hold my peace, ill fellow?

HE: 'T would be a marvel.

SHE: Wherefore?

HE: Thou'rt a woman.

SHE: And thou a man, ill-tongued, ill-beseen, ill-mannered, unlovely,
and I like thee not!

HE: And what is worse, the fish bite not.

Now here, and very suddenly, she fell a-weeping, to the Knight's no small discomfiture, though she wept in fashion wondrous apt and pretty; wherefore Sir Pertinax glanced at her once, looked twice and, looking, scratched his ear, rubbed his chin and finally questioned her in turn:

HE: Distressful damosel, wherefore this dole? SHE: For that I am weary, woeful and solitary. And thou—thou'rt harsh of look, rough of tongue, ungentle of—HE: Misfortunate maiden, thy loneliness is soon amended, get thee to thy friends—thy gossips, thy—

SHE: I have none. And thou'rt fierce and ungentle of face.

Here she wept the more piteously and Sir Pertinax, viewing her distress, forgot his hook and worm, wherefore a fish nibbled it slyly, while the
Knight questioned her further:

HE: Woeful virgin, whence comest thou?

SHE: From afar. And thou art ofeatures grim and—

HE: And whither would'st journey?

SHE: No where! And thou art—

HE: Nay, here is thing impossible, since being here thou art somewhere and that within three bowshots of the goodly town of Canalise wherein thou shalt doubtless come by comfort and succour.

SHE: Never! Never! Here will I weep and moan and perish. And thou—

HE: And wherefore moan and perish?

SHE: For that I am so minded, being a maid forlorn and desolate, a poor wanderer destitute of kith, of kin, of hope, of love, and all that maketh life sweet. And thou art sour-faced and—

HE: Grievous maid, is, among thy many wants, a lack of money?

SHE: That also. And thou art cold of eye, fierce of mouth, hooked of nose, flinty of heart, stony of soul, and I a perishing maid.

At this Sir Pertinax blinked and caught his breath; thereafter he laid down his rod, whereupon the fish incontinent filched his worm all unnoticed while the Knight opened the wallet at his girdle and took thence certain monies.

HE: Dolorous damsel, behold six good, gold pieces! Take them and go, get thee to eat—eat much, so shall thy dolour wax less, eat beef— since beef is a rare lightener of sorrow, by beef shall thy woes be comforted.

SHE: Alas! I love not beef.

Now here Sir Pertinax was dumb a space for wonder at her saying, while she stole a glance at him betwixt slender fingers.

HE (*after some while*): Maid, I tell thee beef, fairly cooked and aptly seasoned, is of itself a virtue whereby the body is strengthened and nourished, whereby cometh content, and with content kindliness, and with kindliness charity, and therewith all other virtues small and eke great; therefore eat beef, maiden, for the good of thy soul.

"How? " said she, viewing him bright-eyed 'twixt her fingers again. "Dost think by beef one may attain to paradise? "

HE: Peradventure.

SHE: Then no beef, for I would not live a saint yet awhile.

HE: Nathless, take thou these monies and go buy what thou wilt.

So saying, Sir Pertinax set the coins beside her shapely foot and took up his neglected rod.

SHE: And is this gold truly mine?

HE: Verily.

SHE: Then I pray thee keep it for me lest I lose it by the way and so— let us begone.

Here Sir Pertinax started.

"Begone? " quoth he. "Begone—in truth? Thou and I in faith? Go whither? "

SHE: Any whither.

HE: Alone? Thou and I?

"Nay, not alone, " she sighed; "let us go together. "

Sir Pertinax dropped his fishing-rod and watched it idly float away down the stream:

"Together, maiden? " said he at last.

"Truly! " she sighed. "For thou art lonely even as I am lonely, and thou art, methinks, one a lonely maid may trust. "

"Ha—trust! " quoth he. "And wherefore would'st trust me, maiden? "

SHE: For two reasons—thou art of age mature and something ill-favoured.

Now, at this Sir Pertinax grew angered, grew thoughtful, grew sad and, beholding his image mirrored in the waters, sighed for his grim, unlovely look and, in his heart, cursed his vile garb anew. At last he spoke:

HE: Truly thou may'st trust me, maiden.

SHE: And wherefore sighest thou, sad soldier?

HE: Verily for thy two reasons. Though, for mine age, I am not forty turned.

Saying which, he sighed again, and stared gloomily into the murmurous waters. But presently, chancing to look aside, he beheld a head low down amid the underwood, a head huge and hairy with small, fierce eyes that watched him right bodefully, and a great mouth that grinned evilly; and now as he stared, amazed by this monstrous head, it nodded grimly, speaking thus:

"Lob, Lobkyn he
Commandeth thee
To let her be
And set her free,
Thou scurvy, cutpurse, outlaw knave,
Lest hanged thou be
Upon a tree
For roguery
And villainy,
Thou knavish, misbegotten slave;
For proud is she
Of high degree,
As unto ye
Explicitly—"

"Ha! " quoth Sir Pertinax, rising and drawing sword. "Now, be thou imp of Satan, fiend accursed, or goblin fell, come forth, and I with steel will try thee, Thing! "

Out from the leaves forthwith crawled a dwarf bowed of leg, mighty of shoulder, humped of back, and with arms very long and thick and hairy. In one great fist he grasped a ponderous club shod with iron spikes, and now, resting his hands on this and his chin on his hands, he scowled at the Knight, yet grinned also.

"Ho! " he cried, rolling big head in threatening fashion:

"Vile dog, thy rogue's sconce cracked shall be, Thy base-born bones be-thwacked shall be. I'll deal thee many a dour ding For that thou darest name me—Thing! "

"Now, as I live! " said Sir Pertinax, scowling also. "Here will I, and with great joyance, cleave me thine impish mazzard and split thee to thy beastly chine. And for thy ill rhyming:

"I with this goodly steel will halve thee
And into clammy goblets carve thee.
So stand, Thing, to thy club betake thee,
And soon, Thing, I will no-thing make thee. "

But, as they closed on each other with eager and deadly intent, the maid stepped lightly betwixt.

"Stay, soldier—hold! " she commanded. "Here is none but Lobkyn Lollo—poor, brave Lob, nor will I suffer him to harm thee. "

"How, maiden? " snorted the good Knight fiercely. "Harm me, say'st thou—yon puny Thing? "

"Truly, soldier! " said she, roguish-eyed. "For though thou art very ungentle, harsh of tongue, of visage grim and manners rude—I would not have Lob harm thee—yet! "

Now hereupon our bold Sir Pertinax
With indignation red of face did wax.
The needful word his tongue was vainly seeking,
Since what he felt was quite beyond the speaking.
Though quick his hand to ward or give a blow,
His tongue all times unready was and slow,
Therefore he speechless looked upon the maid,
Who viewed him 'neath her lashes' dusky shade,
Whence Eros launched a sudden beamy dart
That 'spite chain-mail did reach and pierce his heart.
And in that instant Pertinax grew wise,
And trembled 'neath this forest-maiden's eyes;
And trembling, knew full well, seek where he might,
No eyes might hold for him such magic light,
No lips might hold for him such sweet allure,
No other hand might his distresses cure,
No other voice might so console and cheer,
No foot, light-treading, be so sweet to hear

The Geste of Duke Jocelyn

As the eyes, lips, hand, voice, foot of her who stood
Before him now, cheek flushing 'neath her hood.
All this Sir Pertinax had in his thought,
And, wishing much to say to her, said nought,
By reason that his tongue was something slow,
And of smooth phrases he did little know.
But yet 't is likely, though he nothing said,
She, maid-like, what he spake not, guessed or read
In his flushed brow, his sudden-gentle eyes,
Since in such things all maids are wondrous wise.

Now suddenly the brawny Dwarf did cry:
"Beware, my old great-grand-dam creepeth nigh! "
Thus speaking, 'mid the bushes pointed he,
Where crook'd old woman crouched beneath a tree
Whence, bowed upon a staff, she towards them came,
An ancient, wrinkled, ragged, hag-like dame
With long, sharp nose that downward curved as though
It fain would, beak-like, peck sharp chin below.
Mutt'ring she came and mowing she drew near,
And straightway seized the Dwarf by hairy ear:
Fast by the ear this ancient dame did tweak him,
And cuffed his head and, cuffing, thus did speak him:

"Ha, dolt! Bad elf, and wilt thou slay, indeed,
This goodly man did aid me in my need?
For this was one that fought within the gate
And from Black Lewin saved thy grannam's pate!
Down, down, fool-lad, upon thy knees, I say,
And full forgiveness of this soldier pray. "

But Sir Pertinax, perceiving how the old dame
did thus tweak and wring at the Dwarf's great,
hairy ear even until his eyes watered, interceded,
saying:

"Good, ancient soul, humble not the sturdy, unlovely,
mis-shapen, rascally imp for such small
matter. "

"Nay, but, " croaked the old woman, tightening
claw-like fingers, "kind master, he would doubtless
have slain thee. " At this, Sir Pertinax scowled,

and would have sworn great oath but, meeting the
maid's bright eyes, checked himself, though with
much ado:

"Art so sure, " he questioned, "so sure man of
my inches may be slain by thing so small? "

At this the maid laughed, and the old woman,
sighing, loosed the ear she clutched:

"Shew thy strength, Lob, " she commanded and,
drawing the maiden out of ear-shot, sat down beside
her on the sward and fell to eager, whispered talk.
Meantime the Dwarf, having cherished his ear,
sulkily though tenderly, seized hold upon his great
club with both hairy hands:

And whirling it aloft, with sudden might
A fair, young tree in sunder he did smite,
That 'neath the blow it swayed and crashing fell.
Quoth Pertinax: "Good Thing, 't is very well.
Par Dex, and by the Holy Rood, " quoth he,
"'T is just as well that I was not yon tree! "
And whirling his long sword as thus he spoke,
Shore through another at a single stroke.
"Here's tree for tree, stout manling! " he did say.
"What other trick canst show to me, I pray? "
Then Lobkyn stooped the broken stump to seize,
Bowed brawny back and with a wondrous ease

Up by the roots the rugged bole he tore
And tossed it far as it had been a straw.
Sad grew our knight this mighty feat perceiving,
Since well he knew't was past his own achieving.

But anon he smiled and clapped the mighty Dwarf on shoulder,
saying:

"Greeting to thee, lusty Lob, for by Our Holy Lady of Shene Chapel
within the Wood, ne'er saw I thine equal, since thou, being man so
small, may do what man o' my goodly inches may nowise perform.
Thou should'st make a right doughty man-at-arms! "

Hereupon the Dwarf cut a caper but sighed thereafter: quoth he:

"Aha, good master, and Oho,
As man-at-arms fain would I go;
Aye, verily, I would be so,
But that my grannam sayeth 'No! '

"And, sir, my grand-dam I obey
Since she's a potent witch, they say;
Can cast ye spells by night or day
And charmeth warts and such away.

"Love philtres too she can supply
For fools that fond and foolish sigh,
That wert thou foul as hog in sty
Fair women must unto thee fly.

"Then deadly potions she can make,
Will turn a man to wriggling snake,
Or slimy worm, or duck, or drake,
Or loathly frog that croaks in lake.

"And she can curse beyond compare,
Can curse ye here, or curse ye there;
She'll curse ye clad or curse ye bare,
In fine, can curse ye anywhere.

"And she can summon, so 't is said,
From fire and water, spirits dread,
Strong charms she hath can wake the dead
And set the living in their stead.

"So thus it is, whate'er she say,
My grand-dam, master, I obey. "

"Now by my head, " quoth Sir Pertinax, "an thy grand-dam hath a
potency in spells and such black arts—the which is an ill thing—thou
hast a powerful gift of versification the which, methinks, is worse.
How cometh this distemper o' the tongue, Lobkyn? "

"O master, " spake the sighful Dwarf forlorn,
"Like many such diseases, 't is inborn.
For even as a baby, I

Did pule in rhyme and versify;
And the stronger that I grew,
My rhyming habit strengthened too,
Until my sad sire in despair
Put me beneath the Church's care.
The holy fathers, 't is confessed,
With belt and sandal did their best,
But, though they often whipped me sore,
I, weeping, did but rhyme the more,
Till, finding all their efforts vain,
They sadly sent me home again. "

"A parlous case, methinks! " said Sir Pertinax, staring at the Dwarf's rueful visage. "Learned ye aught of the holy fathers? "

"Aye, sir, they taught me truth to tell,
To cipher and to read right well;
They taught me Latin, sir, and Greek,
Though even then in rhyme I'd speak. "

"And thou canst read and write! " exclaimed Sir Pertinax. "So can not I! "

Cried LOB:

"What matter that? Heaven save the mark,
Far better be a soldier than a clerk,
Far rather had I be a fighter
Than learned reader or a writer,
Since they who'd read must mope in schools,
And they that write be mostly fools.
So 'stead of pen give me a sword,
And set me where the battle's toward,
Where blood—"

But the ancient dame who had risen and approached silently, now very suddenly took Lobkyn by the ear again.

"Talk not of blood and battles, naughty one! " she cried. "Think not to leave thy old grannam lone and lorn and helpless—nor this our fair maid. Shame on thee, Lob, O shame! " saying the which she cuffed him again and
soundly.

59

"Master, " he sighed, "thou seest I may not go,
Since that my grand-dam will not have it so. "

"Good mother, wise mother, " said the maid, viewing Sir Pertinax smilingly askance, "why doth poor soldier go bedight in fine linen 'neath rusty hauberk? Why doth poor soldier wear knightly chain about his neck and swear by knightly oath? Good mother, wise mother, rede me this. "

The old woman viewed Pertinax with her bright, quick eyes, but, ere she could answer, he sheathed sword, drew ragged mantle about him, and made to go, but, turning to the maid, bent steel-clad head.

"Most fair damosel, " said he gently, "evening cometh on, and now, since thou art no longer forlorn, I will away. "

"Nay, first, I pray thee, what is thy name? "

"Pertinax, madam. "

"So then doth Melissa thank Pertinax. And now—out alas! Will Pertinax leave Melissa, having but found her? "

Sir Pertinax looked up, looked down, fidgeted with his cloak, and knew not how to answer; wherefore she sighed again, though with eyes full merry 'neath drooping lashes and reached out to him her slender hand. "Aye me, and shall we meet no more, poor soldier? " she questioned softly.

"This I know not, " he answered.

"For thy brave rescue I do give thee my humble thanks, poor soldier. "

"Thy rescue, child? " cried the old woman. "Alack and wert thou seen? Thy rescue, say'st thou? "

"Indeed, good mother, from Sir Agramore's rough foresters. But for thee, thou needy soldier, my gratitude is thine henceforth. Had I aught else to give thee, that were thine also. Is there aught I may? Speak. "

Now Sir Pertinax could not but heed all the rich, warm beauty of her—these eyes so sombrely sweet, her delicate nose, the temptation of her vivid lips—and so spake hot with impulse:

"Aye, truly, sweet maid, truly I would have of thee a—" Her eyes grew bright with laughter, a dimple played wanton in her cheek, and Sir Pertinax was all suddenly abashed, faint-hearted and unsure; thus, looking down, he chanced to espy a strange jewel that hung tremulous upon her moving bosom: a crowned heart within a heart of crystal.

"Well, thou staid and sorry soldier, what would'st have of me? " she questioned.

"Verily, " he muttered, "I would have of thee yon trinket from thy bosom. " Now at his words she started, caught her breath and stared at him wide-eyed; but, seeing his abashment, laughed and loosed off the jewel with quick, small fingers.

"Be it so! " said she. But hereupon the old woman reached out sudden hand.

"Child! " she croaked, "Art mad? Mind ye not the prophecy? Beware the prophecy—beware!

'He that taketh Crystal Heart,
Taketh all and every part! '

Beware, I say, Oh, beware! "

"Nay, good mother, have I not promised? And for this crystal it hath brought me nought but unease hitherto. Take it, soldier, and for the sake of this poor maid that giveth, break it not, dishonour it not, and give it to none but can define for thee the secret thereof—and so, poor, brave, fearful soldier—fare thee well! "

Saying which this fair maiden turned, and clasping the Witch's bony arm about her slender loveliness, passed away into the denser wood with Lobkyn Lollo marching grimly behind, his mighty club across his shoulder.

Long stood Sir Pertinax, staring down at the strange jewel in his hand yet seeing it not, for, lost in his dreams, he beheld again two eyes, dusky-lashed and softly bright, a slender hand, a shapelyfoot, while in his ears was again the soft murmur of a maid's voice, a trill of girlish laughter. So lost in meditation was he that becoming aware of a shadow athwart the level sunset-glory, he started, glanced up and into the face of a horseman who had ridden up unheard upon the velvet ling; and this man was tall and armed at points like a knight; the vizor of his plumed casque was lifted, and Sir Pertinax saw a ruddy face, keen-eyed, hawk-nosed, thin-lipped.

"Fellow," questioned the haughty knight, "what hold ye there?"

"Fellow," quoth Sir Pertinax, haughty and gruff also, "'t is no matter to thee!" And speaking, he buttoned the jewel into the wallet at his belt.

"Fool!" exclaimed the Knight, staring in amaze, "wilt dare name me 'fellow'? Tell me, didst see three foresters hereabout?"

"Poltroon, I did."

"Knave, wilt defy me?"

"Rogue, I do!"

"Slave, what did these foresters?"

"Villain, they ran away!"

"Ha, varlet! and wherefore?"

"Caitiff, I drubbed them shrewdly."

"Dared ye withstand them, dog?"

"Minion, I did."

"Saw ye not the badge they bore?" demanded the fierce stranger-knight.

"'T was the like of that upon thy shield!" nodded Sir Pertinax grimly.

"Know ye who and what I am, dunghill rogue?"

The Geste of Duke Jocelyn

"No, dog's-breakfast—nor care! " growled Sir Pertinax, whereat the stranger-knight grew sudden red and clenched mailed fist.

"Know then, thou kennel-scourer, that I am Sir

Agramore of Biename, Lord of Swanscote and Hoccom, Lord Seneschal of Tissingors and the March. "

"Ha! " quoth Sir Pertinax, scowling. "So do I know thee for a very rogue ingrain and villain manifest. "

"How! " roared Sir Agramore. "This to my face, thou vile creeper of ditches, thou unsavoury tavern-haunter—this in my teeth! "

"Heartily, heartily! " nodded Sir Pertinax. "And may it choke thee for the knavish carcass thou art. "

At this, and very suddenly, the Knight loosed mace from saddle-bow, and therewith smote Sir Pertinax on rusty bascinet, and tumbled him backward among the bracken. Which done, Sir Agramore laughed full loud and, spurring his charger, galloped furiously away. And after some while Sir Pertinax arose, albeit unsteadily, but finding his legs weak, sat him down again; thereafter with fumbling hands he did off dinted bascinet and viewed it thoughtfully, felt his head tenderly and, crawling to the stream, bathed it solicitously; then, being greatly heartened, he arose and drawing sword, set it upright in the ling and, kneeling, clasped his hands and spake as follows:

"Here and now, upon my good cross-hilt I swear I will with joy and zeal unremitting, seek me out one Sir Agramore of Biename. Then will I incontinent with any, all, or whatsoever weapon he chooseth fall upon him and, for this felon stroke, for his ungentle dealing with the maid, I will forthwith gore, rend, tear, pierce, batter, bruise and otherwise use the body of the said Sir Agramore until, growing aweary of its vile tenement, his viler soul shall flee hence to consume evermore with such unholy knaves as he. And this is the oath of me, Sir Pertinax,

Knight of Shene, Lord of Westover, Framling, Bracton and Deepdene, to the which oath may the Saints bend gracious ear, in especial Our Holy Lady of Shene Chapel within the Wood—Amen! "

Having registered the which most solemn oath, Sir Pertinax arose, sheathed his sword, and strode blithely towards the fair and prosperous town of Canalise. But, being come within the gate, he was aware of much riot and confusion in the square and streets beyond, and hasting forward, beheld a wild concourse, a pushing, jostling throng of people making great clamour and outcry, above which hubbub ever and anon rose such shouts, as:
"Murderer! Thief! Away with him! Death to him! "

By dint of sharp elbow and brawny shoulder our good knight forced himself a way until—surrounded by men-at-arms, his limbs fast bound, his motley torn and bloody, his battered fool's-cap all awry— he beheld Duke Jocelyn haled and dragged along by fierce hands. For a moment Sir Pertinax stood dumb with horror and amaze, then, roaring, clapped hand to sword. Now, hearing this fierce and well-known battle shout, Duke Jocelyn turned and, beholding the Knight, shook bloody head in warning and slowly closed one bright, blue eye; and so, while Sir Pertinax stood rigid and dumb, was dragged away and lost in the fierce, jostling throng.

My daughter GILLIAN propoundeth:

GILL: Father, when you began this Geste, I thought
It was a poem of a sort.

MYSELF: A sort, Miss Pert! A sort, indeed?

GILL: Of course—the sort folks love to read.
But in the last part we have heard
Of poetry there's scarce a word.

MYSELF: My dear, if you the early Geste-books read,
You'll find that, oft as not, indeed,
The wearied Gestours, when by rhyming stumped,
Into plain prose quite often jumped.

GILL: But, father, dear, the last part seems to me
All prose—as prosy as can be—

MYSELF: Ha, prosy, miss! How, do you then suggest
Our Geste for you lacks interest?

GILL: Not for a moment, father, though

Sir Pertinax was much too slow.
When fair Melissa "laughing stood, "
He should have kissed—you know he
should—Because, of course, she wished him to.

MYSELF: Hum! Girl, I wonder if that's true?

GILL: O father, yes! Of course I'm right,
And you're as slow as your slow knight.
Were you as slow when you were young?

MYSELF: Hush, madam! Hold that saucy tongue.
You may be sure, in my young days,
I was most dutiful always.
Grown up, I was, it seems to me,
No slower than I ought to be.
And now, miss, since you pine for verse,
Rhyme with my prose I'll intersperse;
And, like a doting father, I
To hold your interest will try.

FYTTE 5

Which of Duke Joc'lyn's woeful plight doth tell,
And all that chanced him pent in dungeon cell.

* * * * *

In gloomy dungeon, scant of air and light,
Duke Joc'lyn lay in sad and woeful plight;
His hands and feet with massy fetters bound,
That clashed, whene'er he moved, with dismal sound;
His back against the clammy wall did rest,
His heavy head was bowed upon his breast,
But, 'neath drawn brows, he watched with wary eye
Three ragged 'wights who, shackled, lay hard by,
Three brawny rogues who, scowling, fiercely eyed him,
And with lewd gibes and mocking gestures plied him.
But Joc'lyn, huddled thus against the wall,
Seemed verily to heed them none at all,
Wherefore a red-haired rogue who thought he slept
With full intent upon him furtive crept.
But, ere he knew, right suddenly he felt
Duke Joc'lyn's battered shoe beneath his belt;
And falling back with sudden strangled cry,
Flat on his back awhile did breathless lie,
Whereat to rage his comrades did begin,
And clashed their fetters with such doleful din
That from a corner dim a fourth man sprang,
And laughed and laughed, until their prison rang.
"Well kicked, Sir Fool! Forsooth, well done! " laughed he,
"Ne'er saw I, Fool, a fool the like o' thee! "

Now beholding this tall fellow, Jocelyn knew him
for that same forest-rogue had wrestled with him
in the green, and sung for his life the "Song of
Roguery. " Wherefore he smiled on the fellow and
the fellow on him:

Quoth JOCELYN: I grieve to see
A man like thee
In such a woeful plight—

Quoth the ROGUE: A Fool in fetters,
Like his betters,
Is yet a rarer sight.

"Ha i' the clout, good fellow, for Folly in fetters is Folly in need, and Folly in need is Folly indeed! But, leaving folly awhile, who art thou and what thy name? "

Saith the ROGUE: Robin I'm named, Sir Fool,
Rob by the few,
Which few are right, methinks, for
so I do.

"Then, Rob, if dost rob thou'rt a robber, and being robber thou'rt perchance in bonds for robbing, Robin? "

"Aye, Fool, I, Rob, do rob and have robbed greater robbers that I might by robbery live to rob like robbers again, as thou, by thy foolish folly, fooleries make, befooling fools lesser than thou, that thou, Fool, by such fool-like fooleries may live to fool like fools again! "

Quoth JOCELYN: Thou robber Rob,
By Hob and Gob,
Though robber-rogue, I swear
That 't is great pity
Rogue so pretty
Must dance upon thin air.

Quoth ROBIN: Since I must die
On gallows high
And wriggle in a noose,
I'll none repine
Nor weep nor whine,
For where would be the use?
Yet sad am I
That I must die
With rogues so base and small,
Sly coney-catchers,
Poor girdle-snatchers,
That do in kennel crawl.

"And yet, " said Jocelyn, "thou thyself art rogue and thief confessed. How then art better than these thy fellows? "

"By degree, Sir Fool. Even as thou'rt Fool o' folly uncommon, so am I no ordinary rogue, being rogue o' rare parts with power of rogues i' the wild wood, while these be but puny rogues of no parts soever. "

"No rogues are we! " the three did loudly cry,

"But sad, poor souls, that perishing do lie! "

  "In me, " quoth one, "behold a man of worth,
By trade a dyer and yclepen Gurth;
In all this world no man, howe'er he try,
Could live a life so innocent as I! "

The second spake: "I am the ploughman Rick,
That ne'er harmed man or woman, maid or chick!
But here in direful dungeon doomed be I,
Yet cannot tell the wherefore nor the why. "

Then spake Red-head, albeit gasping still:
"An honest tanner I, my name is Will;
'T was me thou kickedst, Fool, in such ill manner,
Of crimes unjust accused—and I, a tanner! "
Here Joc'lyn smiled. "Most saintly rogues, " said he;
"The Saints, methinks, were rogues compared with ye,
And one must needs in prison come who'd find
The noblest, worthiest, best of all mankind.
Poor, ill-used knaves, to lie in dungeon pent,
Rogues sin-less quite, and eke so innocent,
What though your looks another tale do tell,
Since I'm your fellow, fellows let us dwell,
For if ye're rogues that thus in bonds do lie,
So I'm a rogue since here in bonds am I,
Thus I, a rogue, do hail ye each a brother,
Like brethren, then, we 'll comfort one another. "

Thus spake Jocelyn, whereafter these "saintly rogues" all three grew mightily peevish and, withal, gloomy, while Robin laughed and laughed at them, nodding head and wagging finger.

"Prithee, good Motley, " he questioned, "what should bring so rare a Fool to lie in dungeon fettered and gyved along of innocent rogues and roguish robber? "

Whereto Duke Jocelyn answered on this wise:
"Hast heard, belike, of Gui the Red? "
(Here went there up a howl)
"A mighty lord of whom't is said,
That few do love and many dread. "
(Here went there up a growl)

"This potent lord I chanced to view,
Behaving as no lord should do,
And thereupon, this lord I threw
In pretty, plashing pool!

"Whereon this dreadful lord did get
Exceeding wroth and very wet;
Wherefore in dungeon here I'm set,
For fierce and froward Fool. "

Here went there up a shout of glee.
Cried Robin: "O sweet Fool,
I would I had been there to see
This haughty lord of high degree
In pretty, plashing pool. "

Here shout of glee became a roar,
That made the dungeon ring;
They laughed, they rolled upon the floor,
Till suddenly the massy door
On creaking hinge did swing;
And to them the head jailer now appeared,
A sombre man who sighed through tangled beard.

"How now, rogue-lads, " said he, "grow ye merry in sooth by reason o' this Fool! Aye me, all men do grow merry save only I, Ranulph, Chief Torturer, Ranulph o' the Keys, o' the Gibbet, o' the City Axe— poor Ranulph the Headsman. Good lack! I've cut off the head o' many a man merrier than I— aye, that have I, and more's the pity! And now, ye that are to die so soon can wax joyous along o' this motley Fool! Why, 't is a manifest good Fool, and rare singer o' songs, 't is said, though malapert, with no respect for his betters and over-quick at dagger-play. So 't is a Fool must die and sing no more, and there's the pity on't for I do love a song, I—being a companionable soul and jovial withal, aye, a very bawcock of a boy, I. To-morrow Red Gui doth hale ye to his Castle o' the Rock, there to die all five for his good pleasure, as is very fitting and proper, so be merry whiles ye may. Meantime, behold here another rogue, a youngling imp. So is five become six, and six may laugh louder than five, methinks, so laugh your best. "

Then Ranulph o' the Keys sighed, closed the great door and went his way, leaving the new captive to their mercies. Fair he was and slender, and of a timid seeming, for now he crouched against the wall, his face hid 'neath the hood of ragged mantle; wherefore the "saintly" three incontinent scowled upon him, roared at him and made a horrid clashing with their fetters:

"Ha, blood and bones! " cried Rick the Ploughman. "What murderous babe art thou to go unshackled in presence o' thy betters? "

"Aye, forsooth, " growled Will the Tanner, "who 'rt thou to come hither distressing the last hours o' we poor, perishing mortals? Discourse, lest I bite the heart o' thee! "

"Pronounce, imp! " roared Gurth the Dyer, "lest I tear thy liver! "

"Sit ye, here beside me, youth, " said Jocelyn, "and presently thou shalt know these tearers of livers and biters of hearts for lambs of innocence and doves of gentleness—by their own confessions. For, remark now, gentle boy, all we are prisoners and therefore guiltless of every offence—indeed, where is the prisoner, but who, according to himself, is not more sinned against than sinner, and where the convicted rogue but, with his tongue, shall disprove all men's testimony? So here sit three guileless men, spotless of soul and beyond all thought innocent of every sin soever. Yonder is Rob, a robber, and here sit I, a Fool. "

"Ha! " cried Rick. "Yet murderous Fool art thou and apt to dagger-play! Belike hast slain a man this day in way o' folly—ha? "

"Two! " answered Jocelyn, nodding. "These two had been more but that my dagger brake. "

Here was silence awhile what time Jocelyn hummed the line of a song and his companions eyed him with looks askance.

"Why then, good Folly, " said Rick at last, "'t is for a little spilling o' blood art here, a little, pretty business o' murder—ha? "

"'T is so they name it, " answered Jocelyn.

"Bones o' me! " growled Will, "I do begin to love this Fool. "

"And didst pronounce thyself our brother, Fool? " questioned Gurth.

"Aye, verily! "

"Then brethren let us be henceforth, and comrades to boot! " cried Rick. "Jolly Clerks o' Saint Nicholas to share and share alike—ha? So then 't is accorded. And now what o' yon lily-livered imp? 'T is a sickly youth and I love him not. But he hath a cloak, look'ee—a cloak forsooth and poor Rick's a-cold! Ho, lad—throw me thy cloak! "

"Beshrew me! " roared Gurth. "But he beareth belt and wallet! Ha, boy, give thy wallet and girdle—bestow! "

"And by sweet Saint Nick, " growled Will, "the dainty youngling disporteth himself to mine eyes in a gold finger-ring! Aha, boy! Give now thy trinket unto an honest tanner. "

Hereupon and with one accord up started the three, fierce-eyed; but Jocelyn, laughing, rose up also.

"Back, corpses! " quoth he, swinging the heavy fetters to and fro between shackled wrists. "Stand, good Masters Dry-bones; of what avail cloak, or wallet, or ring to ye that are dead men? Now, since corpses ye are insomuch as concerneth this world, be ye reasonable and kindly corpses. Sit ye then, Masters Dust-and-Ashes, and I will incontinent sing ye, chant or intone ye a little song of organs and graves and the gallows-tree whereon we must dance anon; as, hearken:

"Sing a song of corpses three
That ere long shall dancing be,
On the merry gallows-tree—
High and low,

To and fro,
Leaping, skipping,
Turning, tripping,
Wriggling, whirling,
Twisting, twirling:
Sing hey for the gallows-tree. "

"Stint—stint thy beastly song now! " cried Will, pale of cheek. But Jocelyn sang the louder:

"Sing a song of dying groans,
Sing a song of cries and moans,
Sing a song of dead men's bones,
That shall rest,
All unblest,
To rot and rot,
Remembered not,
For dogs to gnaw
And battle for,
Sing hey for the dead rogue's bones. "

"Abate—ha—abate thy fiendish rant! " cried Rick, glancing fearfully over shoulder.

"Aye, Fool—beseech thee! Fair flesh may not abide it! " cried Gurth, shivering, while Robin grinned no more and the fearful youth leaned wide-eyed to behold the singer, this strange, scarred face beneath its battered cock's-comb, these joyous eyes, these smiling lips as Jocelyn continued:

"Now ends my song with ghosts forlorn,
Three gibbering ghosts that mope and mourn,
Then shrieking, flee at breath of dawn,
Where creatures fell
In torment dwell,
Blind things and foul,
That creep and howl,
That rend and bite
And claw and fight.
Where fires red-hot
Consume them not,
And they in anguish
Writhe and languish

And groan in pain
For night again.
Sing hey for pale ghosts forlorn. "

Now when the song was ended, the three looked dismally on one
another and, bethinking them of their cruel end, they groaned and
sighed lamentably:

My daughter GILLIAN interposeth:

    GILL: Father, I like that song, it's fine;
    But let me ask about this line:
    "Blind things and foul,
    That creep and howl. "
    Now tell me, please, if you don't mind,
    Why were the little horrors blind?

    MYSELF: The beastly things, as I surmise,
    Had scratched out one another's eyes.

    GILL:
    I suppose this place where creatures fell
    In torments dwell is meant for—

    MYSELF:
    Well,
    I think, my Gill, the place you've guessed,
    So let me get on with our Geste.

... they groaned and sighed lamentably—

My daughter GILLIAN interjecteth:

    GILL: Father—now don't get in a huff—
    But don't you think they've groaned enough?

    MYSELF: My Gillian—no! Leave well alone;
    This is the place for them to groan.

    Lamentably they did together moan,
    And uttered each full many a hollow groan.

My daughter GILLIAN interposeth:

> GILL: But, father, groans are so distressing,
> And groans in verse are most depressing—

> MYSELF:
> Then peace, child, and in common prose
> I'll let the poor rogues vent their woes:

... they groaned and they sighed lamentably—

My daughter GILLIAN interrupteth:

> GILL: What, father, are they groaning still?

> MYSELF:
> Of course they are, and so they will,
> And so shall I; so, girl, take heed,
> And cease their groaning to impede.
> Is it agreed?

> GILL: Oh, yes, indeed!

> MYSELF: Then with our Geste I will proceed.

... they groaned and sighed lamentably.

"Alack! " cried Gurth, "I had not greatly minded till now, but this vile-tongued Fool hath stirred Fear to wakefulness within me. Here's me, scarce thirty turned, hale and hearty, yet must die woefully and with a maid as do love me grievously! "

"And me! " groaned Rick. "No more than twenty and five, I—a very lad—and with two maids as do languish for me fain and fond! "

"Ha, and what o' me? " mourned dismal, redheaded Will. "A lusty, proper fellow I be and wi' maids a score as do sigh continual. And me to die—O woe! And I a tanner! "

"Content ye, brothers! " said Jocelyn. "Look now, here's Gurth hath lived but thirty years, and now must die—good: so shall he die weighted with less of sin than had he lived thirty more. Be ye comforted in this, distressful rogues, the shorter our life the less we sin, the which is a fair, good thing. As for these shackles, though our bodies be 'prisoned our souls go free, thus, while we languish here, our souls astride a sunbeam may mount aloft, 'bove all pains and tribulations soever. Thus if we must dance together in noose, our souls, I say, escaping these fleshy bonds, shall wing away to freedom everlasting. Bethink ye of this, grievous knaves, and take heart. Regarding the which same truths I will, for thy greater comforting, incontinent make ye a song—hearken!

"Let Folly sing a song to cheer
All poor rogues that languish here,
Doomed in dismal dungeon drear,
Doomed in dungeon dim.

"Though flesh full soon beneath the sod
Doth perish and decay,
Though cherished body is but clod,
Yet in his soul man is a God,
To do and live alway.
So hence with gloom and banish fear,
Come Mirth and Jollity,
Since, though we pine in dungeon drear,
Though these, our bodies, languish here,
We in our minds go free. "

Thus cheerily sang Jocelyn until, chancing to see how the youth leaned forward great-eyed, watching as he sung, he broke off to question him blithely:

"How now, good youth, hast a leaning to Folly e'en though Folly go fettered, and thyself in dungeon? "

"Fool, " answered the youth, soft-voiced, "me-thinks 't is strange Folly can sing thus in chains! Hast thou no fear of death? "

"Why truly I love it no more than my fellow-fools. But I, being fool uncommon, am wise enough to know that Death, howsoe'er he come, may come but once—and there's a comfortable thought! "

So saying, Jocelyn seated himself beside the youth and watched him keen-eyed.

"And thou canst sing of Freedom, Fool, to the jangle of thy fetters? "

"Truly, youth, 't is but my baser part lieth shackled, thus while body pineth here, soul walketh i' the kindly sun—aye, e'en now as I do gaze on thee, I, in my thought, do stand in a fair garden—beside a lily-pool, where she I love cometh shy-footed to meet me, tall and gracious and sweet, as her flowers. A dream, belike, yet in this dream she looketh on me with eyes of love and love is on her lips and in her heart—so is my dream very precious. "

At this, the youth shrank beneath his cloak while in an adjacent corner the three rolled dice with Robin and quarrelled hoarse and loud.

"Youth, " said Jocelyn, "I pray thee, tell me thy name. "

Without lifting head the youth answered:

"Hugo! "

"Look up, Hugo! " But Hugo bowed his head the lower.

"Hast wondrous hair, Hugo—red gold 'neath thy hood! "

Here came a slim, white hand to order the rebellious tress but, finding none, trembled and hid itself. Then very suddenly Jocelyn leaned near and caught this hand, clasping it fast yet with fingers very gentle, and spake quick and eager:

"Hugo—alas, Hugo! What bringeth thee in this evil place? Art in danger? Speak, speak! "

"Nay, here is no harm for me, Joconde. And I am hither come for sake of a poor Fool that is braver than the bravest—one did jeopardise his foolish life for sake of a maid, wherefore I, Hugo, do give him life. Take now this wallet, within is good store of gold and better—a potent charm to close all watchful eyes. Hist, Joconde, and mark me well! Ranulph o' the Axe is a mighty drinker—to-night, drawn by fame of thy wit, he cometh with his fellows. This money shall buy them wine, in the wine cast this powder so shall they sleep and thou go free. "

"Aye! " said Jocelyn, "and then? "

76

"There will meet thee a dwarf shall free thee of thy fetters, and by secret ways set thee without the city—then, tarry not, but flee for thy life—"

"Now by the Holy Rood! " quoth Jocelyn softly, "never in all this world was there prisoner so happy as this poor Fool! But, Hugo, an I win free by reason of a brave and noble lady, so long as she bide in Canalise, so long must I—"

My daughter GILLIAN interposeth:

GILL: O, father, now I understand—
Of course, this Hugo is Yolande!

MYSELF: Exactly, miss, the fact is clear;
But how on earth did she get here?
I don't want her here—

GILL: Why not?

MYSELF: Because, being here, she spoils my plot,
Which would drive any author frantic—

GILL: I think it's fine, and most romantic.
Besides, you know, you wrote her there—

MYSELF: She came—before I was aware—

GILL: She couldn't, father, for just think,
You've made her all of pen and ink.
So you, of course, can make her do
Exactly as you want her to.

MYSELF: Dear innocent! You little know
The trials poor authors undergo.
How heroines, when they break loose,
Are apt to play the very deuce,
Dragging their authors to and fro,
And where he wills—they will not go.

GILL: Well, since she's here, please let her be,
She wants to set Duke Joc'lyn free.

MYSELF: Enough—enough, my plans are made,
I'll set him free without her aid,
And in a manner, I apprise you,
As will, I fancy, quite surprise you.
Besides, a dungeon no fit place is
For a dainty lady's graces.
So, since she's in, 't is very plain
I now must get her out again.

"To bide in Canalise, 't is folly! " cried Hugo. "O, 't were a madness fond! "

"Aye, " sighed Jocelyn, "some do call love a madness—thus mad am I, forsooth! "

"Hush! " whispered Hugo, as from without came the tramp of heavy feet. "Fare-thee-well and—ah, be not mad, Joconde! "

The door creaked open, and six soldiers entered bringing a prisoner, chained and fettered, and therewith fast bound and gagged, whom they set ungently upon the stone floor; then straightway seizing upon Robin, they haled him to his feet.

"Come, rogue, " said one, "thou art to hang at cockcrow! " "Is't so, good fellows? " quoth Robin,

"Then cock be curst
That croweth first!

As for thee, good Motley, peradventure when, by hangman's noose, our souls enfranchised go, they shall company together, thine and mine! Till then —farewell, Folly! "

So Robin was led forth of the dungeon and the heavy door crashed shut; but when Jocelyn looked for Hugo—lo! he was gone also.

Evening was come and the light began to fail, therefore Jocelyn crouched beneath the narrow loophole and taking from his bosom the wallet, found therein good store of money together with the charm or philtre: and bowing his head above this little wallet, he fell to profound meditation.

But presently, roused by hoarse laughter, he glanced up to find the three plaguing the helpless prisoner with sundry kicks and buffets;

so Jocelyn crossed the dungeon, and putting the tormentors aside, stood amazed to behold in this latest captive none other than Sir Pertinax. Straightway he loosed off the gag, whereupon the good knight incontinent swore a gasping oath and prayed his limbs might be loosed also; the which done, he forthwith sprang up, and falling on the astonished three, he beat and clouted them with fist and manacles, and drave them to and fro about the dungeon.

"Ha, dogs! Wilt spurn me with they vile feet, buffet me with thy beastly hands, forsooth! " roared he and kicked and cuffed them so that they, thinking him mad, cried aloud in fear until Sir Pertinax, growing a-weary, seated himself against the wall, and folding his arms, scowled indignant upon Jocelyn who greeted him merrily:

"Hail and greeting to thee, my Pertinax; thy gloomy visage is a joy! "

Sir Pertinax snorted, but spake not; wherefore the Duke questioned him full blithe: "What fair, good wind hath blown thee dungeon-wards, sweet soul? "

"Ha! " quoth the knight. "Fetters, see'st thou, a dungeon, and these foul knaves for company—the which cometh of thy fool's folly, messire! So prithee ha' done with it! "

"Stay, gentle gossip, thou'rt foolish, methinks; thou frettest 'gainst fate, thou kickest unwisely 'gainst the pricks, thou ragest pitifully 'gainst circumstance—in fine, thou'rt a very Pertinax, my Pertinax! "

"Aye troth, that am I and no dog to lie thus chained in noisome pit, par Dex! So let us out, messire, and that incontinent! "

"Why here is a bright thought, sweet lad, let us out forthwith—but how? "

"Summon the town-reeve, messire, the burgesses, the council, declare thy rank, so shall we go free—none shall dare hold thus a prince of thy exalted state and potent might! Declare thyself, lord. "

"This were simple matter, Pertinax, but shall they believe us other than we seem, think ye? "

Quoth Pertinax: "We can try! "

"Verily, " said Jocelyn, "this very moment! " So saying, he turned to the three who sat in a corner muttering together.

"Good brothers, gentle rogues, " said he, "behold and regard well this sturdy cut-throat fellow that sitteth beside me, big of body, unseemly of habit, fierce and unlovely of look—one to yield the wall unto, see ye! And yet—now heed me well, this fellow, ragged and unkempt, this ill-looking haunter of bye-ways, this furtive snatcher of purses (hold thy peace, Pertinax!). I say this unsavoury-seeming clapper-claw is yet neither one nor other, but a goodly knight, famous in battle, joust and tourney, a potent lord of noble heritage, known to the world as Sir Pertinax of Shene Castle and divers rich manors and demesnes. Furthermore, I that do seem a sorry jesting-fellow, I that in antic habit go, that cut ye capers with ass's ears a-dangle and languish here your fellow in bonds, am yet no antic, no poor, motley Fool, but a duke and lord of many fair towns and rich cities beyond Morfeville and the Southward March. How say ye, brothers? "

"That thou'rt a fool! " quoth Rick.

"True! " nodded Jocelyn.

"Most true! " sighed Sir Pertinax.

"And a liar! " growled Gurth.

"And a murderous rogue! " cried Will, "and shall hang, along of us—as I'm a tanner! "

"Alack, Sir Knight, " smiled Jocelyn, "of what avail rank or fame or both 'gainst a motley habit and a ragged mantle. Thus, Pertinax, thou art no more than what thou seemest, to wit—a poor, fierce rogue, and I, a beggarly stroller. "

"And like to have our necks stretched, lord, by reason of a fond and foolish whim! "

"Unless, Pertinax, having naught to depend on but our native wit we, by our wit, win free. Other poor rogues in like case have broke prison ere now, and 'tis pity and shame in us if thou, a knight so potent and high-born, and I, a prince, may not do the like. "

The Geste of Duke Jocelyn

"Messire, unlearned am I in the breaking o' prisons so when my time cometh to die in a noose I can but die as knight should—though I had rather 't were in honest fight. "

"Spoken like the very fool of a knight! " quoth Jocelyn. "So now will I show thee how by the wit of a brave and noble lady we may yet 'scape the hangman. Hearken in thine ear! "

But, when Jocelyn had told him all and shown money and sleeping-charm, Sir Pertinax grew thoughtful, sighing deep and oft, yet speaking not, wherefore the Duke questioned him.

"Good gossip, gasp not! " quoth he. "How think'st thou of prison-breaking now—expound! "

"Why, sir, I think when all do charmed and spellbound
snore,
Then will we shrewdly choke them that they wake
no more! "

"Nay, Pertinax, here shall be no need of choking, forsooth! " Sir Pertinax bowed chin on fist and sighed again.

"Pertinax, prithee puff not! Yet, an puff ye will, pronounce me then the why and wherefore of thy puffing. "

"Lord, here is neither gasp nor puff, here is honest sighing. I can sigh as well as another. "

"Since when hast learned this so tender art, my Pertinax? "

"And I do sigh by reason of memory. "

"As what, Pertinax? "

"Eyes, lord—her eyes so darkly bright and, as I do think—black! "

"Nay, blue, Pertinax—blue as heaven! "

"Black, messire, black as—as black! "

"Blue, boy, blue! "

"Lord, they are black! "

"Speak'st thou of Yolande? "

"Messire, of one I speak, but whom, I know not. She came to me i' the greenwood as I sat a-fishing. Her hair long and black—ay, black and curled, her eyes dark, and for beauty ne'er saw I her like. "

"And yet hast seen my Lady Yolande oft! "

"Her voice, messire, her voice soft and sweet as the murmur of waters, and very full of allure. "

"Why, how now! " cried Jocelyn. "Art thou—thou, my Pertinax, become at last one of Cupid's humble following? All joy to thee, my lovely lover—here in truth is added bond betwixt us! For since thou dost love a maid, even as I do love a maid, so being lovers twain needs must we love each other the better therefore. "

"Nay, out alack, my lord! " sighed Sir Pertinax. "For though I do love her, she, by reason o' my ill-favoured looks, the which, woe's me, I may not alter, loveth not me, as I do judge. "

"How judge ye this? "

"Lord, she giveth me hard names. She, all in a breath, hath pictured me thus: 'Hooked of nose, fierce-eyed, of aspect grim—ungentle, unlovely, harsh o' tongue, dour o' visage, hard o' heart, flinty o' soul and of manners rude. '"

"Good! But was this all, my Pertinax? "

"Nay, lord, and with a wannion—there was more to like purpose. "

"Excellent, my lovely knight—let hope sing in thee. For look now, if she named thee hooked of nose, fierce-eyed and of aspect grim—she speaketh very truth, for so thou art, my Pertinax. Now truth is a fair virtue in man or maid, so is she both virtuous and fair! Nay, puff not, sighful Pertinax, but for thy comforting mark this—she hath viewed and heeded thy outward man narrowly—so shall she not forget thee soon; she with woman's eye hath marked the great heart of thee through sorry habit and rusty mail, and found therein the love thy harsh tongue might not utter; and thus, methinks, she hath thee in mind—aye, even now, mayhap. Lastly, good, lovely blunderbore—mark this! 'Tis better to win a maid's anger than she should heed thee none at all. Let love carol i' thy heart and be ye worthy, so, when ye shall meet again, 'tis like enough, despite thy hooked nose, she shall find thine eyes gentle, thy unloveliness lovely, thy harsh tongue wondrous tender and thy flinty soul the soul of a man. "

"Why, faith, lord, " quoth Pertinax, his grim lips softening to a smile, "despite her words, she spake in voice full sweet, and her eyes—ah, messire, her eyes were wondrous kind—gentle eyes—aye, her eyes were—"

"Eyes, my Pertinax—black eyes! "

"And gentle! By which same token, lord, she did give to me this token—this most strange trinket. "

But all at once, was the creak of hinges, and the ponderous door opening, Ranulph o' the Axe appeared, followed by divers of the warders bearing torches.

"Oho! " sighed Ranulph, doleful of visage. "Aha, good bawcocks, here come I, and these my fellows, for love o' thee, good Fool, thy quips, thy quirks, thy songs and antics capersome. For troth I'm a merry dog, I—a wanton wag, a bully boy and jovial, though woeful o' look! "

"Wherefore woeful! "

"For that I am not joyous, good Motley. Look 'ee—here's me born with a rare, merry heart, but sad and sober of head! Here's a heart bubbling with kindliness and soft and tender as sucking lamb, wedded to head and face full o' gloom! Here's laughter within me and woe without me, so am I ever at odds with myself—and there's my sorrow. Regarding the which same I will now chaunt ye song I made on myself; 'twas meant for merry song and blithe, but of itself turned mournful song anon as ye shall hear. "

So saying, Ranulph o' the Axe threw back grim head and sang gruff, albeit plaintive, thus:

"O! merry I am and right merry I'll be,
Ho-ho for block, gibbet and rack—oho!

To hang or behead ye there's none like to me,
For I'm headsman, tormentor, and hangman, all three,
And never for work do I lack—oho!

"I live but to torture since torment's my trade,
But my torment well meant is, I trow;
If I hang or behead ye, it can't be gainsaid,
Though my head for the head of a headsman was made,
Still I'm all loving-kindness below.

"But if ever I strive merry story to tell,
Full of japeful and humorsome graces,
'T is as though I were tolling a funeral bell
As if dismally, dolefully tolling a knell,
So solemn and sad grow all faces.

"I hang, burn and torture the best that I may,
Ho pincers and thumbscrews and rack—oho!
And all heads I cut off in a headsmanlike way;
So I'll hang, burn and torment 'till cometh the day
That my kind heart within me shall crack—oho!
Well-a-wey! Well-a-wey!
Woe is me for the day
That my poor heart inside me shall crack! Oho!

"So there's my song! 'T is dull song and, striving to be merry song, is sad song, yet might be worse song, for I have heard a worse song, ere now—but 't is poor song. So come, Fool, do thou sing us merry song to cheer us 'gainst my sad song. "

"Why truly, Sir Headsman, " said Jocelyn, "here be songs a-many, yet if thou 'rt for songs, songs will we sing thee, each and every of us. But first, behold here is money shall buy us wine in plenty that we may grow merry withal in very sooth. "

"Oho! " cried Ranulph. "Spoken like a noble Motley, a fair, sweet Fool! Go thou, Bertram, obey this lord-like Fool—bring wine, good wine and much, and haste thee, for night draweth on and at cock-crow I must away. "

"Aye, " nodded Jocelyn, "in the matter of one—Robin? "

"Verily, Fool. A cheery soul is Robin, though an outlaw, and well beloved in Canalise. So is he to hang at cock-crow lest folk make disturbance. "

"Where lieth he now? "

"Where but in the watch-house beside the gallows 'neath Black Lewin's charge. But come, good Motley, sing—a pretty song, a merry ditty, ha! "

So forthwith Jocelyn took his lute and sang:

"With dainty ditty
Quaint and pretty
I will fit ye,
So heed and mark me well,
And who we be
That here ye see
Now unto ye
Explicit I will tell:

"Then here first behold one Gurth, a worthy, dying
Dyer,
Since he by dyeing liveth, so to dye is his desire:
For being thus a very Dyer, he liveth but to dye,
And dyeing daily he doth all his daily wants
supply.
Full often hath he dyed ere now to earn his
daily bread,
Thus, dyeing not, this worthy Dyer must soon,
alas! be dead.

"Here's Rick—a saintly ploughman, he
Hath guided plough so well,
That here, with rogues the like of me,
He pines in dungeon cell.

"Here's Red-haired Will—O fie!
That Will should fettered lie
In such base, cruel manner!
For though his hair be red,
Brave Will, when all is said,
Is—hark 'ee—Will's a tanner! "

"Enough, Fool!" cried Will. "An thou must sing, sing of thyself, for thyself, to thyself, and I will sing of myself an' need be!"

Laughed JOCELYN:

  Why then, brave Will,
  Come, sing thy fill.

Whereupon Will cleared his throat, squared his shoulders, and rumbling a note or so to fix the key, burst into songful roar:

  "A tanner I, a lusty man,
  A tanner men call Will,
  And being tanner true, I tan,
  Would I were tanning still;
  Ho derry, derry down,
  Hey derry down,
  Would I were tanning still."

"Aye, verily!" growled Sir Pertinax. "And choked in thy vile tan-pit, for
scurvier song was never heard, par Dex!"

"Why 'tis heard, forsooth," said Jocelyn, "and might be heard a mile hence!
Chant on, brave Will."

The Tanner, nothing loth, wiped his mouth, clenched his fists and standing
square and rigid, continued:

  "How gaily I a-tanning went,
  No tanner blithe as I,
  No tanner e'er so innocent,
  Though here in chains I lie.
  Ho derry down,
  Hey derry down,
  In grievous chains I lie.

  "No more, alack, poor Will will tan,
  Since Will will, all unwilling,
  Though tanner he and proper man,
  A gloomy grave be filling.

Hey derry down,
Ho derry down,
A gloomy grave be filling. "

"Now out upon thee, Tanner! " sighed Ranulph. "Here's sad song, a song o' graves, and therefore most unlovely, a song I—Saints and Angels! " he gasped:

And pointed where Sir Pertinax did stand,
The Heart of Crystal shining in his hand.
"The Heart-in-Heart! The Crystal Heart! " cried he,
And crying thus, sank down on bended knee,
While jailers all and scurvy knaves, pell-mell,
Betook them to their marrow-bones as well;
Whereat Sir Pertinax oped wond'ring eyes,
And questioned him 'twixt anger and surprise.
Then answered Ranulph, "Sir, though chained ye go,
Yet to thee we do all obedience owe
By reason of that sacred amulet,
That crystal heart in heart of crystal set:

'For he that holdeth Crystal Heart
Holdeth all and every part,
And by night or eke by day
The Heart-in-Heart all must obey! "'

"Obey? " quoth Pertinax. "Ha! Let us see
If in thy vaunt there aught of virtue be:
For by this Heart of Crystal that I bear,
I charge ye loose the chains the Fool doth wear,
Then off with these accursèd gyves of mine,
Or—"

Ranulph to the warders gave a sign,
And they to work did go with such good speed,
That Joc'lyn soon with Pertinax stood freed,
"Now by my halidome! " quoth Pertinax,
"This talisman methinks no magic lacks,
So knaves, I bid ye—by this magic Heart,
Draw bolt and bar that hence we may depart—"
But now the scurvy knaves made dismal cry.
"Good sir! " they wailed, "Ah, leave us not to die! "
"Aye, by Heav'n's light! " fierce quoth Sir Pertinax,

"Ye're better dead by gibbet or by axe,
Since naught but scurvy, coward rogues are ye,
And so be hanged—be hanged to ye, all three! "

"Knight! " Joc'lyn sighed, "'neath Heaven's light
somewhere
Doth live a dark-eyed maid with black-curled hair—
Her voice is soft and full of sweet allure,
And thou, perchance, one day may humbly woo her;
So these poor rogues now woo their lives of thee,
Show mercy then and mercy find of she. "

At this Sir Pertinax rubbed chin and frowned,
Red grew his cheek, his fierce eyes sought the ground,
Then, even as he thus pinched chin and scowled,
"Loose, then, the dismal knaves! " at last he
growled.
But now grim Ranulph tangled beard tore
And wrung his hands and sighed and groaned and
swore
With loud complaints and woeful lamentations,
With muttered oaths and murmured objurgations,
With curses dire and impious imprecations.

"Beshrew me, masters all! " quoth he. "Now here's ill prank to play a
poor hangman, may I ne'er quaff good liquor more, let me languish
o' the quartern ague and die o' the doleful dumps if I ever saw the
like o' this! For look 'ee now, if I set these three rogues free, how may
I hang 'em as hang 'em I must, since I by hanging live to hang again,
and if I don't hang 'em whom shall I hang since hang I must, I being
hangman? Bethink ye o' this, sirs, and show a little pity to a poor
hangman. "

"Why then, mark ye this, hangman, " said Jocelyn, "since on hanging
doth thy hangman's reputation hang, then hang thou must;
therefore, an ye lack rogue to hang, go hang thyself, so, hanging,
shall thy hanging be done with and thou having lived a hangman,
hangman die, thus, hangman hanging hangman, hangman hanging
shall be hangman still, and being still, thus hanging, shall hang no
more. "

The Geste of Duke Jocelyn

"Aye, verily! " quoth Sir Pertinax, "there it is in a nutshell—
hangman, be hanged to thee! So off with their fetters, Master
Gallows, by Crystal Heart I charge thee! "

Hereupon the scurvy knaves were freed, to their great joy, and
following the bold knight, made haste to quit their gloomy dungeon.
Reaching the guardroom above, Sir Pertinax called lustily for sword
and bascinet, and thereafter chose divers likely weapons for his
companions who, with axe and pike and guisarme on shoulder,
followed him out into the free air.

Now it was night and very dark, but Gurth, who was a man of the
town, brought them by dim and lonely alleys and crooked ways
until at last they halted within a certain dark and narrow street.

"Whither now? " questioned Sir Pertinax.

"Verily, " said Jocelyn, "where but to the gatehouse—"

"Not so, " muttered Gurth, "'tis overly well guarded—"

"Aye, " growled Will, "which is true, as I'm a tanner! "

"Howbeit, " said Jocelyn, "I'm for the gatehouse! "

"And wherefore? " demanded Sir Pertinax.

"In cause of one Rob, a robber. "

"Aye, but, " said Gurth, "he is to hang at crow-o'-cock and 'tis nigh
cock-crow now. "

"The more need for haste, " said Jocelyn.

> But, even now, as they together spoke,
> A sullen tramp the sleeping echoes woke,
> Behind them in the gloom dim forms they saw,
> While others grimly barred the way before;
> And so, by reason that they could not fly,
> They grasped their weapons and prepared to die.
> Then in the darkness of that narrow street,
> Broad axe and pike and flashing sword did meet.
> Duke Jocelyn full many a thrust drave home,

Till whirling pike-staff smote him on cock's-comb,
And staggering back to an adjacent wall,
In deep-sunk doorway groaning he did fall.

My daughter GILLIAN remonstrateth:

GILL: Now, father, please don't let him die—

MYSELF: No, no, indeed, my Gill, not I,
My heroes take a lot of killing—

GILL: Then go on quick, it's very thrilling!
I hope he vanquishes his foes,
And let him do it, please, in prose.

"O woe! " said a quavering voice. "Alack, and well-a-wey—"

My daughter GILLIAN demurreth:

GILL: No, father—that's not right at all.
You'd got to where you'd made him fall.

MYSELF: Well, then, Duke Joc'lyn, from his swoon awaking,
Found that his head confoundedly was aching;
Found he was bruised all down from top to toe—

GILL: A bruise, father, and he a duke? No, no!
Besides, you make
A frightful mistake—
A hero's head should never ache;
And, father, now, whoever knew
A hero beaten black and blue?
And then a bruise, it seems to me,
Is unromantic as can be.
He can't be bruised,
And shan't be bruised,
For, if you bruise him,
And ill-use him,
I'll refuse him—
No reader, I am sure, would choose
A hero any one can bruise.
So, father, if you want him read,
Don't bruise him, please—

MYSELF: Enough is said!

At this, Jocelyn sat up and wondered to find himself in a small chamber
dim-lit by a smoking cresset. On one side of him leaned an ancient woman,
a very hag-like dame

> With long, sharp nose that downward curved as though
> It fain would, beak-like, peck sharp chin below;

and upon his other side a young damsel of a wondrous dark beauty.

"Lady, " said he, "where am I? "

"Hush, poor Motley! " whispered the maid. "Thou didst fall 'gainst the door yonder. But speak low, they that seek thy life may yet be nigh. "

"Nay, then, " quoth Jocelyn, reaching for his sword, "I must out and aid my comrades. "

"Alack! " sighed the old woman. "Thy comrades do without lie all slain save one that groaneth—hearken! "

"O, woe! " mourned a quavering voice beyond the door. "O, woe, sore hurted I be, and like to die—and I a tanner! "

Very heedfully, Jocelyn unbarred the door, and peering into the narrow street, found it deserted and empty save for certain outstretched forms that stirred not; looking down on these dim shapes he knew one for Rick the Ploughman, whose ploughing days were sped and, huddled in a corner hard by, he found Will the Tanner, who groaned fitfully; but of Sir Pertinax and Gurth he saw nothing. So Jocelyn made shift to bear the Tanner within the house, and here Will, finding his hurts of small account, sat up, and while the wise old woman bandaged his wound, answered Jocelyn's eager questions, and told how Sir Pertinax and Gurth the Dyer had broken through their assailants and made good their escape.

Now, when the old woman had thus cherished their hurts, Jocelyn would fain have given her money, but she mumbled and mowed and cracked her finger-joints and shook grey head.

"Not so, good Fool! " she croaked, "for I do know thee for that same gentle Motley did save me from Black Lewin—a murrain seize him! So now will I save thee—behold! " So saying she set bony hand to wall; and lo! in the wall yawned a square opening narrow and dark, whence issued a cold wind. "Begone, thou brave merryman! " quoth she. "Yonder safety lieth; this darksome way shall carry thee out beneath the city wall! "

"Gramercy, thou kindly Witch! " said Jocelyn. "Yet first must I to the watch-house beside the gate for one Robin that lieth 'prisoned there. "

"How, Fool, dost mean Robin-a-Green that is to hang? "

"In truth! "

"But Rob o' the Green is outlawed, banned o' Church, a very rogue! "

"But a man, wherefore I would save him alive. "

"Nay, Fool, o' thy folly be wise and seek ye safety instead. Would'st peril thy body for a thief? "

"Verily, dame, even as I did for a Witch. "

Now, here the old woman scowled and mumbled and cracked her finger-bones angrily. But the beauteous young maid viewed Jocelyn with bright, approving eyes:

"But, Fool, " cried she, "O wondrous Fool, wilt adventure thyself in cause so desperate? "

"Blithely, fair lady! "

"But, alas! the guards be many and thou but one—"

"Nay! " cried a voice:

"For thou may'st see
That two are we! "

And forth of the dark opening in the wall strode Lobkyn Lollo the Dwarf, his great, spiked club on brawny shoulder. Jocelyn viewed the monstrous little man in awed wonder; but beholding his mighty girth and determined aspect, wonder changed to kindliness; quoth he:

"Fair greeting, comrade! If thou'rt for a little bickering and disputation with that goodly club o' thine, come thy ways for methinks I do smell the dawn. "

"Aha, thou naughty little one! " cried the Witch, shaking bony fist. "Art for fighting for rogue's life along of a Fool, then? "

Quoth LOBKYN:

Aye, grannam, though ye slap me, still,
Fight and aid this Fool I will—

"And talking o' Will, " quoth Will, "what o' me, for though I'm a tanner I'm a man, aye, verily, as I'm a tanner. "

"And methinks a better man than tanner! " said Jocelyn. "So here we stand three goodly wights and well armed. Let's away—"

"Nay, then, wild Madcap, " croaked the Witch, "an my Lobkyn go I go, and, though I be old and feeble, shalt find my craft more potent than sword or club—wait! "

Here the old woman, opening a dingy cupboard, took thence a small crock over which she muttered spells and incantations with look and gesture so evil that Lobkyn eyed her askance, Will the Tanner cowered and whispered fragments of prayers, and even Jocelyn crossed himself.

"Come! " croaked the Witch. "Now do I go to save rogue from gallows for sake of thee, tall Fool. Come ye, come and do as I bid ye in all things—come! "

FYTTE 6

Tells how for Robin a good fight was fought
And our old Witch a spell mysterious wrought.

* * * * *

Phoebus, the young and gladsome god of day,
His fiery steeds had yoked to flaming car
(By which, my Gill, you may surmise
The sun was just about to rise)
And that be-feathered, crook-billed harbinger,
The rosy-wattled herald of the dawn,
Red comb aflaunt, bold-eyed and spurred for strife,
Brave Chanticleer, his strident summons raised
(By which fine phrase I'd have you know,
The cock had just begun to crow)
And gentle Zephyr, child of Boreas,
Stole soft the hush of dewy leaves,
And passing kissed the flowers to wakefulness.
Thus, laden with their sweetness, Zephyr came
O'er hill and dale, o'er battlement and wall,
Into the sleeping town of Canalise,
Through open lattice and through prison-bars,
To kiss the cheek of sleeping Innocence
And fevered brows of prisoners forlorn,
Who, stirring 'neath sweet Zephyr's soft caress,
Dreamed themselves young, with all their sins unwrought.
So, gentle Zephyr, messenger of dawn,
Fresh as the day-spring, of earth redolent,
Through narrow loophole into dungeon stole,
Where Robin the bold outlaw fettered lay,
Who, sighing, woke to feel her fragrant kiss,

And, breathing in this perfume-laden air,
He seemed to smell those thousand woodland scents
He oft had known, yet, knowing, never heeded:
Of lofty bracken, golden in the sun,
Of dewy violets shy that bloomed dim-seen
Beside some merry-laughing, woodland brook

The Geste of Duke Jocelyn

Which, bubbling, with soft music filled the air;
The fragrant reek of smouldering camp-fire
Aglow beside some dark, sequestered pool
Whose placid waters a dim mirror made
To hold the glister of some lonely star;
He seemed to see again in sunny glade
The silky coats of yellow-dappled deer,
With branching antlers gallantly upborne;
To hear the twang of bow, the whizz of shaft,
And cheery sound of distant-winded horn.
Of this and more than this, bold Robin thought,
And, in his dungeon's gloomy solitude,
He groaned full deep and, since no eye could see,
Shed bitter tears.

My daughter GILLIAN supplicateth:

GILL: Poor Robin! Father, promise me
To save him from the gallows-tree.
He's much too nice a man to kill;
So save him, father; say you will!

MYSELF: But think of poor Ranulph with no one to hang!

GILL: Ranulph's song was top-hole, but—

MYSELF: You know I hate slang—

GILL: Yes, father—but then I hate Ranulph much more,
With his nasty great beard that in tangles he wore.
So, father, if you must have some one to slay,
Instead of poor Robin, hang Ranulph—

MYSELF: Why, pray?

GILL: In nice books the nasty folks only should die;
Those are the kind of books nice people buy.
I like a book that makes me glad,
And loathe a book that makes me sad;
So, as this Geste is made for me,
Make it as happy as can be.

95

MYSELF: And is it, so far, as you'd wish?

GILL: Well, father, though it's rather swish,
I think it needs a deal more love—

MYSELF: Swish? How—what's this? Great heavens
above!
Will you, pray, miss, explain to me
How any story "swish" may be?
And why, my daughter, you must choose
A frightful word like "swish" to use?
What hideous language are you talking?

GILL: Sorrow, father! "Swish" means "corking. "
I think our Geste is "out of sight, "
Except that, to please me, you might
Put in more love—

MYSELF: Now, how can Joc'lyn go love-making
When his head is sore and aching?
Besides, this is no place to woo;
He'll love-make when I want him to.

GILL: But, father, think—in all this time,
In all this blank-verse, prose and rhyme,
The fair Yolande he's never kissed,
And you've done nothing to assist;
And, as I'm sure they're both inclined,
I think your treatment most unkind.

MYSELF: This Geste I'll write in my own way,
That is, sweet Prattler, if I may;
When I'm ready for them to kiss,
Then kiss they shall; I promise this.
Now I'll to Rob return, if you,
My Gillian, will permit me to!

Thus in his prison pent, poor woeful Rob,
Since none might see or hear, scorned not to sob,
And mightily, in stricken heart, did grieve
That he so soon so fair a world must leave.
And all because the morning wind had brought
Earth's dewy fragrance with sweet mem'ries fraught.

So Robin wept nor sought his grief to stay,
Yearning amain for joys of yesterday;
Till, hearing nigh the warder's heavy tread,
He sobbed no more but strove to sing instead.

"A bow for me, a bow for me,
All underneath the greenwood tree,
Where slaves are men, and men are free;
Give me a bow!

"Give me a bow, a bow of yew,
Good hempen cord and arrows true,
When foes be thick and friends be few,
Give me a bow! "

Thus cheerily sang Robin the while he dried his bitter tears, as the door of his prison was flung wide and Black Lewin strode in and with him men-at-arms bearing torches.

"What ho, rogue Robin! " cried he. "The cock hath crowed. Ha! Will ye sing, knave, will ye sing, in faith? "

"In faith, that will I! " laughed Robin.

"Here come we to bring ye to the gallows, Robin—how say ye? "

"The more reason for singing since my singing must soon be done! " So, with pikemen before him and behind, bold Robin marched forth to die, yet sang full blithely as he went:

"So lay my bones 'neath good yew-tree,
Thus Rob and yew soon one shall be,
Where all true men may find o' we
A trusty bow! "

"Ha' done! " growled Black Lewin, shivering in the chilly air of dawn. "Quit—quit thy singing, rogue, or by the foul fiend I—"

"Who dareth name the fiend? " croaked an awful voice, whereat Black Lewin halted, gaped and stood a-tremble, while beneath steel cap and bascinet all men's hair stirred and rose with horror; for before them was a ghastly shape, a shape that crouched in the gloom with dreadful face aflame with smouldering green fire.

"Woe! " cried the voice. "Woe unto thee, Lewin the Black, that calleth on fiend o' the pit! "

And now came a fiery hand that, hovering in the air, pointed lambent finger at gaping Lewin and at each of the shivering pike-men in turn.

"Woe—sorrow and woe to one and all, ye men of blood, plague and pest, pain o' flesh, and grief of soul seize ye, be accursed and so—begone! Hence ho—away!

"Rommani hi! Avaunt, I say,
Prendraxon!
Thus direst curse on ye I lay
Shall make flesh shrink and bone decay,
To rot and rot by night and day
Till flesh and bone do fall away,
Mud unto mud and clay to clay.
A spell I cast,
Shall all men blast.
Hark ye,
Mark ye,
Rommani hi—prendraxon! "

Down fell pike and guisarme from nerveless fingers and, gasping with fear, Black Lewin and his fellows turned and fled nor stayed for one look behind; only Robin stood there (since he might not run away by reason of his bonds) babbling prayers between chattering teeth and with all his fingers crossed.

"Oho, Fool, aha! " cried the voice. "Thus have I, a poor, feeble old woman, wrought better than all thy valiance or Lobkyn's strength. So, by potency of my spells and magic are we quits, thou and I. Bring, then, thy rogue outlaw and haste ye! "

So saying the old Witch muffled her awful, fiery face in ragged mantle and turned away; and in that moment Robin was aware of three forms about him in the grey dawn-light, felt his bonds loosed off by quick, strong hands and drew a great, joyous breath.

98

"How, Fool, thou brave and noble Motley, " quoth he, "is it thou again? And I to live? "

"Aye, marry, Robin! But come apace, the day breaketh and the city is astir—hark to yon shouts! Follow! "

So with the Tanner on one side and Lobkyn on the other, Robin ran, hard on Jocelyn's heels; and ever the dawn brightened until up came the sun chasing away sullen shadow and filling street and alley with his glory.

But now, and just as they reached that narrow street where safety lay, they heard a shout, a scream, a rush of feet and roar of fierce voices and beheld, amid a surge of armed men, the old woman struggling in the cruel grip of Black Lewin who (like many others I wot of, my Gill) was brave enough by daylight. Vainly the old creature strove, screaming for mercy as Black Lewin whirled aloft his sword; but his blade clashed upon another as Jocelyn sprang, and for a while the air rang with the sound of fierce-smiting steel until, throwing up his arms, Black Lewin fell and lay there. But, roaring vengeance, the soldiery closed about Jocelyn who, beset by blows on every side, sank in turn, yet, even as he fell, two short though mighty legs bestrode his prostrate form and Lobkyn Lollo, whirling huge club, smote down the foremost assailant and, ever as he smote, he versified and chanted—thus:

"I'm Lollo hight,
Brave Lobkyn Lollo, I,
I'm Lollo hight,
'Tis my delight
By day or night
In honest fight
With main and might
Good blows to smite,
And where they light
'Tis sorry plight
For that poor wight,
Brave Lobkyn Lollo, I.

"Bows, swords and staves,
Come, lusty knaves,
And fit for graves
Brave Lobkyn soon will make ye;

So fight, say I,
Nor turn and fly,
Or, when ye die,
Then may old Horny take ye. "

Fierce raged the conflict, but in that narrow street they made good play against their many assailants, the valiant Dwarf's mighty club, backed by the Tanner's darting pike and Robin's flashing sword, which he had snatched from a loosened grasp. But Jocelyn lay prone upon his face, between Lobkyn's firm-planted feet, and stirred not. So club whirled, sword flashed and pike darted while, high above the tumult, rose Lobkyn's fierce chant:

"Hot blood I quaff,
At death I laugh,
Brave Lobkyn Lollo, I.
Come all that may,
And all I'll slay,
And teach ye how to die. "

"Lob—Lobkyn! " screamed the Witch. "Thou that drinkest nought but milk—talk not of blood, thou naughty poppet. Back now—stand back, I do command thee! "

Lobkyn smote a man to earth and, sighing regretful, stepped aside.

"Back! " screamed the Witch. "Stand back, I say, all three,
And leave this wicked rabblement to me.
Now shall they learn the terror of my curse,
Black magic shall they feel—and something worse! "

Then uttered she a sudden, hideous cry,
And, leaping, whirled her bony hands on high,
And lo! a choking dust-cloud filled the air;
That wreathed in whirling eddies here and there.

"Perendewix! " she cried. "Oh Radzywin—
Thraxa! Behold, my witchcraft doth begin! "
Back shrank their foes, back reeled they one and all,
They choked, they gasped, they let their weapons fall;
And some did groan, and some did fiercely sneeze,
And some fell prone, some writhed upon their knees;
Some strove to wipe the tears from blinded eyes,
But one and all gave voice to awful cries.

"Come! " cried the Witch, "to the door—the door. Lobkyn, bear ye the brave Fool—and tenderly! Haste, naughty bantling, haste—I hear the tread of more soldiers! "

So Lobkyn stooped and, lifting Jocelyn's inanimate form, tucked it beneath one arm, and with Robin and Will the Tanner, followed the old Witch into the house.

My daughter GILLIAN commandeth:

GILL: Go on, father, do; why will you keep stopping?
I think the old Witch is just perfectly topping.
And what frightful words she uses for curses!

MYSELF: Very frightful, indeed, though your slang still much worse is,
With your "topping, " "top-holing, " your "swishing" and "clipping, "

GILL: Well, I merely intended to say it was ripping;
But, if you object to my praises—

MYSELF: I only object to your phrases,
For there's no author but will own
He "liveth not by bread alone. "
As for myself, if what I write
Doth please—then praise with all your might.

GILL: Well, then, the Witch is splendid, though
I'm very curious to know
Just how her face all fiery grew,
And what the stuff was that she threw—
The stuff that made the soldiers sneeze
And brought them choking to their knees
It sounds as though it might be snuff.

MYSELF: My dear, they'd not found out such stuff.
But grisly witches long ago
Did many strange devices know.
Indeed, my Gill, they knew much more
Than wise folk gave them credit for.

GILL: Well, what was it? You haven't said.

MYSELF: I'll get on with our Geste instead.

FYTTE 7

That telleth to the patient reader nought,
Save how the Duke was to the wild-wood brought.

* * * * *

With sleepy eyes Duke Jocelyn watched afar,
In deep, blue void a solitary star,
That, like some bright and wakeful eye, did seem
To watch him where he lay 'twixt sleep and dream.
And, as he viewed it winking high above,
He needs must think of Yolande and his love,
And how, while he this twinkling star did view,
She, wakeful lying, might behold it too,
Whereas she lay a spotless maid and fair,
Clothed in the red-gold glory of her hair;
And, thinking thus, needs must he fondly sigh,
Then frowned to hear a lusty snore hard by—

—and looking whence came this sound, the Duke sat up and his
wonder grew; for by light of a fire that glowed in a blackened fissure
of rock he beheld himself couched on a bed of bracken within a
roomy cave. Beside the fire leaned a mighty, iron-shod club, and
beyond this, curled up like a dog, snored Lobkyn Lollo, the Dwarf.
Hereupon Jocelyn reached out and shook Lob to wakefulness, who
grunted sleepily, rubbed his eyes drowsily and yawned mightily:

Quoth JOCELYN: Good Dwarf, where am I?

Answered LOBKYN:
Safe, Fool, safe art thou, I trow,
Where none but Lob and friends do know.

JOCELYN: But how am I hither?

LOBKYN: Why, truly thou art hither, Fool,
Because thou art not thither, Fool!
In these two arms, thy life to save,
I bore thee to this goodly cave.

JOCELYN: How may one of thy inches bear man of mine so far?

The Geste of Duke Jocelyn

LOBKYN: Why, Fool, though I of inches lack,
I'm mighty strong, both arm and back,
Thou that art longer man than me,
Yet I am stronger man than thee,
Though, lusty Fool, big fool you be,
I'd bear thee, Fool, if thou wert three.
And mark, Fool, if my grammar seemeth weak,
Pray license it since I in verse must speak.

JOCELYN: And pray why must thou speak in verse?

LOBKYN: Nature hath on me laid this curse,
And, though to speak plain prose I yearn,
My prose to verse doth ever turn.
Therefore I grieve, as well I might,
Because of my poetic plight—
Though bards and rhymers all I scorn,
Alack! I was a rhymer born.

JOCELYN: Alack! poor Dwarf, as thou must versify,
By way of courtesy, then, so will I.

LOBKYN: How, Fool, then canst thou rhyme?

JOCELYN: Aye, Dwarf, at any time!
In dark, in light,
By day, by night,
Standing, sitting,
As be fitting,
Verses witty,
Quaint or pretty,
Incontinent I'll find.
Verses glad, Dwarf,
Verses sad, Dwarf,
Every sort, Lob,
Long or short, Lob
Or verses ill,
Yet verses still
Which might be worse,
I can rehearse
When I'm for verse inclined.
So, Lob, first speak me what became
Of our old Witch, that potent dame.

LOBKYN: Why, Fool, in faith she wrought so well
With direful curse and blasting spell
That every howling soldier-knave,
Every rogue and base-born slave
That by chance I did not slay,
From my grand-dam ran away.

JOCELYN: A noble Witch! Now, Lobkyn, tell
What hap'd when in the fight I fell,
And how alive I chance to be.

LOBKYN: Fool, I was there to succour thee.
I smote those pike-men hip and thigh,
That they did mangled pike-men lie;
Their arms, their legs, their skulls I broke,
Two, three, and four at every stroke.
I drave them here, I smote them there,
I smote, I slew, I none did spare,
I laughed, I sang, I—

"Ha, Lob! " growled a sleepy voice. "Now, as I'm a tanner, here's a-
many I's! By Saint Crispin, meseemeth thou'rt all I's—for as thou
fought I fought, or thought I fought, forsooth! "

LOBKYN: True, Will, did'st fight in goodly manner,
Though fightedst, Will, like any tanner;
But I did fight, or I'm forsworn,
Like one unto the manner born.
I fought, forsooth, with such good will,
'Tis marvel I'm not fighting still.
And so I should be, by my fay,
An I had any left to slay;
But since I slew them all—

"Hold there! " cried the Tanner. "I slew one or two, Lob, and Robin
likewise. Thou'rt a lusty fighter, but what o' me and Robin—ha,
what o' we? "

LOBKYN: In faith, ye're proper men and tall,
And I'm squat man, my stature small,
Nath'less, though small and squat I be,
I am the best man of the three.

"Why, as to that, " quoth the Tanner, "'tis but you says so! As to me I think what I will, and I do think—"

But here Lobkyn started up and seized the great club; quoth he:

"Hark and mark,
Heard ye nought there i' the dark? "

"Not I! " answered Will.

"Methought I heard an owl hoot, " said Jocelyn.

"Aye, " nodded Lobkyn:

"Aye, Fool, and yet this owl I 'll swear,
Hath ne'er a feather anywhere.
This owl hath ne'er a wing to fly,
But goes afoot like thou and I.
Now mark,
And hark! "

Hereupon the Dwarf laid finger to lip and uttered an owl-cry so dismal, so tremulous and withal so true to nature that it was wonder to hear. Instantly, from the dimness beyond the cavern-mouth, the cry was repeated, and presently was heard a panting and 'plaining, a snuffling and a shuffling, and into the light of the fire hobbled the old Witch. Beholding Jocelyn sitting cross-legged on his couch of fern, she paused and, leaning on her crooked stick, viewed him with her wise, old eyes.

"Aha, Motley! " she croaked. "Oho, thou flaunting jackanapes, didst peril thy foolish flesh for me that am poor and old and feeble, and cursed by all for witchcraft! So have I with my potions ministered to thee in thy sickness, and behold thou'rt alive, hale and strong again. Give me thy hand! Aha, here's cool, unfevered blood! Show me thy tongue. Oho! Aha! A little sup o' my black decoction—roots gathered at full o' moon—a little sup and shall be thyself by to-morrow's dawn. But—as for thee, thou good-for-naught, thou wicked elf—aha! would'st dare leave thy poor old grannam weak and 'fenceless? Give me thy rogue-ear! " Obediently, the mighty Dwarf arose and sighfully suffered the old woman to grasp him by the ear and to tweak and wring and twist it as she would.

"What dost thou here i' the wild-wood, thou imp, thou poppet o' plagues, thou naughty wap-de-staldees? "

To which Lobkyn, writhing and watering at the eyes, answered thus:

"Stay, prithee grannam, loose thy hold!
I would but be an outlaw bold,
An outlaw fierce that men shall fear—
Beseech thee, grand-dam, loose mine ear! "

"An outlaw, naughty one! " screeched the Witch, tweaking ear the harder. "Dare ye tell me so, elf? "

LOBKIN: Aye, grand-dam—cuff me an ye will,
Nath'less an outlaw I'll be still,
And many a wicked rogue I'll kill—
O grand-dam, loose mine ear!
And day and night I'll slay until
All rogues my name do fear.

For grand-dam, I'm a fighter—O,
Beseech thee, let my ear go!
And bones shall crack and blood shall flow,
If any dare resist me.
And all the world my name shall know,
Pray by the ear don't twist me!

All men before my club shall fly,
All on their knees shall "mercy" cry,
Or mangled in their gore shall lie—
Ah, grand-dam, pray don't clout me!
Don't beat me, grannam dear, but try
To do awhile without me—

"Without thee, thou piece o' naughtiness? " screamed the old woman. "Now will I lay my stick about thee—hold still, Rogue! "

Saying which, she proceeded to belabour the poor Dwarf with her knotted stick, clutching him fast by his ear the while. Thus she be-thwacked him soundly until he roared for mercy.

"Why, how now—how now? " cried a merry voice, and Robin strode into the firelight. "Gentle Witch, sweet dame, " quoth he, "what do ye with poor Lob? "

"Thwack him shrewdly! "

"Which is, Witch, that which none but witch the like o' thee might do, for lustier fighter and mightier dwarf never was. Thus, but for thy witch-like witcheries, the which, Witch, witch do prove thee, but for this and the power and potency of thy spells, now might he crack out thy life 'twixt finger and thumb—"

"Ha, forest-rogue, 'tis a bad brat, a very naughty elf would run off into the wild to be rogue like thee—an outlaw, forsooth! "

"Forsooth, Witch, " laughed Robin, "outlaw is he in very truth, in sooth and by my troth! Outlaw is Lob, banned by Church and Council of Ten, and so proclaimed i' the market square of Canalise this very morn by sound o' trumpet and—"

"How? How? " cried the old woman, wringing her trembling hands. "My Lobkyn outlawed? My babe, my lovely brat, my pretty bantling, woe and alas! My dear ugly one an outlaw? "

"Aye, marry is he, Witch, outlaw proclaimed, acclaimed, announced, pronounced and denounced; as such described, ascribed and proscribed by Master Gregory Bax, the port-reeve, for the late slaying and maiming of divers of the city guard. So outlaw is Lobkyn, his life henceforth forfeit even as mine. "

"My Lobkyn an hairy outlaw i' the wild-wood! Out alas! And what of his poor old grannam? What o' me—? "

"Content thee, sweet hag, since thou'rt outlawed along with him and, as witch, doomed to die unpleasantly by fire and flame and faggot, if thou'rt caught. "

"Alack! Wala-wa! Woe 's me! " groaned the Witch, cracking her finger-bones. "And all this by reason o' the Fool yonder. "

"Why, the Fool is dubbed outlaw likewise, Witch, " quoth Robin. "Outlaw is he along o' thee and Tanner Will. "

"And all by reason that this Fool must needs peril our lives for sake of rogue-outlaw, of forest-robber, of knavish woodland-lurker—"

"Hight Robin! " laughed Robin, leaning on his long bow-stave. "Now, this brave Fool having saved Robin his life, Witch, the which, Witch, was good thing for Robin, our Fool next saved thee, Witch, which was nought to Robin, in the which, Witch, Robin did not joy; for thou, old Witch, being witch, art therefore full o' witcheries which be apt to be-devil a man and fright his reason, for the which reason, being reasonable man, I reason, for this reason, that, so reasoning, I love thee not. But thou art old, Witch, which is good reason to reasonably reason thou art wise, Witch, and, being wise, I on this wise would seek counsel of thy wisdom, Witch. Imprimis, then—"

"Hold! " commanded the Witch; "here's a whirl o' windy wind! Hast more of such-like, forester? "

"Some little, Witch, which I will now, Witch—"

"Nay, then, Robin-a-Green, suffer me to rest my old bones whiles thy mill clacks. " Hereupon the old Witch seated herself beside the fire, with bony knees up-drawn to bony chin. "Speak, outlaw Robin, " she croaked, blinking her red eyes, "and speak ye plain. "

"Why, then, wise Witch, look 'ee: since we be outlaws each and every, with all men's hands against us, with none to succour, and death watchful for us, 'tis plain, and very plain, we, for our harbourage and defence, must in the wild-wood bide—"

"Ho! " cried Lobkyn:

"It soundeth good,
The brave wild-wood,
Where flowers do spring
And birds do sing.
To slay the deer
And make good cheer,
With mead and beer,
The livelong year,
And—"

"Roar not, toad! " cried the Witch. "Say on—Rogue-Robin! "

"Why, mark me, good Witch, here's where buskin chafeth! Not long since I ruled i' the wild-wood, a very king, with ten-score lusty outlaw-rogues to do my will. To-day is there never an one, and for this reasonable reason—to wit, I am hanged, and, being hanged, am dead, and, being dead, am not, and thus Robin is nobody; and yet again, perceive me, Witch, being Robin, I am therefore somebody; thus is nobody somebody, and yet somebody that nobody will believe anybody. The which, Witch, is a parlous case, methinks, for here am I, somebody, nobody and Robin altogether and at the same time; therefore, Witch, o' thy witchful wisdom—who am I, what and which, Witch? "

Here the Witch blinked and mowed, and cracked her finger-bones one after another. Quoth she:

"For thy first, thou'rt thyself; for the second, a rogue; and for the third, a wind-bag. I would thy second might tie up thy first in thy third. "

"So should Robin choke Robin with Robin. But hark 'ee again, good, patient dame. It seemeth that Ranulph the executioner betaketh him at cock-crow to hang poor me; but, finding me not, made great outcry, insomuch that the city guard, such as mighty Lob and Will had left alive, sought counsel together; and taking one of their slain fellows, Ranulph hanged him in my stead, and there he hangeth now, above the city gate, his face so marred that he might be me or any other. "

"Ha, Robin—well? "

"This day, at sunset, came I unto the trysting-oak, and by blast of horn summoned me my outlaw company. They came apace and in great wonderment, for, seeing me, they fell to great awe and dread, thinking me dead, since many had seen my body a-dangle on the gallows; wherefore, seeing me manifestly alive, they took me for ghoulish ghost 'stead o' good flesh and blood, and fled from me amain. So, by reason of my dead body, that is no body o' mine, yet that nobody will believe is no body o' mine, they believe that this my body is yet no body, but a phantom; the which is out of reason; yet thus unreasonably do the rogues reason by reason of the body that hangeth in place of my body above the city gate. Wherefore I reason there is yet reason in their unreason, seeing this body was somebody, yet no body o' mine, but which nobody among them can swear to. Which, Witch, is a matter which none but wise witch may counsel me in. How say'st thou, Witch? "

But for a while the old Witch scowled on the fire, bony chin on bony knees, and dreamily cracked her finger-joints.

"Oho! " she cried suddenly. "Aha—a body that nobody's is, yet body that everybody knoweth for body o' thine—aha! So must nobody know that nobody's body is not thy body. Dost see my meaning, Robin-a-Green? "

"No whit, Witch! Thou growest involved, thy talk diffuse, abstruse and altogether beyond one so obtuse as simple Rob—"

"Then hark 'ee again, Addlepate! Everybodymust believe nobody's body thy body, so by dead body will I make thy live body of so great account to everybody that nobody henceforth shall doubt dead body made live body, by my witchcraft, and thou be feared, therefore, of everybody. Dost follow me now, numskull? "

"Aye, truly, mother! And truly 'tis a rare subtlety, a notable wile, and thou a right cunning witch and wise. But how wilt achieve this wonder? "

"Since dead thou art, I to life will bring thee. Oho, I will summon thee through fire and flame; aha, I will make thee more dreaded than heretofore; thy fame shall fill the wild-wood and beyond. Know'st thou the Haunted Wood, hard by Thraxby Waste? "

Now here Robin's merry smile languished, and he rubbed nose with dubious finger.

"Aye, I do, " quoth he sombrely; "an ill place and—demon-rid, they say—"

"Come ye there to-morrow at midnight. "

"Alone? " says Robin, starting.

"Alone! "

"Nay, good Witch, most gentle, potent dame, I—though phantom accounted, I love not phantoms, and Thraxby Waste—"

"Come ye there—at midnight! "

"Why, then, good Witch, an come I must, suffer that I bring the valiant Fool and mighty Lob—prithee, now! "

At this the old Witch scowled and mumbled and crackled her finger-bones louder than ever.

"Oho! " cried she at last, "thou great child, afraid-o'-the-dark, bring these an ye will—but none other! "

"Good mother, I thank thee! "

"Tchak! " cried the Witch, and, struggling to her feet, hobbled to Jocelyn and laid bony finger on wrist and brow, nodded, mumbled, and so, bent on her staff, hobbled away; but, reaching the cave-mouth, she paused, and smote stick to earth fiercely.

"To-morrow! " she croaked. "Midnight! Re—member! "

FYTTE 8

Tells how the Witch, with incantations dire,
In life to life brought Robin through the fire.

* * * * *

The wind was cold—indeed 'twas plaguy chill—
That furtive crept and crept, like something ill
Stealing with dreadful purpose in the dark,
With scarce a sound its stealthy course to mark;
While pallid moon did seem to swoon, as though
It ghastly things beheld on earth below;
And Robin gripped the good sword by his side,
And Joc'lyn looked about him watchful-eyed;
While Lobkyn Lollo felt and looked the bolder
By reason of the club across his shoulder.

"Here, " whispered Robin, peering through the gloom,
"Is dismal place, I've heard, of death and doom.
Here do be ghosts and goblins, so 'tis said,
Demons, phantoms, spectres of the dead—"
"Aye, verily, " quoth Lob, "and what is worse,
'Tis here my grand-dam oft doth come to curse,
And haunteth it with spiteful toads and bats,
With serpents fell, with ewts and clawful cats.
Here doth she revel hold o' moony nights,
With grave-rank ghouls and moaning spectral sprites;
And... Saints! what's that?
A hook-winged bat?
Not so; perchance, within its hairy body fell
Is man or maid transformed by magic spell.
O, brothers, heedful be, and careful tread
Lest magic gin should catch and strike us dead!
O would my grannam might go with us here.
Since, being witch, she doth no witchcraft fear. "

So came the three at last to Haunted Wood,
Where mighty trees in gloomy grandeur stood,
Their wide-flung boughs so closely interweaving
Scarce space between for ghostly moonbeams leaving;
But, snake-like, round each other closely twined,

The Geste of Duke Jocelyn

In shuddering wind did mournful voices find,
And, groaning, writhed together to and fro
Like souls that did the fiery torment know.
Thus, in the wood, 'twas dark and cold and dank,
And breathed an air of things long dead and rank;
While shapes, dim-seen, did creep and flit and fly
With sudden squeak, and bodeful, wailing cry.

At last they reached a clearing in the wood,
Where, all at once, as 'mid the leaves they stood,
From Lobkyn's lips, loud, tremulous, and high,
There rose and swelled the owlet's shuddering cry.
Scarce on the air this dismal sound had died,
When they the Witch's hobbling form espied.
Beholding Robin, by the arm she caught him,
And to a place of rocks in haste she brought him;
And here, where bosky thickets burgeoned round,
She pointed to a chasm in the ground.

"Go down! " she hissed. "Go down, thou thing of clay,
Thou that art dead—into thy grave I say.
Since thou 'rt hanged, a dead man shalt thou be
Till from thy grave my spells shall summon thee—"
"My grave? " gasped Robin, blenching from her frown.
"Aye, Rogue! " she croaked. "Behold thy grave! Go down! "
So shiv'ring Robin, in most woeful plight,
Crept into gloom and vanished from their sight.
"O, Robin, Robin! " the old Witch softly cried,
"Alack, I'm here! " faint voice, below, replied.
"Thou dead, " croaked she, "thou ghostly shade forlorn,
From charnel-vault sound now thy spectral horn,
Sound now thy rallying-note, then silent be
Till from thy mouldering tomb I summon thee! "

Now, on the stillness rose the ghostly sound
Of Robin's hunting horn that through the ground
Rang thin and high, unearthly-shrill and clear,
That thrilled the shivering woodland far and near,
And shuddering to silence, left behind
A whisper as of leaves in stealthy wind.
A rustling 'mid the underbrush they heard
Where, in the gloom about them, dim things stirred—
Vague, stealing shapes that softly nearer drew,

Till from the tree-gloom crept a ragged crew,
Wild men and fierce, a threatening, grimly herd,
Who stood like shadows, speaking not a word;
And the pale moon in fitful flashes played
On sword and headpiece, pike and broad axe-blade.
While the old hag, o'er witch-fire crouching low,
Puffed at the charcoal till it was aglow;
Then hobbling round and round her crackling fire,
She thus began her incantations dire:

"Come ye long-dead,
Ye spirits dread,

Ye things of quaking fear,
Ye poor, lost souls,
Ye ghosts, ye ghouls,
Haxwiggin bids ye here!
By one by two, by two by three,
Spirits of Night, I summon ye,
By three by four, by four by five,
Come ye now dead that were alive,
Come now I bid ye
From grave-clods rid ye,
Come!
From South and North,
I bid ye forth,
From East, from West,
At my behest—
Come!
Come great, come small,
Come one, come all,
Heed ye my call,
List to my call, I say,
From pitchy gloom
Of mouldered tomb
Here find ye room
For sport and holiday.
Come grisly ghosts and goblins pale,
Come spirits black and grey,
Ye shrouded spectres—Hail, O Hail!
Ho! 'tis your holiday.

Come wriggling snakes
From thorny brakes,
Hail!
Come grimly things
With horny wings,
That flit, that fly,
That croak, that cry,
Hail!

"Come ghouls, come demons one and all,
Here revel whiles ye may;
Ye noisome things that creep and crawl,
Come, sport and round me play.
Ho, claw and wing and hoof and horn,
Here revel till the clammy dawn.

"Peeping, creeping,
Flying, crying,
Fighting, biting,
Groaning, moaning,
Ailing, wailing,
Spirits fell,
Come to my spell,
Ho! 'tis your holiday!
So, are ye there,
High up in air,
The moonbeams riding
'Mid shadows hiding?

"Now gather round, ye spectral crew,
This night have we brave work to do—
Bold Robin o' the Green, 'tis said,
On gallows hangeth cold and dead
Beneath the sky
On gibbet high,
They in a noose did swing him.
Go, goblins, go,
And ere they know,
Unto me hither bring him. "

Here paused the Witch to mend her glowing fire,
While each man to his neighbour shuffled nigher,
As witch-flame leapt and ever brighter grew,

Till, to their horror, sudden it burned blue;
Whereat each silent, fearful beholder
Felt in the gloom to touch his fellow's shoulder,
Yet, in that moment, knew an added dread
To see the fire from blue turn ghastly red;
Then, as the Witch did o'er it crooning lean,
Behold! it changed again to baleful green.
Whereat the Witch flung bony arms on high,
As though with claw-like hands she'd rend the sky;
And while the lurid flames leapt ever higher,
She thus invoked the Spirit of the Fire.

"As fire doth change, yet, changed, unchanged doth burn,
By fiery spell shall dead to life return!

"Ho, goblins yonder—'neath the moon,
Have ye brought me the dead so soon?
Ha! is it Bxibin that ye bring,
That pale, that stiff, that clammy thing?
Now work we spell with might and main,
Shall make it live and breathe again.

"Now in and out,
And round about,
Ye wriggling rout,
With hoof and claw and wing;
Now high, now low,
Now fast, now slow,
Now to and fro
Tread we a magic ring.

"Thus, while the frighted moon doth peep,
We'll wake this cold, dead thing from sleep,
Till Robin back to life shall leap.
And when he from the fire shall spring,
Ye outlaws hail him for your King.

"For on that wight
Who, day or night,
Shall Robin disobey
With purpose fell
I'll cast a spell
Shall wither him away.

116

"Ho, Robin! Ope thy death-cold eyes,
Ho, Robin! From thy grave arise,
Ho, Robin! Robin, ho!
Robin that doth bide so near me,
Robin, Robin, wake and hear me,
Ho, Robin! Robin, ho!

"Back to life I summon thee,
Through the fire thy path must be,
Through the fire that shall not harm thee,
Through flame that back to life shall charm thee,
Shall warm thy body all a-cold,
And make grim Death loose clammy hold.
Ho, Robin-a-Green,
Ho, Robin-a-Green,
Leap back to life by all men seen! "

Through curling smoke-wreaths and through writhing flame,
With mighty bound, bold Robin leaping came,
And by the Witch did in the fire-light stand,
Sword by his side and bugle-horn in hand,
And laughed full blithe as he was wont to do,
And, joyous, hailed his wild and ragged crew:

"What lads, are ye there forsooth? Is't Myles I see with lusty Watt
and John and Hal o' the Quarterstaff? God den t' ye, friends, and
merry hunting to one and all, for by oak and ash and thorn here
stand I to live with thee, aye, good lads, and to die with ye here in
the good greenwood—"

But now and all at once from that grim and silent company a
mighty shout went up:

"'Tis Robin—'tis Robin, 'tis bold Robin-a-Green! 'Tis our Robin
himself come back to us! "

And fearful no longer, they hasted to him and clasped him in
brawny arms, hugging him mightily and making great rejoicing
over him.

FYTTE 9

That tells almost as fully as it should,
The joys of living in the good greenwood.

* * * * *

Deep-hidden in the trackless wild the outlaws had made them a
haven of refuge, a camp remote and well sequestered. Here were
mossy, fern-clad rocks that soared aloft, and here green lawns where
ran a blithesome brook; it was indeed a very pleasant place shut in
by mighty trees. Within this leafy boskage stood huts of wattle,
cunningly wrought; beneath the steep were many caves carpeted
with dried fern and fragrant mosses, while everywhere, above and
around, the trees spread mighty boughs, through which the sun
darted golden beams be-dappling the sward, and in whose leafy
mysteries the birds made joyous carolling.

And here beneath bending willows arched over this merry brook,
one sun-bright morning riotous with song of birds, sat Jocelyn with
Robin a-sprawl beside him.

"O brother, " says Robin, "O brother, 't is a fair place the greenwood,
a fair, sweet place to live—aye, or to die in methinks, this good
greenwood, whereof I have made a song—hark 'ee! "

"Oho, it is a right good thing
When trees do bud and flowers do spring
All in the wood, the fair, green wood,
To hear the birds so blithely sing,
Adown, adown, hey derry down,
All in the good, green wood.

"Who cometh here leaves grief behind,
Here broken man hath welcome kind,
All in the wood, the fair, green wood.
The hopeless here new hope may find,
Adown, adown, hey derry down,
All in the kind, green wood.

"Ho, friend, 'tis pleasant life we lead,
No laws have we, no laws we need

Here i' the good, green wood.
For every man's a man indeed,
Adown, adown, hey derry down,
Here i' the good, green wood.

"All travellers that come this way
Must something in fair tribute pay
Unto the wood, the fair, green wood.
Or here in bonds is like to stay,
Adown, adown, hey derry down,
Lost in the good, green wood.

"Full many a lord, in boastful pride,
This tribute, scornful, hath denied
Unto the wood, the fair, green wood.
And thereupon hath sudden died,
Adown, adown, hey derry down,
All in the fair, green wood.

"And when our time shall come to die
Methinks we here may softly lie
Deep in the fair, green wood.
With birds to sing us lullaby,
Adown, adown, hey derry down,
All in the good, green wood. "

"So there it is, brother—and life and death in a nutshell, as 'twere. Now, wherefore wilt not join us and turn outlaw, good Fool? "

"For that I am a fool belike, Robin. Howbeit, I'm better Fool than outlaw. "

"Say, rather, greater fool, Fool, for foresters' life is better than life o' folly, and payeth better to boot, what with booty—ha! Moreover, I do love thee, since, Fool, though fool, art wise in counsel and valiant beyond thought—so 'tis I would not lose thee. Stay, therefore, and live my comrade and brother, equal with me in all things. How say'st thou? "

"Why, Robin, I say this: True friendship is a goodly thing and a rare in this world, and, therefore, to be treasured; 'tis thing no man may buy or seek, since itself is seeker and cometh of itself; 'tis a prop—a staff in stony ways, a shield 'gainst foes, a light i' the dark. So do I love friendship, Robin, and thou'rt my friend, yet must leave thee, though friendship shall abide. "

Quoth ROBIN: How abide an we be parted?

"In heart and mind and memory, Robin. Moreover, though I go, yet will I return anon, an life be mine. "

"And wherefore go ye, brother? "

"First to seek my comrade. "

"Thy comrade—ha! I mind him, a fierce great fellow with hawk's beak and a fighting eye. And whither trend ye? "

"To Canalise. "

"Art crazed, brother? 'Tis there death waiteth thee! "

"Yet must I go, Robin, since there my heart waiteth me. "

"A maid, brother? "

"A maid, Robin. "

"Heigho! So wilt thou go, come joy, come pain, come life or death, since a maid is made to make man saint or devil, some days glad and some days sad, but ever and always a fool. And thou art Fool by profession, and, being lover professed and confessed, art doubly a fool; and since, good Folly, love's but folly and thou, a Fool, art deep in folly, so is thy state most melancholy. "

"And dost think love so great folly, Robin? " said a soft voice, and, looking round, they beheld the lovely, dark-tressed Melissa, who viewed them bright-eyed and pouted red mouth, frowning a little.

"Aye, verily, lady, " laughed Robin, as she sank on the grass beside them. "Forsooth, 'tis a madness fond. For see, now, a man being in love is out of all else. "

"As how, Sir Outlaw? "

"Marry, on this wise—when man's in love he mopeth apart and is ill company, so is he out o' friends; he hangeth humble head abashed, so is he out o' countenance; he uttereth frequent, windy, sighful suspirations, so is he out o' breath; he lavisheth lucre on his love, so is he out o' pocket; he forsweareth food, despiseth drink, scorneth sleep, so is he out o' health—in fine, he is out of all things, so is he out of himself; therefore he is mad, and so may go hang himself! "

MELISSA: And hast thou loved, Robin?

ROBIN: Ever and always, and none but Robin!

MELISSA: And none more worthy, Robin?

ROBIN: And none more, as I am worthy Robin.

MELISSA: Lovest thou not Love, Robin?

ROBIN: Love, love not I.

MELISSA: Then Love canst thou know not.

ROBIN: Then if I love Love for Love's sake, must Love then love me, therefore?

MELISSA: If thy love for Love be true love, so shall Love love thee true.

ROBIN: Then if Love should love me for my sake, then would I love Love for Love's sake; but since Love ne'er hath sought me for my sake, ne'er will I seek Love for Love's sake for my sake, since Love, though plaguy sweet, is a sweet plague, I judge and, so judging, will by my judgment stand.

MELISBA: And how think you, Sir Fool?

JOCELYN: I think if Love find Robin and Robin, so found of Love, shall learn to love Love for Love's sake, Love shall teach Robin how, hi loving Love—Love, if a plague, doth but plague him lovingly to his better judgment of Love, till, being on this wise, wise—he shall judge of Love lovingly, loving Love at last for Love's own lovely sake, rather than for his own selfish self. For as there is the passion of love, the which is a love selfish, so there is the true Spirit of Love, the which forgetteth self in Love's self, thus, self-forgotten, Love is crowned by Love's true self.

MELISSA: How think ye of this, Robin?

ROBIN: By Cupid, we are so deep in love that we are like to drown of love
and we be not wary. Here hath my lovely jowlopped-crested brother so beset
poor Robin with Love and self and Robin, that Robin kens not which is Love,
Love's self or himself.

MELISSA: And yet I do think 'tis very plain! Yet an thou canst express this
plainer, prithee do, Sir Fool.

"Blithely, sweet lady, here will I frame my meaning in a rhyme, thus:

"Who loveth Love himself above,
With Love base self transcending
Love, Love shall teach how Love may reach
The Love that hath no ending.

"'Tis thus Love-true, Love shall renew,
Love's love thus waning never,
So love each morn of Love new-born,
Love shall live loving ever. "

ROBIN: Aye, verily, there's Love and yet such a love as no man may find methinks, brother.

JOCELYN: Never, Robin, until it find him. For true love, like friendship, cometh unsought, like all other good things.

ROBIN: 'Las! then needs must I be no good thing since I am sought e'en now of old Mopsa the Witch yonder!

And he pointed where the old creature hobbled towards them bent on her crooked staff. Up rose Robin and, hasting to meet her, louted full low, since she was held in great respect of all men by reason of her potent spells. Chuckling evilly, she drew down Robin's tall head to whisper in his ear, whereupon he laughed, clapped hand to brawny thigh, and taking old Mopsa's feeble arm, hastened away with her. But Melissa, reclining 'neath the willow-shade, gazed down into the murmurous waters of the brook with eyes of dream whiles Jocelyn struck soft, sweet chords upon his lute. And presently she turned to view him thoughtfully—his strange, marred face; his eyes so quick and keen 'neath battered cock's-comb; his high, proud bearing despite his frayed and motley habit; and ever her wonder grew until, at last, she must needs question him:

"Fools, Sir Fool, have I seen a-many, both in the motley and out, but thou art rare among all fools, I do think. "

JOCELYN: Gramercy, lady! Truly fool am I of all fools singular.

MELISSA: Thou'rt he I heard, upon a day, sing strange, sweet songs, within the marketplace of Canalise!

JOCELYN: The same, lady.

MELISSA: That soused my lord Gui head over ears in a lily-pool?

JOCELYN: Verily, lady.

MELISSA: O! Would one might do as much for Sir Agramore of Bie4name!

JOCELYN: One doubtless will, lady.

MELISSA: Thyself?

JOCELYN: Nay—one that loveth the disputatious bickering of sharp steel better than I—one had rather fight than eat, and rather fight three men than one—

"Three men? " cried Melissa, starting.

"Aye, lady—and six men than three! "

"There was such an one, Fool, in truth a very brave man, did fight three of my Lord Agramore's foresters on my behalf. Dost know of such an one, Fool? "

"Methinks he is my comrade, Lady."

"Thy comrade—in truth? Then, pray you, speak me what seeming hath he."

"Ill, lady."

"How so, Fool?"

"A great, fierce rogue is he, unlovely of look, bleak of eye, harsh of tongue, hooked of nose, flinty of soul, stony of heart, of aspect grim and manners rude!"

"Then, verily, thy comrade have I never seen!" quoth Melissa, flushing and with head up-flung. "He that saved me is nothing the like of this."

"And yet," said Jocelyn slyly, "'tis thus he hath been named ere now!"

"Nay, Fool, indeed he that saved me was tall and seemly man, very fierce and strong in fight, but to me wondrous gentle—in truth, something timorous, and, 'spite rusty mail, spake and looked like a noble knight."

"Then forsooth, lady, thy champion is no comrade of mine, for he is but a poor rogue, ill-beseen, ill-kempt, ill-spoken, ill-mannered and altogether ill, save only that he is my friend—"

"And thou speakest ill of thy ill friend, the which is ill in thee—ill Fool!" and the fair Melissa rose.

"And pray, lady, didst learn thy preserver's name?"

"Indeed, for I asked him."

"And it was—?"

"Pertinax!" she sighed.

"Pertinax!" said Jocelyn, both in the same moment; the dark-browed Melissa
sat down again.

"So thy comrade and—he are one, Fool? "

"Indeed, lady. Yet here we have him, on the one hand, a man noble and seemly, and, on the other, a poor rogue, hook-nosed, ill-beseen, ill—"

"'Tis thou hast miscalled him, Fool! " said she, frowning.

"Not I, lady. "

"Who, then? "

"A maid—"

"Ah! " said Melissa, frowning blacker than ever. "A maid, Fool? What maid? "

"A wandering gipsy o' the wood, lady—a dark-eyed damsel with long, black curling hair and 'voice of sweet allure'—'tis so he named her—"

"This was belike some wicked witch! " said Melissa, clenching white fist.

"Aye, belike it was, lady, for she bestowed on him a strange jewel, a heart in heart of crystal, that wrought for us in Canalise marvels great as our wondrous Witch herself. "

Now here the lovely Melissa's frown vanished, and her red lips curved to sudden smile.

"Belike this was no witch after all! " said she gently.

"Howbeit, lady, " quoth Jocelyn slyly, "my poor comrade is surely bewitched by her none the less. She hath wrought on him spell so potent that he groweth mopish and talketh of her eyes, her hair, her sweet and gentle voice, her little foot, forsooth. "

"And doth he so, indeed? " said Melissa softly, and, twiddling one of her own pretty feet, she smiled at it. "Doth he sigh o'er much? " she questioned.

"Consumedly! By the minute! "

"Poor soldier! " she murmured.

"Aye, poor rogue! " said Jocelyn; whereupon she frowned again, and turned
her back upon him.

"And he is thy comrade. "

"Even so—poor knave! "

"And destitute—even as thou? "

"Aye, a sorry clapper-claw—even as I, lady. "

"Then, pray thee, why doth he wear gold chain about his neck? "

"Chain, lady—? "

"Such as only knights do wear! "

"Belike he stole it, lady—"

"Aye—belike he did! " said she, rising; then she sighed and laughed, and so turned and left him.

And in a while Jocelyn rose also, and went on beside the brook; but as he walked deep in thought, there met him Robin, he full of mirth and laughter.

"Oho, brother, good brother! " cried he joyfully, clapping hand on Jocelyn's broad shoulder, "come away, now, and see what the good wind hath blown hither—come thy ways and see! "

So came they where rose a great tree of huge girth, whose gnarled branches spread far and wide, a veryforest of leaves, beneath whose shade were many of the outlaws grouped about one who crouched miserably on his knees, his arms fast bound and a halter about his neck; and, as obedient to Robin's words the fierce company fell back, Jocelyn saw this torn and pallid captive was none other than Ranulph the Hangman.

"Woe's me, my masters! " quoth he 'twixt chattering teeth. "'Tis pity poor Ranulph must die before his time, for ne'er shall be found hangman, headsman or torturer the like o' Ranulph—so dainty i' the nice adjustment o' noose! So clean and delicate wi' the axe! So tender and thoughtful wi' pincers, thumbscrew, rack or red-hot iron! A hangman so kindly o' soul, so merry o' heart, alack, so free, so gay, so merry—forsooth a very wanton, waggish, jovial bawcock-lad—"

"Why, then, good, merry wag, " laughed Robin, "now shalt thou cut us an antic aloft in air, shalt caper and dance in noose to our joyance! Up with him, bully lads, and gently, that he may dance the longer! "

But as Ranulph was dragged, shivering, to his feet, Jocelyn stepped forward.

"Stay! " he cried. "Look, now, here's hangman did but hang since hang he must; must he hang therefore? "

ROBIN: Aye, marry, since hanging shall his hanging end!

JOCELYN: But if to hang his duty is, must he for duty hang? Moreover, if ye hang this hangman, unhanged hangmen shall hang still, and since ye may not all hangmen hang, wherefore should this hangman hang?

ROBIN: Brother, an this hangman hang, fewer hangmen shall there be to hang, forsooth.

JOCELYN: Not so, Robin, for hangman dead begetteth hangman new; this hangman hanged, hangman in his place shall hang men after him. Shall this hangman hang for hanging as in duty bound, whiles other hangmen, unhanged, hang still? Here, methinks, is small wisdom, little reason, and less of justice, Robin.

ROBIN: Beshrew me, brother—but here's so much of hanging hanging on hanging plaguy hangman that hang me if I get the hang on't—

JOCELYN: Plainly, Robin—wilt hang a man for doing his duty?

ROBIN: Plainly, brother—no. But—

JOCELYN: Then canst not hang this hangman, since hanging his duty is—

ROBIN: Yet 'tis base, vile duty —

JOCELYN: Yet duty it is—wherefore, an there be any justice in the good greenwood, this hangman unhanged must go.

Now here Robin scowled, and his brawny fellows scowled likewise, and began to mutter and murmur against Jocelyn, who, leaning back to tree, strummed his lute and sang:

"O, Life is sweet, but Life is fleet,
O'er quick to go, alack!
And once 'tis spilt, try as thou wilt,
Thou canst not call it back!

"So bethink thee, bold Robin, and, as thou 'rt king o' the wild-wood, be thou just king and merciful—"

"Now out upon thee, brother! " cried Robin, forgetting to scowl. "Out on thee with thy honied phrases, thy quipsome lilting rhymes! Here go I to do a thing I ha' no lust to do—and all by reason o' thee! Off—off wi' the halter, lads—loose the hangman-claws of him! Hereafter, since he can pay no ransom, he shall be our serf; to have a hangman fetch and carry shall be rare, methinks! "

Quoth JOCELYN: How much should hangman's flesh be worth i' the greenwood, Robin?

"Why, brother, 'tis poor, sad and dismal knave; five gold pieces shall buy him, aye—halter and all, and 'tis fair, good halter, look you! "

"Why, then, " said Jocelyn, opening his wallet, "behold the monies, so do I buy him of thee—"

"Now, by Saint Nick! " cried Robin, amazed. "Nay, brother, an thou'lt buy so sorry a thing, give thy money to the merry lads; I'll none on't. And now, " said he, the money duly paid, "what wilt do wi' thy hangman? "

"Sir Fool, " cried Ranulph, falling on his knees at Jocelyn's feet, "fain would I serve thee—e'en to the peril o' the life thou hast saved. Bid me labour for thee and in labour shall be my joy, bid me fight for thee and I will fight whiles life is in me; bid me follow thee and I will follow even unto—"

"Nay, hangman, " said Jocelyn, "I bid thee rise and sing for us, and so be gone wheresoever thou wilt. "

Then Ranulph arose and glancing round upon the fierce company, from the noose at his feet to Jocelyn's scarred face, he drew a great breath; quoth he:

"Sir Fool, since 'tis thy will fain would I give thee song blithe and joyful since joy is in my heart, but alack, though my songs begin in merry vein they do grow mournful anon; howbeit, for thy joy now will I sing my cheeriest; " whereupon Ranulph brake into song thus:

"I am forsooth a merry soul,
Hey deny down, ho ho!
I love a merry song to troll,
I love to quaff a cheery bowl,
And yet thinks I, alas!
Such things too soon do pass,
And proudest flesh is grass.
Alack-a-day and woe,
Alack it should be so!

"A goodly lover I might be,
Merrily, ho ho!
But pretty maids in terror flee,
When this my hangman's head they see.
But woe it is, thinks I,
All fair, sweet dames must die,
And pale, sad corpses lie.
Alack-a-day and woe,
Alack it should be so!

"Fairest beauty is but dust,
Shining armour soon will rust,
All good things soon perish must,
Look around, thinks I, and see
All that, one day, dead must be,
King and slave and you and me.
Alack-a-day and woe,
Alack it must be so! "

"Out! " cried Robin. "Here forsooth is dolorous doleful dirge—out on thee for sad and sorry snuffler! "

"Aye, verily, " sighed Ranulph, "'tis my curse. I begin with laugh and end in groan. I did mean this for merry song, yet it turned of itself sad song despite poor I, and there's the pity on't—"

"Enough! " growled Robin, "away with him. Brand, do you hoodwink him in his 'kerchief and give him safe conduct to beyond the ford, and so set Master Hangman Grimglum-grief on his road—"

"Sir Fool, " cried Ranulph, "God den t'ye and gramercy. Should it be e'er thy fate to die o' the gallows, may I have thy despatching—I will contrive it so sweetly shalt know nought of it—oho! 'twould be my joy. "

"Off! " cried Robin. "Off, thou pestiferous fungus lest I tread on thee—hence, away! "

So the outlaws blindfolded Ranulph and led him off at speed.

"Away, " quoth Jocelyn, nodding, "so now in faith must I, Robin—"

"What, is't indeed farewell, brother? "

"Aye, Robin. "

"Why, then, what may I give thee in way o' love and friendship? "

"Thy hand. "

"Behold it, brother! And what beside? Here is purse o' good pieces—ha? "

"Nay, Robin, prithee keep them for those whose need is greater. "

"Can I nought bestow—dost lack for nothing, brother? "

"What thou, methinks, may not supply—"

"And that? "

"Horse and armour! " Now at this, Robin laughed and clapped hand to thigh;

quoth he:

"Come with Robin, brother! " So he brought Jocelyn into a cave beneath the steep and, lighting a torch from fire that burned there, led him on through other caves and winding passages rough-hewn in the rock, and so at last to a vasty cavern.

And here was great store of merchandise of every sort, —velvets, silks, and rich carpets from the Orient; vases of gold and silver, and coffers strong-clamped with many iron bands. And here also, hanging against the rocky walls, were many and divers suits of armour with helms and shields set up in gallant array; beholding all of which Jocelyn paused to eye merry Robin askance; quoth he soberly:

"Sir Rogue, how came ye by all this goodly furniture? "

"By purest chance, brolher, " laughed Robin, "for hark 'ee —

   "Chance is a wind to outlaws kind,
   And many fair things blows us,
   It—merchants, priors, lords, knights and squires,
   And like good things bestows us—"

"Aye, " said Jocelyn, "but what of all those knights and squires whose armour hangeth here? "

"Here or there, brother, they come and they go. Ha, yonder soundeth Ralfwyn's horn—three blasts which do signify some right fair windfall. Come, let us see what this jolly wind hath blown us this time! " So saying, Robin laughed and led the way out into the sunny green. And here, surrounded by a ring of merry forest rogues, they beheld a knight right gallantly mounted and equipped, his armour blazing in the sun, his gaudy bannerole a-flutter from long lance, his shield gaudy and brave with new paint; beholding which, Robin chuckled gleefully; quoth he:

"Oho! On a field vert three falcons gules, proper, charged with heart ensanguined—aha, here's good booty, methinks! "

Now, as this splendid knight rode nearer, contemptuous of his brawny captors, Robin stared to see that on his helmet he wore a wreath of flowers, while lance and sword, mace and battle-axe were wreathed in blooming roses.

"Ho, Jenkyn, Cuthbert! " cried Robin, "what Sir Daintiness have ye here? " But ere his grinning captors could make reply, the knight himself spake thus:

"Behold a very gentle knight,
Sir Palamon of Tong,
A gentle knight in sorry plight,
That loveth love and hateth fight,
A knight than fight had rather write,
And strophes to fair dames indite,
Or sing a sighful song.

"By divers braggarts I'm abused,
'Tis so as I've heard tell,
Because, since I'm to fight unused,
I many a fight have bold refused,
And, thereby, saved my bones unbruised,
Which pleaseth me right well.

"No joy have I in steed that prances,
True gentle man am I
To tread to lutes slow, stately dances.
'Stead of your brutish swords and lances,
I love love's lureful looks and glances,
When hand to hand, unseen, advances,
And eye caresseth eye. "

"And how a plague, Sir Gentleness, " questioned Robin, "may eye caress eye? "

"E'en as lips voiceless may wooing speak, Sir Roguery, and tongue unwagging tell tales o' love, Sir Ferocity. "

ROBIN: Then had I the trick o' voiceless speech, now would I, with silly tongue, tell thee thou art our prisoner to ransom, Sir Silken Softness.

SIR PALAMON: And I joy therefore, Sir Forest Fiend.

ROBIN: And wherefore therefore?

SIR PALAMON: For that therefore I need not to the joust, to that bone-shattering sport of boastful, brutal braggadocios, but here, lapped soft in the gentle green, woo the fair Yolande—

JOCELYN: How, knight, the fair lady Yolande, say'st thou?

SIR PALAMON: Even she.

JOCELYN: But here she is not and thou art, how then may one that is, woo one is not?

SIR PALAMON: Gross mountebank, by thought—I woo in thought, breathe my thought upon the balmy air and air beareth it to her feet.

ROBIN: And she treadeth on't, so there's an end o' thy love! But pray you, Sir Downy Daintiness, how come ye that are so gentle so ungently dight? Discourse, Sir Dove!

SIR PALAMON: In two words then, thou lewd lurcher o' the thickets; I ride thus in steely panoply—the which doth irk me sore— by reason of the tongue of my mother (good soul!) the which doth irk me more. For she (worthy lady!) full-fed o' fatuous fantasies and fables fond, fuddled i' faith o' faddling fictions as—gestes of jongleurs, tales told by tramping troubadours, ballades of babbling braggarts, romances of roysterous rhymers, she (good gossip!) as I say, having hearkened to and perused the works of such-like pelting, paltry prosers and poets wherein sweep of sword and lunge o' lance is accompted of worthier repute than the penning of dainty distich and pretty poesies pleasingly passionate. She, I say—my mother (God rest her!), e'en she with tongue most harsh, most bitter and most unwearying, hath enforced me, her son (whom Venus bless!)— e'en I that am soul most transcendental—I that am a very wing-ed Mercury—me, I say she hath, by torrential tongueful tumult (gentle lady!), constrained to don the habit of a base, brawling, beefy and most material Mars! Wherefore at my mother's behest (gracious dame!) I ride nothing joyful to be bruised and battered by any base, brutal braggart that hath the mind to try a tilt with me. Moreover—

ROBIN: Hold! Take breath, gentle sir, for thine own sweet sake draw thy wind.

SIR PALAMON: 'Tis done, fellow, 'tis done! And now in three words will I—

ROBIN: Cry ye mercy, sir, thy two words do yet halloo "Buzz-buzz" in mine ears.

SIR PALAMON: Faith, robber-rogue, since I a tongue possess —

ROBIN: Therein thou art very son o' thy mother (whom St. Anthony cherish!).

SIR PALAMON: With this rare difference, outlaw — for whereas her tongue (honoured relict!) is tipped with gall, wormwood, henbane, hemlock, bitter-aloes and verjuice, and stingeth like the adder, the asp, the toad, the newt, the wasp, and snaky-haired head of Medusa, mine —

ROBIN: Buzzeth, buzz, O buzz!

SIR PALAMON: Mine, thou paltry knave, I say mine —

ROBIN: Buzz — ha — buzz!

JOCELYN: I pray you, Sir Knight, doth the Red Gui tilt at to-morrow's joust?

SIR PALAMON: Base mime, he doth! My Lord Gui of Ells, Lord Seneschal of Raddemore, is myfriend, a very mirror of knightly prowess, the sure might of whose lance none may abide. He is, in very truth, the doughtiest champion in all this fair country, matchless at any and every weapon, a-horse or a-foot, in sooth a very Ajax, Achilles, Hector, Roland and Oliver together and at once, one and indivisible, aye — by Cupid a very paladin!

"'Tis so I've heard, " said Jocelyn thoughtfully.

SIR PALAMON: Two knights only there are might cope with him, and one Sir Agramore and one Jocelyn of the Helm, Duke of Brocelaunde. The fame of which last rumour hath so puffed up that thrice my Lord Gui hath sent his cartel of defiance, but the said Duke, intent on paltry battles beyond his marches, hath thrice refused, and wisely — so 'tis said.

"Aye me, messire, " quoth Jocelyn, strumming his lute, "and so bloweth the wind. Yet mayhap these twain shall meet one day. "

ROBIN: And heaven send me there to see! Now as to thee, Sir Softly Sweet, fair Lord of Tong, thy goodly horse and armour are mine henceforth, first because thy need of them is nothing, secondly because thou art my prisoner—

SIR PALAMON: And thirdly, Sir Riotous Roughness, I do freely on thee bestow them, hide and hair, bolt and rivet.

ROBIN: Now as to thy ransom, Sir Mildly-Meek, at what price dost rate thy value, spiritual and corporeal?

SIR PALAMON: Fellow, though youthful, well-favoured and poet esteemed, I am yet marvellous modest! 'Tis true I am knight of lineage lofty, of patrimony proud, of manors many—

ROBIN: Even as of thy words, Sir Emptiness.

SIR PALAMON: 'Tis also true, thou ignorant atomy, I, like Demosthenes, am blessed with a wonder o' words and glory o' sweet phrase, and yet, and here's the enduring wonder—I am still but man, though man blessed with so much profundity, fecundity, and redundity of thought and expression, and therefore a facile scribe or speaker, able to create, relate, formulate or postulate any truth, axiomatic, sophistry subtle, or, in other words, I can narrate—

ROBIN: Verily Sir Windbag thou dost, to narrate, thyself with wind inflate, and, being thus thyself inflate of air, thou dost thyself deflate of airy sounds which be words o' wind, and windy words is emptiness—thus by thy inflatings and deflatings cometh nought but wind bred o' wind, and nought is nothing, so nought is thy relation or narration; whereof make now a cessation, so will I, in due form, formulate, postulate and deliberate. Thus, with my good rogues' approbation and acclamation, I will of thy just valuation make tabulation, and give demonstration in relation to thy liberation from this thy situation, as namely, viz. and to-wit: First thou art a poet; in this is thy marketable value to us nought, for poets do go empty of aught but thought of sort when wrought, unbought; thus go they short which doth import they're empty, purse and belly. Second, upon thy testimony thou'rt a man. Go to! Here we be out again, for on the score of manliness thou art not. Yet thou art flesh and blood— good! for here we deal in such. Not that we yearn for thy flesh and blood, but, being thine, they are to thee dear, perchance, and thou would'st fain keep them alive a little longer; wherefore thou shalt for thy loved flesh and blood pay—purchasing the same of us. And, as flesh varies, so do our prices vary; we do sell a man his own flesh and blood at certain rateable values. Thus unto a hangman we did of late sell a hangman, in fair good halter, and he a hangman brawny, for no more than five gold pieces, the which was cheap, methinks, considering the goodly halter, and he a lusty, manly rogue to boot. Now as for thee, thou'rt soft and of a manlihood indifferent, so would I rate thee at one gold piece.

SIR PALAMON: Ignorant grub! Am I less than base hangman—I, a knight—

ROBIN: True, Sir Knight, thou'rt a knight for no reason but that thou art knight born and thus, by nought but being born, hath won to thyself nobility, riches and honours such as no man may win either by courage, skill, or learning, since highborn fool and noble rogue do rank high 'bove such. So *thou* art knight, Sir Knight, and for thy knighthood, thy lineage lofty, thy manors many, mulcted thou shalt be in noble fashion. For thy manhood I assess thee at one gold piece, but, since thou'rt son o' thy dam (whom the Saints pity!) we do fine thee five thousand gold pieces—thy body ours until the purchase made. Away with him, lads; cherish him kindly, unarm him gently, and set him a-grinding corn till his ransom be paid—away!

Now here was mighty roar of laughter and acclaim from all who heard, only Sir Palamon scowled, and, for once mute and tongue-tied, was led incontinent away to his labours.

"And now, brother, " quoth Robin, turning where Jocelyn stood smiling and merry-eyed, "what o' this armour dost seek, and wherefore? "

"Art a lovely robber, Robin, " said he; "a very various rogue, yet no rogue born, methinks! "

"I was not always outlaw, brother—howbeit, what would a Fool with horse and knightly arms? "

Now Jocelyn, bending close, whispered somewhatin Robin's ear, whereon he clapped hand to thigh, and laughed and laughed until the air rang again.

"Oho, a jape—a jape indeed! " he roared. "O lovely brother, to see proud knight unhorsed by prancing motley Fool! Hey, how my heart doth jump for gladness! An thou wilt a-tilting ride, I will squire thee—a Fool of a knight tended by Rogue of a squire. O, rare—aha! oho! Come thy ways, sweet brother, and let us set about this joyous jape forthwith! "

And thus it was that, as evening fell, there rode, through bowery bracken and grassy glade, two horsemen full blithe and merry, and the setting sun flashed back in glory from their glittering armour.

FYTTE 10

How Red Gui sore smitten was in fight
By motley Fool in borrowed armour dight.

* * * * *

Now shrill tucket and clarion, trumpet and horn
With their cheery summons saluted the morn,
Where the sun, in his splendour but newly put on,
Still more splendid made pennon and brave gonfalon
That with banners and pennoncelles fluttered and flew
High o'er tent and pavilion of every hue.
For the lists were placed here, for the tournament set,
Where already a bustling concourse was met;
Here were poor folk and rich folk, lord, lady and squire,
Clad in leather, in cloth and in silken attire;
Here folk pushed and folk jostled, as people still do
When the sitters be many, the seats scant and few;
Here was babble of voices and merry uproar,
For while some folk laughed loud, some lost tempers and swore.
Until on a sudden this tumult and riot
Was hushed to a murmur that sank into quiet
As forth into the lists, stern of air, grave of face,
Five fine heralds, with tabard and trumpet, did pace
With their Lion-at-arms, or Chief Herald, before;
And a look most portentous this Chief Herald wore,
And, though portly his shape and a little too round,
Sure a haughtier Chief Herald could nowhere be found.
So aloof was his look and so grave his demeanour,
Humble folk grew abashed, and mean folk felt the meaner;
When once more the loud clarions had all echoes woke
This Chief Herald in voice deep and sonorous spoke:

"Good people all,
Both great and small,
Oyez!
Ye noble dames of high degree
Your pretty ears now lend to me,
And much I will declare to ye.
Oyez! Oyez!
Ye dainty lords of might and fame,

Ye potent gentles, do the same,
Ye puissant peers of noble name,
Now unto ye I do proclaim:
Oyez! Oyez! Oyez! "

Here pealed the trumpets, ringing loud and clear,
That deafened folk who chanced to stand too near.
In special one—a bent and hag-like dame,
Who bent o'er crooked staff as she were lame;
Her long, sharp nose—but no, her nose none saw,
Since it was hidden 'neath the hood she wore
But from this hood she watched with glittering eye
Four lusty men-at-arms who lolled hard by,
Who, 'bove their armour, bore on back and breast
A bloody hand—Lord Gui's well-hated crest,
And who, unwitting of the hooded hag,
On sundry matters let their lewd tongues wag:

THE FIRST SOLDIER: Why, she scorned him, 'tis well beknown!

THE SECOND SOLDIER: Aye, and it doth not do to scorn the Red Gui, look 'ee!

THE THIBD SOLDIER: She'll lie snug in his arms yet, her pride humbled, her proud spirit broke, I'll warrant me!

THE FOURTH SOLDIER: She rideth hence in her litter, d'ye see; and with but scant few light-armed knaves attendant.

THE FIRST SOLDIER: Aye, and our signal my lord's hunting-horn thrice winded—

Thus did they talk, with laughter loud and deep,
While nearer yet the hooded hag did creep;
But: —
Now blew the brazen clarions might and main,
Which done, the portly Herald spake again:

"Good people, all ye lords and ladies fair,
Oyez!
Now unto ye forthwith I do declare
The charms of two fair dames beyond compare.
Oyez! Oyez! Oyez!

The first, our Duchess—Benedicta hight,
That late from Tissingors, her town, took flight,
To-day, returning here, doth bless our sight,
And view the prowess of each valiant knight;
Each champ-i-on, in shining armour dight,
With blunted weapons gallantly shall fight.
And, watched by eyes of ladies beamy-bright,
Inspired and strengthened by this sweet eye-light,
Shall quit themselves with very main and might;
The second: —in her beauty Beauty's peer,
Yolande the Fair, unto our Duchess dear,
For whose sweet charms hath splintered many a spear,
Throned with our lovely Duchess, sitteth here
With her bright charms all gallant hearts to cheer.
Now, ye brave knights, that nought but Cupid fear,
To these sweet dames give eye, to me give ear!
Oyez!
'Tis now declared—"

My daughter GILLIAN expostulateth:

GILL: O, father, now
You must allow
That your herald is rather a bore.
He talks such a lot,
And it seems frightful rot—

MYSELF: I hate slang, miss! I told you before!
If my herald says much,
Yet he only says such
As by heralds was said in those days;
Though their trumpets they blew,
It is none the less true
That they blew them in other folks' praise.
If my herald verbose is
And gives us large doses
Of high-sounding rodomontade,
You'll find they spoke so
In the long, long ago,
So blame not—O, blame not the bard.
But while we are prating
Our herald stands waiting
In a perfectly terrible fume,

So, my dear, here and now,
The poor chap we'll allow
His long-winded speech to resume:

"'Tis here declared by order of the Ten,
Fair Benedicta's guardians—worthy men!
Thus they decree—ye lovers all rejoice!
She shall by their command, this day make choice
Of him—O, him! O blest, thrice blessed he
Who must anon her lord and husband be.
'Tis so pronounced by her grave guardians ten,
By them made law—and they right reverend men!
And this the law—our lady, be it said,
This day shall choose the husband she must wed;
And he who wins our Duchess for his own
Crowned by her love shall mount to ducal throne,
So let each knight, by valiant prowess, prove
Himself most worthy to our lady's love.
Now make I here an end, and ending, pray
Ye quit you all like val'rous knights this day. "

Thus spake the Chief Herald and so paced solemnly down the lists
while the long clarions filled the air with gallant music. But the
lovely Benedicta, throned beneath silken canopy, knit her black
brows and clenched slender hands and stamped dainty foot, yet
laughed thereafter, whereupon Yolande, leaning to kiss her flushed
cheek, questioned her, wondering:

"How say'st thou to this, my loved Benedicta? "

Quoth the DUCHESS:

"I say, my sweeting, 'tis quite plain
That I must run away again!

Howbeit I care not one rush for their laws! Marry forsooth—a fig! Let
them make laws an they will, these reverend, right troublesome
grey-beards of mine, they shall never wed me but to such a man as
Love shall choose me, and loving him—him only will I wed, be he
great or lowly, rich or poor, worthy or unworthy, so I do love him, as
is the sweet and wondrous way of love. "

"Ah, Benedicta! what is love? "

141

"A joy that cometh but of itself, all unsought! This wisdom had I of a Fool i' the forest. Go learn you of this same Fool and sigh not, dear wench. "

"Nay, but, " sighed Yolande, lovely cheeks a-flush, "what of Sir Agramore—hath he not sworn to wed thee? "

"I do fear Sir Agramore no longer, Yolande, since I have found me one may cope with him perchance—even as did a Fool with my Lord Gui of Ells upon a tune. Art sighing again, sweet maid? "

"Nay, indeed—and wherefore should I sigh? "

"At mention of a Fool, belike. "

"Ah, no, no, 'twere shame in me, Benedicta! A Fool forsooth! "

"Yet Fool of all fools singular, Yolande. And for all his motley a very man, methinks, and of a proud, high bearing. "

Here Yolande's soft cheek grew rosy again:

"Yet is he but motley Fool—and his face—marred hatefully—"

"Hast seen him smile, Yolande, for then—how, dost sigh again, my sweet? "

"Nay, indeed; but talk we of other matters—thy so sudden flight— tell me all that chanced thee, dearest Benedicta. "

"Why first—in thine ear, Yolande—my jewel is not—see! "

"How—how, alas! O most sweet lady—hast lost it? Thy royal amulet? "

"Bestowed it, Yolande. "

"Benedicta! On whom? "

"A poor soldier. One that saved me i' the forest from many of Sir Agramore's verderers—a man very tall and strong and brave, but dight in ragged cloak and rusty mail—"

"Ragged? A thief—"

"Mayhap! "

"An outlaw—"

"Mayhap! "

"A wolf's-head—a wild man and fierce. "

"True he is very wild and very fierce, but very, very gentle—"

"And didst give to such thy jewel? O Benedicta! The Heart-in-heart? "

"Freely—gladly! He begged it of me very humbly and all unknowing what it signified—"

"O my loved Benedicta, alas! "

"O my sweet Yolande, joy! "

"But if he should claim thee, and he so poor and wild and ragged—"

"If he should, Yolande, if he should—

  'He that taketh Heart-in-heart,
  Taketh all and every part. '

O, if he should, Yolande, then I—must fulfil the prophecy. Nay, dear my friend, stare not so great and sadly-eyed, he knoweth not the virtue of the jewel nor have I seen him these many days. "

"And must thou sigh therefore, Benedicta? "

But now the trumpets blew a fanfare, and forth rode divers gallant knights, who, spurring rearing steeds, charged amain to gore, to smite and batter each other with right good will while the concourse shouted, caps waved and scarves and ribands fluttered.

  But here, methinks, it booteth not to tell
  Of every fierce encounter that befell;
  How knight 'gainst knight drove fierce with pointless spear
  And met with shock that echoed far and near;

Or how, though they with blunted swords did smite,
Sore battered was full many a luckless wight.
But as the day advanced and sun rose high
Full often rose the shout: "A Gui—A Gui! "
For many a proud (though bruised and breathless) lord,
Red Gui's tough lance smote reeling on the sward;
And ever as these plaudits shook the air,
Through vizored casque at Yolande he would stare.

And beholding all the beauty of her he smiled evilly and muttered to himself, glancing from her to certain lusty men-at-arms who, lolling 'gainst the barriers, bore at back and breast his badge of the bloody hand.

But the fair Yolande heeded him none at all, sitting with eyes a-dream and sighing ever and anon; insomuch that the Duchess, watching her slyly, sighed amain also and presently spake:

"Indeed, and O verily, Yolande, meseemeth we do sigh and for ever sigh, thou and I, like two poor, love-sick maids. How think'st thou? "

"Nay, O Benedicta, hearken! See, who rideth yonder? "

Now even as thus fair Yolanda spoke,
A horn's shrill note on all men's hearing broke,
And all eyes turned where rode a gallant knight,
In burnished armour sumptuously bedight.
His scarlet plumes 'bove gleaming helm a-dance,
His bannerole a-flutter from long lance,
His gaudy shield with new-popped blazon glowed:
Three stooping falcons that on field vert showed;
But close-shut vizor hid from all his face
As thus he rode at easy, ambling pace.

"Now as I live! " cried Benedicta. "By his device yon should be that foolish knight Sir Palamon of Tong! "

"Aye, truly! " sighed Yolande. "Though he wear no motley hither rideth indeed a very fool. And look, Benedicta—look! O, sure never rode knight in like array—see how the very populace groweth dumb in its amaze! "

For now the crowd in wonderment grew mute,
To see this knight before him bare a lute,
While blooming roses his great helmet crowned,
They wreathed his sword, his mighty lance around.
Thus decked rode he in rosy pageantry,
And up the lists he ambled leisurely;
Till, all at once, from the astonied crowd
There brake a hum that swelled to laughter loud;
But on he rode, nor seemed to reck or heed,
Till 'neath the balcony he checked his steed.
Then, handing lance unto his tall esquire,
He sudden struck sweet chord upon his lyre,
And thus, serene, his lute he plucked until
The laughter died and all stood hushed and still;
Then, hollow in his helm, a clear voice rang,
As, through his lowered vizor, thus he sang:

"A gentle knight behold in me,
(Unless my blazon lie!)
For on my shield behold and see,
Upon field vert, gules falcons three,
Surcharged with heart ensanguiney,
To prove to one and all of ye,
A love-lorn knight am I. "

But now cometh (and almost in haste) the haughty and right
dignified Chief Herald with pursuivants attendant, which latter
having trumpeted amain, the Herald challenged thus:

"Messire, by the device upon thy shield,
We know my Lord of Tong is in the field;
But pray thee now declare, pronounce, expound,
Why thus ye ride with foolish roses crowned? "

Whereto the Knight maketh answer forthwith:

"If foolish be these flowers I bear,
Then fool am I, I trow.
Yet, in my folly, fool doth swear,
These flowers to fool an emblem rare
Of one, to fool, more sweet, more fair,
E'en she that is beyond compare,
A flower perchance for fool to wear,

Who shall his foolish love declare
Till she, mayhap, fool's life may share,
Nor shall this fool of love despair,
Till foolish hie shall go.

"For life were empty, life were vain,
If true love come not nigh,
Though honours, fortune, all I gain,
Yet poorer I than poor remain,
If true-love from me fly;
So here I pray,
If that thou may,
Ah—never pass me by! "

Here the Chief Herald frowned, puffing his cheeks, and waved his ebony staff authoritatively.

Quoth he: "Enough, Sir Knight! Here is no place for love! For inasmuch as we—"

THE KNIGHT: Gentle Herald, I being here, here is Love, since I am lover, therefore love-full, thus where I go goeth Love—

The Herald: Apprehend me, Sir Knight! For whereas love hath no part in—

The Knight: Noble Herald, Love hath every part within me and without, thus I, from Love apart, have no part, and my love no part apart from my every part; wherefore, for my part, and on my part, ne'er will I with Love part for thy part and this to thee do I impart—

"Sweet Saints aid us! " The Chief Herald clasped his massy brow and gazed with eye distraught. "Sir Knight—messire—my very good and noble Lord of Tong—I grope! Here is that which hath a seeming... thy so many parts portend somewhat... and yet... I excogitate... yet grope I still ... impart, part... thy part and its part... so many parts... and roses ... and songs o' love... a lute! O, thundering Mars, I... Sound, trumpets! "

But the Duchess up-starting, silenced Herald and trumpeters with imperious hand.

146

"Sir Knight of Tong, " said she, "'tis told thou'rt of nimble tongue and a maker of songs, so we bid thee sing if thy song be of Love—for Love is a thing little known and seldom understood these days. Here be very many noble knights wondrous learned in the smiting of buffets, but little else; here be noble dames very apt at the play of eyes, the twining of fingers, the languishment of sighs, that, seeking True-love, find but its shadow; and here also grey beards that have forgot the very name of Love. So we bid thee sing us of Love—True-love, what it is. Our ears attend thee! "

"Gracious lady, " answered the Knight, "gladly do I obey. But Love is mighty and I lowly, and may speak of Love but from mine own humility. And though much might be said of Love since Love's empire is the universe and Love immortal, yet will I strive to portray this mighty thing that is True-love in few, poor words. "

Then, plucking sweet melody from his lute, the Knight sang as here followeth:

"What is Love? 'Tis this, I say,
Flower that springeth in a day
Ne'er to die or fade away
Since True-love dieth never.

"Though youth, alas! too soon shall wane,
Though friend prove false and effort vain,
True-love all changeless doth remain
The same to-day and ever. "

Now while the clarions rang out proclaiming Sir Palamon's defiance, Benedicta looked on Yolande and Yolande on Benedicta:

"O, wonderful! " cried the Duchess. "My Lord of Tong hath found him manhood and therewith a wisdom beyond most and singeth such love as methought only angels knew and maids might vision in their dreams. Ah, Yolande—that such a love could be... e'en though he went ragged and poor in all but love.... "

"Benedicta, " sighed Yolande, hands clasped on swelling bosom, "O Benedicta, here is no foolish Lord of Tong... and yet... O, I am mad! "

"Why, then, 'tis sweet madness! So, my Yolande, let us be mad awhile together... thou—a Fool... and I—a beggar-rogue! "

"Nay—alas, dear Benedicta! This were shame—"

"And forsooth is it shame doth swell thy heart, Yolande, light the glamour in thine eyes and set thee a-tremble—e'en as I? Nay indeed, thou'rt a-thrill with Folly... and I, with Roguery. Loved Folly! Sweet Roguery! O Yolande, let us fly from empty state, from this mockery of life and learn the sweet joys of... of beggary, and, crowned with poverty, clasp life—"

> MYSELF, myself interrupting:
> By the way, my dear, you'll understand,
> Though this is very fine,
> Still, her Grace's counsel to Yolande
> Must not be in your line!
> Not that I'd have you wed for wealth,
> Or many a beggar-man by stealth,
> But I would have you, if you can—
>
> GILL: Marry some strong, stern, silent man,
> Named Mark, and with hair slightly gray by the ears!
> Now he's just the sort who would bore me to tears.
> If I for a husband feel ever inclined,
> I shall choose quite an ordin'ry husband—the kind
> With plenty of money and nothing to do,
> With a nice, comfy house, and a motor or two—
>
> MYSELF: That's all very fine, miss, but what would you do
> If he, by some ill-chance, quite penniless grew?
>
> GILL: Oh, why then—why, of course,
> I should get a divorce—
>
> MYSELF: A divorce? Gracious heaven! For goodness' sake—
>
> GILL: 'Twould be the most dignified action to take!
>
>
> MYSELF: Pray, what in the world of such things do you know?
>
> GILL: Well, father, like you—each day older I grow.
> But, instead of discussing poor me,
> I think you would much nicer be

To get on with our Geste.

MYSELF: I obey your behest!

Said Yolande to the duchess, said she:

"Nay, my Benedicta, these be only dreams, but life is real and dreams a very emptiness! "

"And is 't so, forsooth? " exclaimed the Duchess. "Then am I nought but a duchess and lonely, thou a maid fearful of her own heart, and yon singer of love only a very futile knight, Sir Palamon of Tong, nothing esteemed by thee for wit or valour and little by his peers— see how his challengers do throng. How think you? " But the lady Yolande sat very still and silent, only she stared, great-eyed, where danced the scarlet plume.

And indeed many and divers were the knights who, beholding the blazon of Tong, sent the bearer their defiance, eager to cope with him; and each and every challenge Sir Palamon accepted by mouth of his tall esquire who (vizor closed, even as his lord's) spake the Chief Herald in loud, merry voice, thus:

"Sir Herald, whereas and forinasmuch as this, my Lord of Tong himself, himself declaring fool, is so himself-like as to meet in combat each and every of his challengers—themselves ten, my lord that is fool, himself himself so declaring, now declareth by me that am no fool but only humble esquire—messire, I say, doth his esquire require that I, the said esquire, should on his part impart as followeth, namely and to wit: That these ten gentle knights, the said challengers, shall forthwith of themselves choose of themselves, themselves among themselves thereto agreeing, which of themselves, among themselves of themselves so chosen, shall first in combat adventure himself against my Lord of Tong himself. And moreover, should Fortune my lord bless with victory, the nine remaining shall among themselves choose, themselves agreeing, which of themselves shall next, thus chosen of themselves, themselves represent in single combat with this very noble, fool-like Lord of Tong, my master. Furthermore, whereas and notwithstanding—"

"Hold, sir! " cried the Chief Herald, fingering harassed brow. "Pray thee 'bate—O, abate thy speechful fervour. Here forsooth and of truth is notable saying—O, most infallibly—and yet perchance something discursive and mayhap a little involved. "

"Nay, Sir Herald, " quoth the esquire, "if involved 'twill be resolved if revolved, thus: Here be ten lords would fight one, and one—that is my lord who is but one—ten fight one by one. But that ten, fighting one, may as one fight, let it be agreed that of these ten one be chosen one to fight, so shall one fight one and every one be satisfied—every one of these ten fighting one, one by one. Thus shall ten be one, and one ten fight one by one till one be discomfited. Shall we accord the matter simply, thus? "

"Sir, " quoth the Chief Herald, gasping a little, "Amen! "

"O! " cried the Duchess, clapping her hands, "O Yolande, hark to this rare esquire! Surely, I have heard yon cunning tongue ere this? "

But Yolande gazed ever where Sir Palamon, having taken his station, set himself in array. For now, the ten knights having chosen one to represent them, forth rode their champion resplendent in shining mail and green surcoat with heralds before to proclaim his name and rank.

"Yolande, " quoth the Duchess softly, "pray—pray this Lord of Tong may tilt as bravely as he doth sing, for Sir Thomas of Thornydyke is a notable jouster. "

The trumpets blew a fanfare and, levelling their pointless lances, both knights gave spur, their great horses reared, broke into a gallop and thundered towards each other.

> But hard midway upon the green surcoat,
> Sir Palamon's stout lance so truly smote,
> That, 'neath the shock, the bold Sir Thomas reeled
> And, losing stirrups, saddle, lance and shield,
> Down, down upon the ling outstretched he fell
> And, losing all, lost breath and speech as well.
> Thus, silent all, the bold Sir Thomas lay,
> Though much, and many things, he yearned to say,
> Which things his squires and pages might surmise
> From the expression of his fish-like eyes
> E'en as they bore him from that doleful place;
> While, near and far, from all the populace,

Rose shout on shout that echoed loud and long:
"Sir Palamon! Sir Palamon of Tong! "
So came these ten good knights, but, one by one,
They fell before this bold Sir Palamon,
Whose lance unerring smote now helm, now shield,
That many an one lay rolling on the field.
But each and all themselves did vanquished yield;
And loud and louder did the plaudits grow,
That one knight should so many overthrow.
Even Sir Gui, within his silken tent
Scowled black in ever-growing wonderment.

But the Knight of Tong, his gaudy shield a little battered, his fine surcoat frayed and torn, leaped from his wearied steed and forthwith mounted one held by his tall esquire, a mighty charger that tossed proud head and champed his bit, pawing impatient hoof.

"Aha! " quoth the esquire, pointing to ten fair steeds held by ten fair pages. "Oho, good brother, most puissant Knight of Tong, here is good and rich booty—let us begone! "

"Nay, " answered the Knight, tossing aside his blunt tilting-spear, "here is an end to sportful dalliance—reach me my lance! "

"Ha, is't now the Red Gui's turn, brother? The Saints aid thee, in especial two, that, being women, are yet no saints yet awhile—see how they watch thee, sweet, gentle dames! Their prayers go with thee, methinks, brother, and mine also, for the Red Gui is forsooth a valiant rogue! "

And now, mounted on the great black war-horse, the Knight of Tong rode up the lists:

His scarlet plume 'bove shining helm a-dance,
His bannerole a-flutter from long lance,
Till he was come where, plain for all to spy,
Was hung the shield and blazon of Sir Gui,
With bends and bars in all their painted glory,
Surcharged with hand ensanguined—gules or gory.

Full upon this bloody hand smote the sharp point of Sir Palamon's lance; whereupon the watching crowd surged and swayed and hummed expectant, since here was to be no play with blunted weapons but a deadly encounter.

Up started Sir Gui and strode forth of his tent, grim-smiling and confident. Quoth he:

"Ha, my Lord of Tong, thou'rt grown presumptuous and over-venturesome, methinks. But since life thou dost hold so cheap prepare ye for death forthright! "

So spake the Lord of Ells and, beckoning to his esquires, did on his great tilting-helm and rode into the lists, whereon was mighty roar of welcome, for, though much hated, he was esteemed mighty at arms, and the accepted champion of the Duchy. So while the people thundered their acclaim the two knights galloped to their stations and, reining about, faced each other from either end of the lists,

> And halted thus, their deadly spears they couched,
> With helms stooped low, behind their shields they crouched;
> Now rang the clarions; goading spurs struck deep,
> The mighty chargers reared with furious leap
> And, like two whirlwinds, met in full career,
> To backward reel 'neath shock of splintering spear:
> But, all unshaken, every eye might see
> The bloody hand, the scarred gules falcons three.
> Thrice thus they met, but at the fourth essay,
> Rose sudden shout of wonder and dismay,
> For, smitten sore through riven shield, Sir Gui
> Thudded to earth there motionless to lie.

Thus Sir Gui, Lord of Ells and Seneschal of Raddemore, wounded and utterly discomfited, was borne raging to his pavilion while the air rang with the blare of trumpet and clarion in honour of the victor. Thereafter, since no other knight thought it prudent to challenge him, Sir Palamon of Tong was declared champion of the tournament, and was summoned by the Chief Herald to receive the victor's crown. But even as he rode towards the silk-curtained balcony, a distant trumpet shrilled defiance, and into the lists galloped a solitary knight.

> Well-armed was he in proud and war-like trim,
> Of stature tall and wondrous long of limb;
> 'Neath red surcoat black was the mail he wore;

His glitt'ring shield a rampant leopard bore,
Beholding which the crowd cried in acclaim,
"Ho for Sir Agramore of Bename! "

But from rosy-red to pale, from pale to rosy-red flushed the Duchess Benedicta, and clenching white teeth, she frowned upon Sir Agramore's fierce and warlike figure. Quoth she:

"Oh, sure there is no man so vile or so unworthy in all Christendom as this vile Lord of Bename! "

"Unless, " said Yolande, frowning also, "unless it be my Lord Gui of Ells! "

"True, my Yolanda! Now, as thou dost hate Sir Gui so hate I Sir Agramore, therefore pray we sweet maid, petition we the good Saints our valiant singer shall serve my hated Sir Agramore as he did thy hated Sir Gui—may he be bruised, may he be battered, may—"

"Oho, 'tis done, my sweeting! A-hee—a-hi, 'tis done! " croaked a voice, and starting about, the Duchess beheld a bent and hag-like creature,

With long, sharp nose that showed beneath her hood,
A nose that curved as every witch's should,
And glittering eye, before whose baleful light,
The fair Yolande shrank back in sudden fright.

"Nay, my Yolande, " cried the Duchess, "hast forgot old Mopsa, my foster- mother, that, being a wise-woman, fools decry as witch, and my ten grave and learned guardians have banished therefor? Hast forgot my loved and faithful Mopsa that is truly the dearest, gentlest, wisest witch that e'er witched rogue or fool? But O Mopsa, wise mother—would'st thou might plague and bewitch in very truth yon base caitiff knight, Sir Agramore of Bename! "

"'Tis done, loved daughter, 'tis done! " chuckled the Witch.

"He groaneth,
He moaneth,
He aileth,
He waileth,
Lying sighing,

Nigh to dying,
Oho,
I know
'Tis so.
With bones right sore,
Both 'hind and fore,
Sir Agramore
Doth ache all o'er.

"He aileth sore yet waileth more—oho! I know, I have seen—in the chalk, in the ink, in the smoke—I looked and saw

"Sir Agramore,
By bold outlaw,
Bethwacked most sore
As told before—"

"Nay, but, good Mopsa, how may this be? Sir Agramore rideth armed yonder, plain to my sight."

"Child, I have told thee sooth," croaked the Witch. "Have patience, watch and be silent, and shalt grow wise as old Mopsa—mayhap—in time.

"For, 'tis written in the chalk,
Sore is he and may not walk.
O, sing heart merrily!
I have seen within the smoke
Bones bethwacked by lusty stroke,
Within the ink I looked and saw,
Swathed in clouts, Sir Agramore;
Dread of him for thee is o'er,
By reason of a bold outlaw.
Sing, heart, and joyful be!"

"Go to, Mopsa, thou'rt mad!" quoth the Duchess. "For yonder is this hated lord very strong and hale, and in well-being whiles thou dost rave! Truly thou'rt run mad, methinks!"

But the old Witch only mumbled and mowed, and cracked her finger-bones as is the custom of witches.

Meantime, Sir Agramore, checking his fiery charger and brandishing heavy lance fiercely aloft, roared loud defiance:

"What ho! Ye knights, lords, esquires, and lovers of lusty blows, hither come I with intent, sincere and hearty, to bicker with, fight, combat and withstand all that will—each and every, a-horse or a-foot, with sword, battleaxe or lance. Now all ye that love good blows—have at ye! "

Here ensued great clamour and a mighty blowing of trumpets that waxed yet louder when it was proclaimed that Sir Palamon, as champion of the day, had accepted Sir Agramore's haughty challenge.

And now all was hushed as these two doughty knights faced each other and, as the trumpets brayed, charged furiously to meet with thunderous shock of breaking lances and reeling horses that, rearing backwards, fell crashing upon the torn and trampled grass. But their riders, leaping clear of lashing hooves, drew their swords and, wasting no breath in words, beset each other forthwith, smiting with right good will.

Sir Agramore's leopard shield was riven in twain by a single stroke, Sir Palamon's scarlet plume was shorn away, but they fought only the fiercer as, all untiring, the long blades whirled and flashed until their armour rang, sparks flew, and the populace rocked and swayed and roared for very joy. Once Sir Agramore was beaten to his knees, but rising, grasped his sword in two hands and smote a mighty swashing blow, a direful stroke that burst the lacing of Sir Palamon's great helm and sent it rolling on the sward. But, beholding thus his adversary's face, Sir Agramore, crying in sudden amaze, sprang back; for men all might see a visage framed in long, black-curled hair, grey-eyed, but a face so direly scarred that none, having seen it but once, might well forget.

"Par Dex! " panted Sir Agramore, lifting his vizor.

"Pertinax! " gasped Duke Jocelyn. "O Pertinax—thou loved and lovely smiter—ne'er have I been so sore battered ere now! "

Hereupon all folk stared in hugeous wonderment to behold these two champions drop their swords and leap to clasp and hug each

The Geste of Duke Jocelyn

other in mighty arms, to pat each other's mailed shoulders and grasp each other's mailed hands. Quoth Sir Pertinax:

"Lord, how came ye in this guise? "

"My Pertinax, whence stole ye that goodly armour? "

"Lord, oath made I to requite one Sir Agramore of Biename for certain felon blow. Him sought I latterly therefore, and this day met him journeying hither, and so, after some disputation, I left him lying by the way, nor shall he need armour awhile, methinks—wherefore I took it and rode hither seeking what might befall—"

But here, Sir Gui, all heedless of his wound, started up from his couch, raising great outcry:

"Ha—roguery, roguery! Ho, there, seize me yon knave that beareth the cognizance of Tong. Ha—treason, treason! " At this, others took up the cry and divers among the throng, beholding Duke Jocelyn's scarred features, made loud tumults: "The Fool! The Fool! 'Tis the Singing Motley! 'Tis the rogue-Fool that broke prison—seize him! Seize him! " And many, together with the soldiery, came running.

"Lord, " quoth Sir Pertinax, catching up his sword, "here now is like to be a notable, sweet affray! " But even as these twain turned to meet their many assailants was thunder of hoofs, a loud, merry voice reached them, and they saw Robin hard by who held two trampling chargers.

"Mount, brothers—mount! " he cried. "Mount, then spur we for the barriers! " So they sprang to saddle and, spurring the rearing horses, galloped for the barriers, all three, nor was there any who dare stay them or abide the sweep of those long swords. Thus, leaping the barriers, they galloped away and left behind roaring tumult and dire confusion.

And amid all this, hid by the silken curtains of her balcony, the Duchess Benedicta uttered a joyous cry and, clasping Yolande in her arms, kissed her rapturously.

"Yolande! " she cried, "O dear my friend, thou didst see—even as did I—a sorry fool and a poor rogue-soldier at hand-strokes with each other—O wise Fool! O knightly Rogue! Come, let us fly,

The Geste of Duke Jocelyn

Yolande, let us to the wild-wood and, lost therein, love, True-love, methinks, shall find us. Nay—ask me nothing, only hear this. Be thou to thine own heart true, be thou brave and Shame shall fly thee since True-love out-faceth Shame! How say'st thou, Mopsa, thou wise witch-mother? "

"Ah, sweet children! " croaked the Witch, touching each with claw-like hand yet hand wondrous gentle. "True-love shall indeed find ye, hide where ye will. For True-love, though blind, they say, hath eyes to see all that is good and sweet and true. A poor man-at-arms in rusty mail may yet be true man and a fool, for all his motley, wise. To love such seemeth great folly, yet to the old, love is but folly. Nath'less, being old I do love ye, and being wise I charge ye:

"Follow Folly and be wise,
In such folly wisdom lies;
Love's blind, they say, but Love hath eyes,
So follow Folly—follow! "

My daughter GILLIAN animadverteth:

GILL: "Stop! Your tournament, father, seems too long drawn out,
With quite too much combating and knocking about.

MYSELF: I hope you're wrong, my dear, although
Who knows? Perhaps, it may be so.

GILL: And such scrappy bits of love-making you write;
You seem to prefer much describing a fight.
All authors should write what their readers like best;
But authors are selfish, yes—even the best
And you are an author!

MYSELF: Alack, that is true,
And, among other things, I'm the author of you.

GILL: Then, being my author, it's plain as can be
That you are to blame if I'm naughty—not me.
But, father, our Geste, though quite corking in places,
Has too many fights and too little embraces.
You've made all our lovers so frightfully slow,
You ought to have married them pages ago.
The books that are nicest are always the sort

157

That, when you have read them, seem always too short!
If you make all your readers impatient like me,
They'll buy none of your books—and then where shall we be?
All people like reading of love when they can,
So write them a lot, father, that is the plan.
Go on to the love, then, for every one's sake,
And end with a wedding—

MYSELF: Your counsel I'll take.
I can woo them and wed them in less than no time,
I can do it in prose, in blank verse, or in rhyme;
But since, my dear, you are for speed,
To end our Geste I will proceed.
In many ways it may be done,
As I have told you—here is one:

A short two years have elapsed and we find our hero Jocelyn
tenderly playing with a golden-haired prattler, his beloved son and
heir, while his beautiful spouse Yolande busied with her needle,
smiles through happy tears.

GILL: O, hush, father! Of course, that is simply absurd!
Such terrible piffle—

MYSELF: I object to that word!

GILL: Well, then, please try a little verse.

MYSELF: With pleasure:

"My own at last!" Duke Joc'lyn fondly cried,
And kissed Yolande, his blooming, blushing bride.
"My own!" he sighed. "My own—my very own!"
"Thine, love!" she murmured. "Thine and thine alone,
Thy very own for days and months and years—"

GILL: O, stop! I think that's even worse!

MYSELF: Beyond measure.

Then here's a style may be admired
Since brevity is so desired:

So he married her and she married him,
and everybody married each other
and lived happy ever after.

Or again, and thus, my daughter,
Versified it may be shorter:

So all was marriage, joy and laughter,
And each lived happy ever after.

Or:
If for High Romance you sigh,
Here's Romance that's over high:

Shy summer swooned to autumn's sun-burned arms,
Swoon, summer, swoon!
While roses bloomed and blushing sighed their pain,
Blush, roses, blush!

Filling the world with perfume languorous,
Sighing forth their souls in fragrant amorousness;
And fair Yolande, amid these bloomful languors,
Blushing as they, as languorous, as sweet,
Sighed in the arms that passioned her around:
O Jocelyn, O lord of my delight,
See how—

GILL: Stop, father, stop, I beg of you.
Such awful stuff will never do,
I suppose you must finish it in your own way—

MYSELF: I suppose that I shall, child, that is—if I may.

GILL: But father, wait—I must insist
Whatever else you do
It's time that somebody was kissed
It doesn't matter who—
I mean either Yolande the Fair
Or else the Duchess—I don't care.

MYSELF: In these next two Fyttes both shall kiss
And be well kissed, I promise this.
Two Fyttes of kisses I will make

One after t' other, for your sake.
Two Fyttes of love I will invent
And make them both quite different,
Which is a trying matter rather
And difficult for any father —
But then, as well you know, my Gillian,
You have a father in a million;
And Oh, methinks 'tis very plain
You ne'er shall meet his like again.

FYTTE 11

How Pertinax fell out with Robin and with Friar, Yet, in that very hour, came by his heart's desire.

The sinking sun had set the West aflame, When our three riders to the wild-wood came, Where a small wind 'mid sun-kissed branches played, And deep'ning shadows a soft twilight made; Where, save for leafy stirrings, all was still, Lulled by the murmur of a bubbling rill That flowed o'ershadowed by a mighty oak, Its massy bole deep-cleft by lightning stroke. Here Robin checked his steed. "Good friends, " quoth he, My daughter Gillian suggesteth:

> Gill: That's rather good,
> But, still, I should
> In prose prefer the rest;
> For if this fytte
> Has love in it,
> Prose is for love the best.
> All ord'nary lovers, as every one knows,
> Make love to each other much better in prose.
> If, at last, our Sir Pertinax means to propose,
> Why then—just to please me,
> Father, prose let it be.

> Myself: Very well, I agree!

    Then said Robin, quoth he:
"Good friends, here are we safe! " And, checking his steed within this pleasant shade, he dismounted.

"Safe, quotha? " said Sir Pertinax, scowling back over shoulder. "Not so! Surely we are close pursued—hark! Yonder be horsemen riding at speed—ha, we are beset! "

"Content you, sir! " answered Robin. "Think you I would leave behind good booty? Yonder come ten noble coursers laden with ten goodly armours the same won a-jousting to-day by this right wondrous Fool, my good gossip—"

"Thy gossip, forsooth! " snorted Sir Pertinax. "But tell me, presumptuous fellow, how shall these ten steeds come a-galloping hither! "

"Marry, on this wise, Sir Simple Innocence—these steeds do gallop for sufficient reason, namely—they are to gallop bidden being ridden, bestridden and chidden by whip and spur applied by certain trusty men o' my company, which men go habited, decked, dressed, clad, guised and disguised as smug, sleek citizens, Sir Innocent Simplicity—"

"Par Dex! " exclaimed Sir Pertinax, scowling. "And who 'rt thou, sirrah, with men at thy beck and call? "

"Behold! " said Robin, unhelming. "Behold the king of all masterless rogues, and thy fellow gallow's-bird, Sir High Mightiness! "

"Ha, is 't thou? " cried Sir Pertinax. "Now a plague on thy kingdom and thee for an unhanged, thieving rogue—"

"E'en as thyself, " nodded Robin, "thou that flaunted thy unlovely carcass in stolen armour. "

"Ha! " roared Sir Pertinax, clapping hand on sword. "A pest—a murrain! This to me, thou dog's-meat? Malediction! Now will I crack thy numbskull for a pestilent malapert—"

"Nay, Sir Grim-and-gory, " laughed Robin, "rather will I now use thee as thou would'st ha' served me on a day but for this generous and kindly Fool, my good comrade! " And speaking, Robin sprang nimbly to the great oak tree and thrusting long arm within the jagged fissure that gaped therein drew forth a hunting-horn and winded it loud and shrill. And presently was a stir, a rustle amid the surrounding brushwood and all about them were outlaws, wild men and fierce of aspect, and each and every grasped long-bow with arrow on string and every arrow was aimed at scowling Sir Pertinax.

"Per Dex! " quoth he, "and is this death, then? "

"Verily! " nodded Robin, "an I do speak the word. "

"So be it—speak! " growled Sir Pertinax. "Come, Death—I fear thee not! "

And out flashed his long sword; but even then it was twisted from his grasp and Lobkyn Lollo, tossing the great blade aloft and, catching it very neatly, laughed and spake:

"Five times, five times ten
Are we, all lusty men.
An hundred twice and fifty deaths are we,
So, an Rob speak, dead thou 'lt as often be. "

"Nay, hold a while, sweet lads! " laughed Robin, "the surly rogue shall sing for his life and our good pleasaunce. "

"Sing? " roared Sir Pertinax. "I sing! I? Ha, dare ye bid me so, base dog? Sing, forsooth? By Og and Gog! By the Seven Champions and all the fiends, rather will I die! " And here, being defenceless, Sir Pertinax clenched mighty fists and swore until he lacked for breath.

Then spake Jocelyn, gentle-voiced.

"Sing, Pertinax, " quoth he.

"Ha—never! Not for all the—"

"I do command thee, Pertinax. As Robin once sang for his life, now must thou sing for thine. Song for song, 't is but just! Sing, Pertinax! "

"Nay, " groaned the proud knight, "I had rather drink water and chew grass like a rabbit. Moreover I ha' no gift o' song—"

"Do thy best! " quoth Robin.

"I'm harsh o' voice—knave! "

"Then croak—rogue! " quoth Robin.

"No song have I—vermin! "

"Make one—carrion! But sing thou shalt though thy song be no better than hog-song which is grunt. Howbeit sing thou must! "

Hereupon Sir Pertinax gnashed his teeth and glaring balefully on Robin lifted hoarse voice and burst forth into fierce song:

"Thou base outlaw,
Vile clapper-claw,
Since I must sing a stave,
Then, here and now,
I do avow
Thou art a scurvy knave!
Thy hang-dog air
Doth plain declare
Thou 'rt very scurvy knave.

"Rogues breed apace
In each vile place,
But this I will avow,
Where e'er rogues be
No man may see
A viler rogue than thou,

Since it were vain
To meet again
A rogue more vile than thou.

"As rogue thou art,
In every part,
Then—"

"Hold there—hold! " cried Robin, stopping his ears. "Thy voice is
unlovely as thy look and thy song as ill as thy voice, so do we forgive
thee the rest. Ha' done thy bellowing and begone—"

"Ha—not so! " quoth Sir Pertinax. "For troth I do sing better than
methought possible, and my rhyming is none so ill! So will I rhyme
thy every knavish part and sing song till song and rhyme be ended.
Have at thee again, base fellow!

Since rogue thou art
In every part—part—

Ha, plague on't, hast put me out, rogue! I was about to hang thy
every roguish part in rhyme, but my rhymes halt by reason o' thee,
rogue. "

"Forsooth! " laughed Robin. "Thus stickest thou, for thy part, at my
every part, the which is well since I am man of parts. Thus then

rhyme thou rhymes upon thyself therefore; thus, thyself rhyming rhymes of thee, thou shalt thyself, rhyming of thyself, thyself pleasure thereby, thou thus rhyming of thee, and thee, thou. Thus thy thee and thou shall be well accorded. How think'st thou? "

But Sir Pertinax, astride his charger that cropped joyously at sweet, cool grass, sat chin on fist, lost in the throes of composition, nothing heeding, even when came the ten steeds with the ten suits of armour.

Now these ten horses bare eleven riders, tall, lusty fellows all, save one shrouded in hood and cloak and whom Jocelyn viewed with quick, keen eyes. And thus he presently whispered Robin who, laughing slyly, made signal to his followers, whereupon, by ones and twos they stole silently away until there none remained save only Sir Pertinax who, wrestling with his muse, stared aloft under knitted brows, all unknowing, and presently brake out singing on this wise:

"All men may see
A man in me,
A man who feareth no man,
Thus, fearless, I
No danger fly—"

"Except it be a woman! " sang a soft, sweet voice hard by, in pretty mockery. Hereat Sir Pertinax started so violently that his mail clashed and he stared about him eager-eyed but, finding himself quite alone, sighed and fell to reverie.

"A woman? " said he aloud. "'Except it be a woman—'"

THE VOICE: Aye—a woman, O craven soldier!

SIR PERTINAX: Why here is strange echo methinks and speaketh— with her voice!

THE VOICE: 'O voice so soft and full of sweet allure! '

SIR PERTINAX: O voice beloved that might my dolour cure!

THE VOICE: O craven soldier! O most timid wooer! SIR PERTINAX: Craven am I, yet lover—'t is most sure.

THE VOICE: But thou 'rt a man—at least meseemeth so.

SIR PERTINAX: And, being man, myself unworthy know,
  Yet must I love and my belovèd seek
  And, finding her, no words of love dare speak.
  For this my love beyond all words doth reach,
  And I'm slow-tongued and lack the trick of speech.
  Nor hope have I that she should stoop to bless,
  A man so full of all unworthiness.
  So am I dumb—

THE VOICE: And yet dost speak indeed,
  Such words, methinks, as any maid might heed.

"Ha, think ye so in verity, sweet voice! " cried Sir Pertinax, and springing lightly to earth, strode forward on eager feet. And lo! from behind a certain tree stepped one who, letting fall shrouding cloak and hood, stood there a maid, dark-haired and darkly bright of eye, very shapely and fair to see in her simple tire. And beholding her thus, the tender curve of scarlet lips, the flutter of slender hands, the languorous bewitchment of her eyes, Sir Pertinax halted.

My daughter GILLIAN interpolateth:

GILL:

What, again? Father, that will never do.
Don't make him halt again, I beg of you.
Sir Pertinax has halted much too long,
To make him do it here would be quite
wrong!

MYSELF:

My child, I wish you would not interrupt
My halting muse in manner so abrupt—

GILL:

But here 's a chance at last to let them kiss,
And now you make him halt!

MYSELF: Exactly, miss!

Sir Pertinax halted and bowed his head abashed.

My daughter GILLIAN persisteth:

GILL:

Well, father, while he halts, then tell me,
pray,
Just what you mean by that line where you
say,
'The languorous bewitchment of her eyes'?

MYSELF:

My child, no child should authors catechise,
Especially, poor fellow, if, like me,
Father and author both at once is he.
Wise authors all such questions strictly ban,
And never answer—even if they can.
If of our good knight's wooing you would
hear,
Keep stilly tongue and hearken well, my
dear.

Sir Pertinax halted and bowed his head, abashed by her beauty.

"Melissa! " he whispered, "O Melissa! " and so stood mute.

"O Pertinax! " she sighed. "Art dumb at sight of me? O Pertinax, and
wherefore? "

"All have I forgot save only thy loveliness, Melissa! "

"Methinks such—forgetfulness becometh thee well. Say on! "

"Ah, Melissa, I—do love thee. "

"Why this I knew when thou didst sit a-fishing! " "But, indeed, then
I dreamed not of loving thee or any maid. "

"Because thou art but a man. "

"Verily, and being man, now came I seeking thee for Love's sweet sake yet, finding thee, know not how to speak thee. Alas, I do fear I am but sorry wooer! "

"Alas, Pertinax, I do fear thou art! Yet thou shalt learn, perchance. How—art dumb again, canst speak me no more? "

"Nought—save only this, thou art beyond all maids fair, Melissa! "

"Why, I do think thou'lt make a wooer some day mayhap, by study diligent. 'T will take long time and yet—I would not have thee learn too soon! And hast thought of me? A little? "

"I have borne thee ever within my heart. "

"And wherefore wilt love maid so lowly? "

"For that thou art thyself and thyself—Melissa. And O, I love thy voice! "

"My voice? And what more? "

"Thine eyes. Thy little, pretty feet. Thy scarlet mouth. Thy gentle, small
hands. Thy hair. All of thee! "

"O, " she murmured a little breathlessly, "if thou dost so love me— woo me—a little! "

"Alas! " he sighed, "I know not how. "

"Hast ne'er wooed maid ere this, big soldier? "

"Never! "

"Thou poor Pertinax! How empty—how drear thy life. For this do I pity thee with pity kin to love—"

"Love? " he whispered. "Ah, Melissa, couldst e'en learn to love one so unlovely, so rude, so rough and unmannered as I? "

"Never! " she sighed, "O, never—unless thou teach me? "

"Would indeed I might, Melissa. Ah, teach me how I may teach thee to love one so unworthy as Pertinax! "

Now hearkening to his harsh voice grown soft and tremulous, beholding the truth in his honest eyes, Melissa smiled, wondrous tender, and reaching out took hold upon his two hands.

"Kneel! " she commanded. "Kneel here upon the grass as I do kneel. Now, lay by thy cumbrous helmet. Now fold thy great, strong hands. Now bow thy tall, grim head and say in sweet, soft accents low and reverent: 'Melissa, I do love thee heart and soul, thee only do I love and thee only will I love now and for ever. So aid me, Love, amen! '" Then, closing his eyes, Sir Pertinax bowed reverent head, and, humbly folding his hands, spake as she bade him. Thereafter opening his eyes, he saw her watching him through gathering tears, and leaning near, he reached out eager arms, yet touched her not. Quoth he: "O maid beloved, what is thy sorrow? "

"'Tis joy—joy, and thou—thou art so strong and fierce yet so gentle and simple of heart! O, may I prove worthy thy love—"

"Worthy? Of my love? " he stammered. "But O Melissa, I am but he thou didst name harsh of tongue. "

"Aye, I did! " she sobbed.

"Hard of heart, flinty of soul, rude, unmannered and unlovely. "

"Aye—I did and—loved thee the while! " she whispered. "So now do I pray that I prove worthy. "

"Worthy? Thou? O my sweet maid—thou that art kin to the holy angels, thou so high and far removed 'bove me that I do tremble and—fear to touch thee—".

"Nay, fear me not, Pertinax, " she sighed, "for though indeed I am all this, yet maid am I also and by times—very human. So Pertinax, thou great, fearless man-at-arms, lay by thy so great fears a while—I do beseech thee. " Then Sir Pertinax, beholding the tender passion of her eyes, forgot his fear in glad wonderment and, reaching out hands that trembled for all their strength, drew her to his close embracement.

And thus, kneeling together upon the sun-dappled sward, they forgot all things in this joyous world save only their love and the glory of it. And when they had kissed each other—

* * * * *

My daughter GILLIAN remonstrateth:

GILL: But, wait, they haven't yet, you know!

MYSELF: Indeed, they have, I've just said so.

GILL: Then, father, please to tell me this:
How can a person say a kiss?
And so, since kisses can't be said,
Please make them do it now instead.

Thus, cradled in his strong arms, she questioned him tenderly:

"Dost mind how, upon a day, my Pertinax, didst ask of me the amulet I bore within my bosom? "

"Aye, " he answered, "and sure 'tis charm of potent magic whose spell brought us out of the dungeon at Canalise—the which is great matter for wonder! But 'tis for thy dear sake I do cherish it—"

"Bear you it yet? "

"Here upon my heart. "

"And if I should ask it of thee again—wouldst render it back to me? "

"Never! " quoth he. "Never, until with it I give thee myself also! "

But presently she stirred in his embrace for upon the air was an approaching clamour, voices, laughter and the ring of mail.

"Come away! " whispered Melissa, upspringing to her feet. "Come, let thou and Love and I hide until these disturbers be gone and the sweet world hold but us three again. "

Now, as they stood, hand in hand, deep hidden 'mid the green, they beheld six merry woodland rogues who led an ambling ass whereon rode a friar portly and perspiring albeit he had a jovial eye. And as he rode he spake his captors thus in voice full-toned and deep:

"Have a care, gentle rogues and brethren, hurry not this ambulant animal unduly, poor, much-enduring beast. Behold the pensive pendulation of these auriculars so forlornly a-dangle! Here is ass that doth out-patience all asses, both four and two-legged. Here is meek ass of leisured soul loving not haste—a very pensive perambulator. So hurry not the ass, my brothers, for these several and distinct reasons or arguments. Firstly, dearly beloved, because I love haste no more than the ass; secondly, brethren, 't is property of Holy Church which is above all argument; and, thirdly, 't is bestridden by one Friar John, my very self, and I am forsooth weighty argument. Fourthly, beloved, 'tis an ass that—ha! O sweet vision for eyes human or divine! Do I see thee in very truth, thou damsel of disobedience, dear dame of discord, sweet, witching, wilful lady—is it thou in very truth, most loved daughter, or wraith conjured of thy magic and my perfervid imaginations—speak! "

"'T is I myself, Reverend Father! " laughed Melissa. "O my dear, good Friar John, methinks the kind Saints have brought thee to my need. "

"Saints, quotha! " exclaimed the Friar, rolling merry eye towards his several captors. "Call ye these—Saints? Long have I sought thee, thou naughty maid, and to-day in my quest these brawny 'saints' beset me with bow and quarterstaff and me constrained hither—but my blessing on them since they have brought me to thee. And now, sweet child and daughter, whiles the news yet runneth hot-foot or, like bird unseen, wingeth from lip to lip, I thy ghostly father have rare good news for thee—"

"Nay, Friar John, I will guess thy tidings: Sir Agramore of Biename lieth sorry and sore of a cudgelling. "

"How! " cried the Friar. "Thou dost know—so soon? "

"Verily, Reverend Father, nor have I or my worthy guardians aught to fear of him hereafter. And now have I right wondrous news for thee, news that none may guess. List, dear Friar John, thou the wisest and best loved of all my guardians ten; to-day ye are absolved henceforth all care of your wilful ward since to-day she passeth from the guardianship of ye ten to the keeping of one. Come forth,

Pertinax, thou only one beloved of me for no reason but that thou art thou and I am I—as is ever the sweet, mad way of True-love—come forth, my dear-loved, poor soldier! " Out from the trees strode Pertinax but, beholding his face, Friar John scowled and, viewing his rich surcoat and goodly armour, fell to perspiring wonder and amaze.

"Now by the sweet Saint Amphibalus! " quoth he. "Surely these be the arms of Sir Agramore, dread Lord of Biename? "

"Most true, dear Friar John, " answered Melissa, "and by this same token Sir Agramore lieth sore bruised e'en now. "

"Aha! " quoth the Friar, mopping moist brow. "'T is well—'t is very well, so shall these two ears of mine, with eighteen others of lesser account, scathless go and all by reason of this good, tall fellow. Howbeit, I do know this same fellow for fellow of none account, and no fit mate for thee, noble daughter, love or no. A fierce, brawling, tatterdemalion this, that erstwhile tramped in company with long-legged ribald—a froward jesting fellow. Wherefore this fellow, though fellow serviceable, no fellow is for thee and for these sufficing reasons. Firstly—"

"Ha—enough! " quoth Sir Pertinax, chin out-thrust. "'Fellow' me no more, Friar—"

"Firstly, " continued Friar John, "because this out-at-elbows fellow is a rogue. "

"'Rogue, ' in thy teeth, Churchman! " growled Sir Pertinax.

"Secondly, " continued Friar John, nothing abashed, "because this rogue-fellow is a runagate roysterer, a nameless knave, a highway-haunter, a filching flick-o'-the-gibbet and a—"

"Friar, " snorted Sir Pertinax, "thou 'rt but a very fat man scant o' breath, moreover thou 'rt a friar, so needs must I leave thee alive to make pestilent the air yet a little until thou chokest of an epithet. Meantime perform now one gracious act in thy so graceless life and wed me with this forest maiden. "

"Forest maiden, forsooth! " cried Friar John. "O Saints! O Martyrs! Forest maid, quotha! And wed her—and unto thee, presumptuous malapert! Ho, begone, thy base blood and nameless rank forbid—"

"Hold there, shaveling! " quoth Sir Pertinax, scowling. "Now mark me this! Though I, being very man, do know myself all unworthy maid so sweet and peerless, yet, and she stoop to wed me, then will I make her lady proud and dame of divers goodly manors and castles, of village and hamlet, pit and gallows, sac and soc, with powers the high, the middle and the low and with ten-score lances in her train. For though in humble guise I went, no nameless rogue am I, but Knight of Shene, Lord of Westover, Framling, Bracton and Deepdene—"

"How! " cried Melissa, pouting rosy lip and frowning a little. "O Pertinax, art indeed a great lord? "

"Why, sooth—forsooth and indeed, " he stammered, "I do fear I am. "

"Then thou 'rt no poor, distressful, ragged, outlaw-soldier? "

"Alack—no! " he groaned, regardful of her frown.

"Then basely hast thou tricked me—O cruel! "

"Nay, Melissa—hear me! " he cried, and, forgetful of friar and gaping outlaws, he clasped her fast 'prisoned 'gainst his heart. "Thee do I love, dear maid, 'bove rank, or fame, or riches, or aught this world may offer. So, an thou wouldst have me ragged and destitute and outlaw, all this will I be for thy sweet sake since life were nought without thee, O maid I do so love—how say'st thou? "

"I say to thee, Pertinax, that thy so great love hath loosed thy tongue at last, Love hath touched thy lips with eloquence beyond all artifice since now, methinks, it is thy very soul doth speak me. And who shall resist such wooing? Surely not I that do—love thee beyond telling. So take me, my lord, thy right hand in mine, the talisman in thy left—so! Now, my Pertinax, speak thy heart's wish. "

"Friar, " quoth Sir Pertinax, holding aloft the Crystal Heart, "as her love is mine and mine hers, wed and unite us in our love—by the magic of this jewel I do command thee! "

Here, beholding the talisman, Friar John gasped and stared round-eyed and incredulous.

"By Holy Rood! " he whispered, "'t is indeed the Crystal Heart! "

"And O! " sighed Melissa, "O Friar John, thou dost mind the saying:

"'He that taketh Crystal Heart,
Taketh all and every part! '"

"Aye, truly—truly! " nodded the Friar.

"'And by night, or eke by day,
The Crystal Heart all must obey! '"

So saying he got him down from the ass and, for all his corpulence, louted full low.

"Sir Knight of Shene, " quoth he, "by reason of this jewel potential thou dost bear, now must I perforce obey thy behest and wed thee unto this our gracious lady Benedicta, Duchess of Ambremont, Canalise, Tissingors, Fordyngstoke and divers other towns, villages and—"

"Duchess—a duchess? " exclaimed Sir Pertinax. "Duchess say'st thou—this, the Duchess Benedicta! O Melissa—thou—thou—a duchess! "

"Sooth and forsooth, " sighed she in pretty mockery, "I do fear I am! "

"Then thou 'rt no humble maid, distressful and forlorn, Melissa? "

"Yea, Pertinax—all this am I indeed unless thou love me, and loving me, wed me, and wedding me love me the better therefor, and loving me ever the better, thou may'st learn a little some day how a woman may love a man. "

"Par Dex! " mumbled Sir Pertinax, kissing her rosy finger-tips, "be thou duchess or witch-maid o' the wood, I do love thee heart and soul, body and mind, now and for ever, Melissa. "

Then Friar John, beholding the radiant joy of their faces, reached forth his hands in blessing.

"Kneel ye, my children! " he sighed. "For here methinks is true-love such as brighteneth this world all too seldom. So here, within the forest, the which is surely God's cathedral, this your love shall be sanctified unto you and the world be the better therefor! Kneel ye, my children! "

And thus, kneeling upon the flower-sprent turf hand in hand and with heads reverently bowed, they were wed, while the six outlaws stared in silent awe and the meek ass cropped the grass busily.

"O Pertinax, " sighed the Duchess as they rose, "so greatly happy am I that I will others shall be happy likewise; let us make this indeed a day of gladness. I pray thee sound the bugle that hangeth within the great oak, yonder. "

So Sir Pertinax took the horn and sounded thereon a mighty blast, loud and long and joyous. And presently came the outlaws, thronging in from all directions, until the sunny glade was full of their wild company, while in the green beyond pike-head twinkled and sword-blades glittered; and foremost was Robin with Lobkyn Lollo beside him.

"Robin, " said the Duchess, beckoning him near with white, imperious finger, "Robin a' Green, thou whose tongue is quick and ready as thy hand, hast ever been gentle to the weak and helpless as I do know, in especial to two women that sought thy protection of late. "

"Why, verily, lady, I mind them well, " nodded Robin, "and one was a maid passing fair and one an ancient dame exceeding wise. To aid such is ever a man's joy—or should be. "

"Knew ye who and what this maid was, Robin? "

"Aye, lady, I knew her then as now for that proud and noble lady the Duchess Benedicta. "

"And yet, Robin, knowing this and having me in thy power didst suffer me to go without let or hindrance or single penny of ransom? "

"My lady Duchess, " answered Robin, glancing round upon his wild company, "we be outlaws, 't is true, and rogues—mayhap, yet are we men and thou a lady passing fair, wherefore—though I knew thee for the Duchess Benedicta, thou wert safe with us since we war not with women and harm no maids be they of high or low degree! "

"Spoke like a very knight! " exclaimed the Duchess. "How think'st thou, my lord? "

"Par Dex! " quoth Sir Pertinax. "Aye, by Our Lady of Shene Chapel within the Wood I swear it—thou 'rt a man, Robin! So now do I sue pardon of thee for my song o' rogues since no rogue art thou. And thou didst aid and shield her—this my wife that is the very eyes of me! So, by my troth, my good friend art thou henceforth, Rob o' the Green! "

"Nay, my lord, " answered Robin slyly, "for I am but Robin, and outlaw, and thou art the Duke! "

"Forsooth—and so I am! " exclaimed Sir Pertinax. "Ha—yet am I still a man, and therefore—"

"Wait, my lord! " said Benedicta. "Robin, give me thy sword! " So she took the weapon and motioning Robin to his knees, set the blade across his shoulder. "Robin a' Green, " said she, "since thou art knightly of word and deed, knight shalt thou be in very truth. Sir Robin a' Forest I make thee and warden over this our forest country. Rise up, Sir Robert. " Then up sprang Robin, bright-eyed and flushed of cheek.

"Dear my lady, " cried he, "since knight hast made me, thy knight will I be henceforth in life or in death—" But here his voice was lost in the joyous acclamations of his followers who shouted amain until the Duchess quelled them with lifted hand.

"Ye men of the wild-wood, " said she, looking round upon them gentle-eyed, "all ye that be homeless and desolate, lying without the law, this day joy hath found me, for this is my wedding-morn. And as I am happy I would see ye happy also. Therefore upon this glad day do we make proclamation, my Lord Duke and I—this day we lift from you each and every, the ban of outlawry—free men are ye to go and come as ye list—free men one and all and good citizens henceforth I pray! " Now here was silence awhile, then a hoarse murmur, swelling to a jubilant shout until the sunny woodland rang with the joy of it, near and far.

"And now, Sir Robert, " laughed the Duchess, "pray you where is this noble Fool, this gentle Motley, this most rare singer of songs and breaker of lances? Bid him to us. "

"Ha—the Fool! " exclaimed Sir Pertinax, starting.

"My lady, " answered Robin, "true, he was here, but when I sought him, a while since, there was Sir Palamon's armour he had worn, but himself gone —"

"Gone—gone say'st thou? " cried Sir Pertinax, glancing about. "Then needs must I go seek him—"

"And wherefore, my lord? " cried the Duchess.

"'T is my—my duty, Melissa! " stammered Sir Pertinax. "He is my—my friend and—sworn brother-in-arms! "

"And am I not thy wife, Pertinax? "

"Aye, most dearly loved, and I, thy husband—and yet—needs must I seek this Fool, Melissa. "

"O Pertinax—wilt leave me? "

"Leave thee? " groaned Sir Pertinax. "Aye—for a while! Leave thee? Aye—though it break my heart needs must I! He, my—brother-in-arms. My duty calleth—"

"And what of thy duty to me? "

Now as Sir Pertinax wrung his hands in an agony of indecision, rose a whisper of sweet sound, the murmur of softly-plucked lute-strings, and into the glade, cock's-comb aflaunt and ass's ears a-dangle Duke Jocelyn strode and sang as he came a song he had made on a time, a familiar air:

"Good Pertinax, why griev'st thou so?
Free of all duty thou dost go,
Save that which thou to Love dost owe,

177

My noble Pertinax. "

"And love from heaven hath stooped thus low To me! " quoth
Pertinax.

But here came Robin with certain of his men leading a snow-white
palfrey richly caparisoned.

"Right noble lady, " said he, "behold here a goodly, fair jennet to thy
gracious acceptance. "

"And indeed—'t is rare, pretty beast! " exclaimed Benedicta. "But
Robin, Robin, O Sir Robert, whence had you this? "

"Lady, upon a time I was an outlaw and lived as outlaws may,
taking such things as Fate bestowed, and, lady:

"Fate is a wind
To outlaws kind:

But now since we be free-men all, I and my fellows, fain would we
march hence in thy train to thy honour and our joyance. Wilt grant
us this boon, lady? "

"Freely, for 'tis rare good thought, Robin! Surely never rode duke
and duchess so attended. How the townsfolk shall throng and stare
to see our wild following, and my worthy guardians gape and pluck
their beards for very amaze! How think you, good Friar John? "

"Why, verily, daughter, I, that am chiefest of thy wardens ten, do
think it wise measure; as for thy other guardians let them pluck and
gape until they choke.

"In especial Greg'ry Bax,
Who both beard and wisdom lacks.

I say 'tis wise, good measure, for these that were outlaws be sturdy
fellows with many friends in town and village, so shall this thy day
of union be for them re-union, and they joy with thee. "

Now being mounted the Duchess rode where stood Jocelyn, and
looked down on him merry-eyed.

"Sir Fool, " said she, "who thou art I know not, but I have hunted in Brocelaunde ere now, and I have eyes. And as thou 'rt friend to my dear lord, friend art thou of mine, so do we give thee joyous welcome to our duchy. And, being thy friend, I pray thou may'st find that wonder of wonders the which hideth but to be found, and once found, shall make wise Fool wiser. "

"Sweet friend and lady, " answered Jocelyn, "surely man so unlovely as I may not know this wonder for his very own until it first seek him. Is 't not so? Let now thy woman's heart counsel me. "

"How, Sir Wise Folly, have I not heard thee preach boldness in love ere now? "

"Aye—for others! " sighed Jocelyn. "But for myself—I fear—behold this motley! This scarred face! "

"Why as to thy motley it becometh thee well—"

"Aye, but my face? O, 't is a hideous face! "

"O Fool! " sighed Benedicta, "know'st thou not that True-love's eyes possess a magic whereby all loved things become fair and beauteous. So take courage, noble Motley, and may thy desires be crowned— even as our own. "

"Gramercy, thou sweet and gentle lady. Happiness companion thee alway and Love sing ever within thee. Now for ye twain is love's springtime, a season of sweet promise, may each promise find fulfilment and so farewell. "

"Why then, Sir Fool, an thou wilt tarry here in the good greenwood a while, may Love guide thee. Now here is my counsel: Follow where thy heart commandeth and—fear not! And now, Sir Robert a' Forest, form thy company, and since this is a day of gladness let them sing as they march. "

"In sooth, dear my lady, that will we! " cried Robin. "There is song o' spring and gladness I made that hath oft been our solace, and moreover it beginneth and endeth with jolly chorus well beknown to all. Ho, pikes to van and rear! Bows to the flanks—fall in! Now trusty friends o' the greenwood, free-men all, henceforth—now march we back to hearth and home and love, so sing ye—sing! "

Hereupon from the ragged, close-ordered ranks burst a shout that swelled to rolling chorus; and these the words:

The Men: Sing high, sing low, sing merrily—hey!
And cheerily let us sing,
While youth is youth then youth is gay
And youth shall have his fling.

Robin: The merry merle on leafy spray,
The lark on fluttering wing
Do pipe a joyous roundelay,
To greet the blithesome spring.

Hence, hence cold Age, black Care—away!
Cold Age black Care doth bring;
When back is bowed and head is grey,
Black Care doth clasp and cling.

Black Care doth rosy Pleasure stay,
Age ageth everything;
'T is farewell sport and holiday,
On flowery mead and ling.

If Death must come, then come he may,
And wed with death-cold ring,
Yet ere our youth and strength decay,
Blithe Joy shall be our king.
The Men: Sing high, sing low, sing merrily—hey!
And cheerily we will sing.

So they marched blithely away, a right joyous company, flashing back the sunset glory from bright headpiece and sword-blade, while Jocelyn stood watching wistful-eyed until they were lost amid the green, until all sounds of their going grew to a hush mingling with the whisper of leaves and murmurous gurgle of the brook; and ever the shadows deepened about him, a purple solitude of misty trees and tangled thickets, depth on depth, fading to a glimmering mystery.

Suddenly amid these glooming shadows a shadow moved, and forth into the darkling glade, mighty club on mighty shoulder, stepped Lobkyn Lollo the Dwarf, and his eyes were pensive and he sighed gustily.

"Alack! " quoth he:

"So here's an end of outlawry,
And all along o' lady,
Yet still an outlaw I will be
Shut in o' shaws so shady.
And yet it is great shame, I trow,
That our good friends should freemen go
And leave us lonely to our woe,
And all along o' lady.

"And plague upon this love, I say,
For stealing thus thy friend away,
And since fast caught and wed is he
Thy friend henceforth is lost to thee,
And thou, poor Fool, dost mope and sigh,
And so a plague on love! say I. "

"Nay, good Lobkyn, what know you of love? " Answered LOBKYN:

"Marry, enough o' love know I
To steal away if love be nigh.

"For love's an ill as light as air,
Yet heavy as a stone;
O, love is joy and love is care,
A song and eke a groan.

"Love is a sickness, I surmise,
Taketh a man first by the eyes,
And stealing thence into his heart,
There gripeth him with bitter smart.
Alas, poor soul,
What bitter dole,
Doth plague his every part!

"From heart to liver next it goes,
And fills him full o' windy woes,

And, being full o' gusty pain,
He groaneth oft, and sighs amain,
Poor soul is he
In verity,
And for his freedom sighs in vain. "

"Miscall not love, Lobkyn, for sure True-love is
every man's birthright. "

Quoth LOBKYN:

"Why then, methinks there's many a wight
That cheated is of his birthright,
As, item first, here's Lobkyn Lollo
To prove thine argument quite hollow.
Dare I at maid to cast mine eye,
She mocketh me, and off doth fly,

And all because I'm humped o' back,
And something to my stature lack.
Thus, though I'm stronger man than three,
No maid may love the likes o' me.
Next, there's thyself—a Fool, I swear,
At fight or song beyond compare.
But—thou 'rt unlovely o' thy look,
And this no maid will ever brook.
So thou and I, for weal or woe,
To our lives' end unloved must go.
But think ye that I grieve or sigh?
Not so! A plague on love, say I! "

Now here Jocelyn sighed amain and, sitting beneath a tree, fell to sad
and wistful thinking.

"Aye, verily, " he repeated, "I am 'unlovely of my
look. '"

Quoth Lobkyn heartily:

"In very sooth,
Fool, that's the truth! "

The Geste of Duke Jocelyn

"Alas! " sighed Jocelyn, "'And this no maid
will ever brook! '"

Answered Lobkyn:

"And there dost speak, wise Fool, again,
A truth right manifest and plain,
Since fairest maids have bat-like eyes,
And see no more than outward lies.
And seeing thus, they nothing see
Of worthiness in you or me.
And so, since love doth pass us by,
The plague o' plagues on love, say I! "

"Nath'less, " cried the Duke, leaping to his feet. "I will put Love to
the test—aye, this very hour! "

Lobkyn: Wilt go, good Motley? Pray thee where?

Jocelyn: To one beyond all ladies fair.

Lobkyn: Then dost thou need a friend about thee
To cheer and comfort when she flout thee.
So, an thou wilt a-wooing wend,
I'll follow thee like trusty friend.
In love or fight thou shalt not lack
A sturdy arm to 'fend thy back.
I'll follow thee in light or dark,
Through good or ill—Saints shield us!
Hark!

And Lobkyn started about, club poised for swift action, for, out-
stealing
from the shadows crept strange and dismal sound, a thin wail that
sank to
awful groaning rumble, and so died away.

"O! " whispered Lobkyn:

"Pray, Fool, pray with all thy might,
Here's goblin foul or woodland sprite
Come for to steal our souls away,
So on thy knees quick, Fool, and pray! "

But, as these dismal sounds brake forth again, Jocelyn stole forward, quarter-staff gripped in ready hand; thus, coming nigh the great oak, he espied a dim, huddled form thereby and, creeping nearer, stared in wonder to behold Mopsa, the old witch, striving might and main to wind the great hunting-horn.

"What, good Witch!" quoth he, "here methinks is that beyond all thy spells to achieve."

"O Fool," she panted, "kind Fool, sound me this horn, for I'm old and scant o' breath. Wind it shrill and loud, good Motley, the rallying-note, for there is ill work afoot this night. Sound me shrewd blast, therefore."

"Nay, 't were labour in vain, Witch; there be no outlaws hereabout, free men are they henceforth and gone, each and every."

"Out alas—alas!" cried the old woman, wringing her hands. "Then woe is me for the fair lady Yolande."

"Ha! What of her, good Witch? Threateneth danger? Speak!"

"Aye, Fool, danger most dire! My Lord Gui yet liveth, and this night divers of his men shall bear her away where he lieth raging for her in his black castle of Ells—"

"Now by heaven's light!" swore Jocelyn, his eyes fierce and keen, "this night shall Fool be crowned of Love or sleep with kindly Death."

"Stay, Fool, thy foes be a many! Wilt cope with them alone?"

"Nay!" cried a voice:

"Not so, grandam
For here I am!"

and Lobkyn stepped forward.

"Aha, my pretty poppet! Loved duck, my downy chick—what wouldst?"

"Fight, grandam,
Smite, grandam,

184

Sweet, blood-begetting blows.
Where Fool goeth
Well Fool knoweth
Lobkyn likewise goes. "

"Why, then, my bantling—loved babe, fight thy fiercest, for these be
wicked men and 't will be an evil fray. And she is sweet and good,
so, Lobkyn, be thy strongest—"

Saith Lobkyn:

"Aye that will I,
Or may I die.
By this good kiss
I vow thee this.

"And here is signal, Fool, shall shew
Each where the other chance to go.

"Croak like a frog,
Bark like a dog,
Grunt like a hog,
I'll know thee.

"Hoot like an owl,
Like grey wolf howl,
Or like bear growl,
'T will shew thee—"

"Then come, trusty Lob, and my thanks to thee! " cried Jocelyn,
catching up his quarter-staff. "But haste ye, for I would be hence ere
the moon get high. Come! "

So Duke Jocelyn strode away with Lobkyn Lollo at his heels; now as
they went, the moon began to rise.

FYTTE 12

Which being the last Fytte of our Geste I hope may please my daughter best.

"O, Wind of Night, soft-creeping,
Sweet charge I give to thee,
Steal where my love lies sleeping
And bear her dreams of me;
And in her dream,
Love, let me seem
All she would have me be.

"Kind sleep! By thee we may attain
To joys long hoped and sought in vain,
By thee we all may find again
Our lost divinity.

"So, Night-wind, softly creeping,
This charge I give to thee,
Go where my love lies sleeping
And bear her dreams of me. "

Hearkening to this singing Yolande shivered, yet not with cold, and casting a cloak about her loveliness came and leaned forth into the warm, still glamour of the night, and saw where stood Jocelyn tall and shapely in the moonlight, but with hateful cock's-comb a-flaunt and ass's ears grotesquely a-dangle; wherefore she sighed and frowned upon him, saying nothing. "Yolande? " he questioned. "O my lady, and wilt frown upon my singing? "

Answered she, leaning dimpled chin upon white fist and frowning yet:

"Nay, not—not thy—singing. "

"Is 't then this cap o' Folly—my ass's ears, Yolande? Then away with them! So shalt jester become very man as thou art very maid! " Forthwith he thrust back his cock's-comb and so stood gazing up at her wide-eyed.

But she, beholding thus his scarred face, shivered again, shrinking a little, whereupon Jocelyn bowed his head, hiding his features in his long, black-curling hair.

"Alas, my lady! " he said, "doth my ill face offend thee? This would I put off also for thy sake an it might be, but since this I may not do, close thou thine eyes a while and hear me speak. For now do I tell thee, Yolande, that I—e'en I that am poor jester—am yet a man loving thee with man's love. I that am one with face thus hatefully scarred do seek thee in thy beauty to my love—"

"Presumptuous Fool, how darest thou speak me thus? " she whispered.

"For that great love dareth greatly, Yolande. "

"And what of thy lord? How of Duke Jocelyn, thy master? "

"He is but man, lady, even as I. Moreover for thee he existeth not since thou hast ne'er beheld him—to thy knowing. "

"Nay, then—what of this? " she questioned, drawing the jewelled picture from her bosom.

"'T is but what it is, lady, a poor thing of paint! "

"But sheweth face of noble beauty, Fool! "

"Aye, nobly painted, Yolande! A thing of daubed colours, seeing naught of thy beauty, speaking thee no word of love, whiles here stand I, a sorry Fool of beauty none, yet therewithal a man to woo thee to my love—"

"Thy love? Ah, wilt so betray thy lord's trust? "

"Blithely, Yolande! For thee I would betray my very self. "

"And thyself art Fool faithless to thy lord, a rhyming jester, a sorry thing for scorn or laughter—and yet—thy shameful habit shames thee not, and thy foolish songs hold naught of idle folly! And thou— thou art the same I saw 'mid gloom of dungeon sing brave song in thy chains! Thou art he that overthrew so many in the lists! O Joconde, my world is upside down by reason of thee. "

"And thou, Yolande, didst stoop to me within my dungeon! And thou didst pray for me, Yolande, and now—now within this sweet night thou dost lean down to me through the glory of thy hair—to me in my very lowliness! And so it is I love thee, Yolande, love thee as none shall ever love thee, for man am I with heart to worship thee, tongue to woo thee, eyes to behold thy beauties, and arms to clasp thee. So am I richer than yon painted duke that needs must woo thee with my lips. And could I but win thee to love—ah, Yolande, could I, despite these foolish trappings, this blemished face, see Love look on me from thine eyes, O—then—"

"How—then—Joconde? "

"Then should Fool, by love exalted, change to man indeed and I—mount up to heaven—thus! " So saying, Jocelyn began to climb by gnarled ivy and carven buttress. And ever as he mounted she watched him through the silken curtain of her hair, wide of eye and with hands tight-clasped.

"Ah, Joconde! " she whispered, "'t is madness—madness! Ah, Joconde! " But swift he came and swung himself upon the balcony beside her and reached out his arms in mute supplication, viewing her wistfully but with scarred face transfigured by smile ineffably tender, and when he spoke his voice was hushed and reverent.

"I am here, Yolande, because methought to read within thy look the wonder of all wonders. But, O my lady, because I am but what I am, fain would I hear thee speak it also. "

"Joconde, " said she in breathless voice, "wouldst shame me—? "

"Shame? " he cried. "Shame? Can there be aught of shame in true love? Or is it that my ass's ears do shame thee, my cock's-comb and garments pied shame the worship of this foolish heart, and I, a Fool, worshipping thee, shame thee by such worship? Then—on, cock's-comb! Ring out, silly bells! Fool's love doth end in folly! Off love—on folly—a Fool can but love and die. "

"Stay, Joconde; ah, how may I tell thee—? Why dost thou start and fumble with thy dagger? "

"Heard you aught, lady? "

"I heard an owl hoot in the shadows yonder, no more. "

"True, lady, but now shall this owl croak like a frog—hearken! Aha—and now shall frog bark like dog—"

"And what meaneth this? "

"That thou, proud lady, must this night choose betwixt knightly rogue and motley Fool—here be two evils with yet a difference—"

"Here is strange, wild talk, Fool! "

"Here shall be wild doings anon, lady, methinks. Hush thee and listen! "

A jangle of bridle-chains, a sound of voices loud and rough, and a tread of heavy feet that, breaking rudely upon the gentle-brooding night, drove the colour from Yolande's soft cheek and hushed her voice to broken whisper:

"Heaven shield us, what now, Joconde? "

"Wolves, lady, wolves that come to raven—see yonder! " Even as he spake they espied armed men who, bold and assured by reason of the solitude, moved in the garden below; and on back and breast of each was the sign of the Bloody Hand.

"My Lord Gui's followers! Alas, Joconde, these mean thee ill—here is death for thee! " Now as she spake, Jocelyn thrilled to the touch of her hand upon his arm, a hand that trembled and stole to clasp his. "Alas, Joconde, they have tracked thee hither to slay thee—"

"And were this so, wouldst fly with me, Yolande? Wouldst trust thy beauties to a Fool's keeping? "

"Nay, nay, this were madness, Joconde; rather will I hide thee—aye, where none shall dare seek thee—come! "

"Yolande, " he questioned, "Yolande, wilt trust thyself to Love and me? " But seeing how she shrank away, his eager arms fell and he bowed his head. "Nay, I am answered, " quoth he, "even while thine eyes look love, thy body abhorreth Fool's embrace—I am answered.

Nay, 't is enough, trouble not for words—ha, methinks it is too late, the wolves be hard upon us—hark ye to their baying! "

And now was sudden uproar, a raving clamour of fierce shouts, and a thundering of blows upon the great door below.

"Yolande—ha, Yolande, yield thee! Open! Open! "

"Ah—mercy of God! Is it me they seek? " she whispered.

"Thee, Yolande! To bear thee to their lord's embraces—"

"Rather will I die! " she cried, and snatched the dagger from his girdle.

"Not so! " quoth he, wresting the weapon from her grasp. "Rather shalt thou live a while—for thou art mine—mine to-night, Yolande—come! " And he clasped her in fierce arms. "Nay, strive not lest I kiss thee to submission, for thou art mine, though it be for one brief hour and death the next! " So, as she struggled for the dagger, he kissed her on mouth and eyes and hair until she lay all unresisting in his embrace; while ever and anon above the thunder of blows the night clamoured with the fierce shout:

"Open—open! Yolande, ha, Yolande! "

"There is death—and worse! " she panted. "Loose me! "

"Stay, " he laughed, "here thou 'rt in thy rightful place at last—upon my heart, Yolande. Now whither shall I bear thee? Where lieth safety? "

"Loose me! " she commanded.

"Never! Hark, there yields the good door at last! "

"Then here will we die! "

"So be it, Yolande! A sweet death thus, heart to heart and lip to lip! "

"O Fool—I hate thee! "

"Howbeit, Yolande—I love thee! "

"Yolande! Ha—Yolande! "

The cry was louder now and so near that she shivered and, hiding her face, spake below her breath:

"The turret-stair—behind the arras of my bed! "

Swiftly, lightly he bore her down the winding stair and by divers passage-ways until, thrusting open a narrow door, he found himself within the garden and, keeping ever amid the darkest shadows, hasted on to the postern hard by the lily-pool.

And now Yolande felt herself swung to lofty saddle, heard Jocelyn's warning shout drowned in a roar of voices and loud-trampling hoofs as the great horse reared, heard a fierce laugh and, looking up, saw the face above her grim and keen-eyed beneath its foolish cock's-comb as his vicious steel flashed to right and left, and ever as he smote he mocked and laughed:

"Ha—well smitten, Lob! Oho, here Folly rides with pointed jest keen and two-edged—make way, knaves—make way for Folly—"

The snorting charger, wheeled by strong hand, broke free, whereon rose an uproar of shouts and cries that sank to a meaningless babble swept backward on the rush of wind. Away, away they sped, through moonlight and shadow, with fast-beating hoofs that rang on paved walk, that thudded on soft grass, that trampled the tender flowers; and Yolande, swaying to the mighty arm that clasped her, saw the fierce, scarred face bent above her with eyes that gleamed under scowling brows and mouth grim-smiling; and shivering, she looked no more.

On they sped with loosened rein, o'er grassy mead, through ferny hollows, o'erleaping chattering rill that babbled to the moon, 'mid swaying reeds and whispering sedge, past crouching bush and stately tree, and so at last they reached the woods. By shadowy brake and thicket, through pools of radiant moonlight, through leafy, whispering glooms they held their way, across broad glade and clearing, on and on until all noise of pursuit was lost and nought was to hear save the sounds of their going.

Thus rode they, and with never a word betwixt them, deep and deeper into the wild until the moon was down and darkness shut them in; wherefore Jocelyn drew rein and sat a while to listen. He heard the good steed, deep-breathing, snuff at dewy grass; a stir and rustle all about him; the drowsy call of a bird afar; the soft ripple of water hard by and, over all, the deep hush of the wild-wood. Then upon this hush stole a whisper:

"O, 'tis very dark! "

He: Dark, Lady? Why so 'tis, and yet 'tis natural, for 'tis night, wherefore 'tis the bright god Phoebus is otherwhere, and Dian, sly-sweet goddess, hath stole her light from heaven, wherefore 'tis 'tis dark, lady.

She: Where are we?

He: The sweet Saints know that, lady—not I!

She (*scornfully*): Verily, thou art no saint—

He: Not yet, lady, not yet—witness these ass's ears.

She: True, thou 'rt very Fool!

He: In very truth, lady, and thou art lost with this same Fool, so art thou in very woeful case. As for me, a lost fool is no matter, wherefore Fool for himself grieveth no whit. But for thee—alas! Thou art a proud lady of high degree, very nice of thy dainty person, soft and delicate of body, so shall the greensward prove for thee uneasy couch, I judge, and thou sleep ill—

She: Sleep? No thought have I of sleep! Ride on, therefore. Why tarry we here?

He: Lady, for three sufficing reasons—our foes pursue not, I'm a-weary, and 'tis very dark—

She: No matter! Ride on, I do command thee.

He: Aye, but whither?

She: I care not so thou leave this place; 'tis an evil place!

He: Why, 'tis good place, very well secluded and with stream hard by that bubbleth. So here will we bide till dawn. Suffer me to aid thee down.

She: Touch me not! Never think I fear thee though I am alone.

He: Alone? Nay, thou 'rt with me, that is—I am with thee and thou art with a Fool. So is Fool care-full Fool since Fool hath care of thee. Suffer me now to aid thee down since here will we wait the day. Come, my arm about thee so, thy hand in mine—

She (*angrily*): O Fool most base—most vile—

He: Nay, hush thee, hush! and listen to yon blithesome, bubblesome, babbling brook how it sigheth 'mid the willows, whispereth under reedy bank and laugheth, rogue-like, in the shallows! Listen how it wooeth thee:

> Though, lady, hard thy couch must be,
> If thou should'st wakeful lie,
> Here, from the dark, I'll sing to thee
> A drowsy lullaby.
> O lady fair—forget thy pride
> Whiles thou within the greenwood bide.

And now suffer me to aid thee down.

She: Why wilt thou stay me in this evil place?

He (*patiently*): The wild is ill travelling in the dark, lady; there be quagmires and perilous ways—wherefore here must we bide till dawn. Suffer me to—

SHE (*breathlessly and shrinking from his touch*): But I fear not quagmires—there be greater perils—more shameful and—and—'tis so dark, so dark! 'Tis hateful place. Ride we till it be day—

He (*mockingly*): Perils, lady? Why certes there be perils—and perils. Perils that creep and crawl, perils that go on four legs and perils two-legged—e'en as I. But I, though two-legged, am but very fool of fools and nothing perilous in blazing day or blackest night. So stint thy fears, lady, for here bide we till dawn!

The Geste of Duke Jocelyn

Herewith he caught her in sudden arms and lifted her to the ground; then, dismounting, he set about watering and cherishing the wearied steed and tethered him beside a dun stream that rippled beneath shadowy willows; and so doing, fell a-singing on this wise:

"'Fair lady, thou 'rt lost! ' quoth he,
Sing derry, derry down.
'And O, 'tis dark—'tis dark! ' quoth she,
'And in the dark dire perils be, '
O, derry, derry down!

"Quoth he: 'Fair lady, stint thy fear, '
Sing derry, derry down.
'I, being Fool, will sit me here,
And, till the kindly sun appear,
Sing derry, derry down.

"'I'll make for thee, like foolish wight,
Hey, derry, derry down,
A song that shall out-last dark night,
And put thy foolish fears to flight
With derry, derry down.

"'For 'tis great shame thou shouldst fear so,
Hey, derry, derry down,
A peril that two-legged doth go,
Since he's but humble Fool, I trow,
With derry, derry down. '"

Thus sang he, a dim figure beside dim stream and, having secured the horse, sat him down thereby and took forth his lute.

But Yolande, though he could not see, clenched white fists and, though he could not hear, stamped slim foot at him.

"Joconde, " quoth she, betwixt clenched teeth, "Joconde, I—scorn thee! "

"Alack! " he sighed. "Alack, and my lute hath taken sore scath of a sword-thrust! "

"Thou'rt hateful—hateful! " she cried. "Aye—hateful as thy hateful song, so do I contemn thee henceforth! "

194

"Say'st thou so, lady, forsooth? " sighed he, busied with his lute. "Now were I other than Fool, here should I judge was hope of winning thy love. But being only Fool I, with aid of woe-begone lute, will sing thee merry song to cheer thee of thy perilous fears—"

"Enough, ill Fool, I'll hear thee not! "

"So be it, dear lady! Then will we sit an list to the song of yon stream, for streams and rivers, like the everlasting hills, are passing wise with length of days—"

"And thou'rt a very Fool! " she cried angrily. "A fond Fool presumptuous in thy folly! "

"As how presumptuous, proud lady? " he questioned humbly.

"In that thou dreamest I—stoop to fear thee! "

"Aye, verily! " sighed he. "Alas, thou poor, solitary, foolish, fearful maid, thou art sick with fear of me! So take now my dagger! Thus Fool offenceless shall lie defenceless at thy mercy and, so lying, sleep until joyous day shall banish thy so virginal fears! " Which saying, he tossed off belt and dagger and setting them beside her, rolled his weather-worn cloak about him, stretched himself beneath the dim willows and straightway fell a-snoring. And after some while she questioned him in voice low and troubled:

"O Joconde, art truly sleeping? "

"Fair lady, " he answered, "let these my so loud snores answer thee. "

Up sprang Yolande and, coming beside him in the gloom, cast back his girdle, speaking quick and passionate:

"Take back thy dagger lest I be tempted to smite it to the cruel, mocking heart of thee! " Then turned she stately back and left him, but, being hid from view, cast herself down full length upon the sward, her pride and stateliness forgotten quite. Now Jocelyn, propped on uneasy elbow, peered amid the gloom for sight of her and hearkened eagerly for sound of her; but finding this vain, arose and, creeping stealthily, presently espied her where she lay, face hidden in the dewy grass. Thus stood he chin in hand disquieted and anxious-eyed and wist not what to do.

"Lady? " he questioned at last; but she stirred not nor spoke. "Yolande! " he murmured, drawing nearer; but still she moved not, though his quick ear caught a sound faint though very pitiful. "Ah, dost thou weep? " he cried. Yolande sobbed again, whereupon down fell he beside her on his knees, "Dear lady, why grievest thou? "

"O Joconde, " she sighed, "I am indeed solitary—and fearful! And thou—thou dost mock me! "

"Forgive me, " he pleaded humbly, "and, since thou'rt solitary, here am I. And, for thy fears, nought is here shall harm thee, here may'st thou sleep secure—"

"Stay, Joconde, the forest is haunted of wolves and—worse, 'tis said! "

"Then will I watch beside thee till the day. And now will I go cut bracken for thy bed. "

"Then will I aid thee. " So she arose forthwith and, amid the fragrant gloom, they laboured together side by side; and oft in the gloom her hand touched his, and oft upon his cheek and brow and lip was the silken touch of her wind-blown hair. Then beneath arching willows they made a bed, high-piled of springy bracken and sweet grasses, whereon she sank nestling, forthwith.

"O, 'tis sweet couch! " she sighed.

"Yet thou'lt be cold mayhap ere dawn, " quoth he, "suffer me to set my cloak about thee. "

"But how of thyself, Joconde? "

"I am a Fool well seasoned of wind and rain, heat and cold, lady, and 'tis night of summer. " So he covered her with his travel-stained cloak and, sitting beneath a tree, fell to his watch. And oft she stirred amid the fern, deep-sighing, and he, broad back against the tree, sighed oftener yet.

"Art there, Joconde? " she questioned softly.

"Here, lady. "

"'Tis very dark, " sighed she, "and yet, methinks, 'tis sweet to lie thus in the greenwood so hushed and still and the stars to watch like eyes of angels. "

"Why, 'tis night of summer, lady, a night soft and languorous and fragrant of sleeping flowers. But how of grim winter, how of rain and wind and lashing tempest—how think you? "

"That summer would come again, Joconde. "

"Truly here is brave thought, lady. "

"Hark, how still is the night, Joconde, and yet full of soft stir, a sighing amid the leaves! 'Tis like the trees whispering one another. O, 'tis sweet night! "

"Soon to pass away, alas! " he sighed, whereupon she, stirring upon her ferny couch, sighed also; thereafter fell they silent awhile hearkening to the leafy stirrings all about them in the dark, and the slumberous murmur of the stream that, ever and anon, brake into faint gurglings like a voice that laughed, soft but roguish.

SHE: I pray thee talk to me.

HE: Whereof, lady?

SHE: Thyself.

HE: I am a Fool—

SHE: And why sit so mumchance?

HE: I think.

SHE: Of what?

HE: Folly.

SHE: And why dost sigh so deep and oft?

HE: I grieve for thee.

SHE: For me! And wherefore?

HE: Being lost with a Fool thou'rt desolate, sad and woeful.

SHE: Am I, Joconde? And how dost know all this?

HE: 'Tis so I do think, lady.

SHE: Then are thy thoughts folly indeed. If thou must sigh, sigh for thyself.

HE: Why so I do, lady, and therewith grieve for myself and thyself, myselfbeing Fool and thyself a dame of high degree, thus, betwixt whiles, I do fear thee also.

SHE: Thou fear! Thou fear me forsooth! And wherefore fear a helpless maid?

HE: There is the reason—she is helpless!

SHE: Ah, there doth Fool speak like chivalrous knight.

HE: Or very fool—a fool that fain would win fair Dian from high heaven. Alas, poor Fool, that, being fool, must needs look and sigh and sigh and look and leave her to the winning of some young Endymion!

SHE (*dreamily*): Endymion was but lowly shepherd, yet was he loved!

HE: Endymion was fair youth comely of feature, lady. Now had he worn ass's ears 'bove visage scarred—how then? On Ida's mount he had been sighing forlorn and lonely yet, methinks. For maids' hearts are ever governed by their eyes—

SHE: Art so wise in maids' hearts, Joconde?

HE: Wise am I in this: No man may ever know the heart of a woman—and woman herself but seldom.

Now here was silence again wherein Yolande, smiling, viewed him a dim shape in the gloom, and he leaned back to watch a star that twinkled through the leafy canopy above.

SHE: Thou art Duke Jocelyn's Fool at court?

198

The Geste of Duke Jocelyn

HE: I am Duke Jocelyn's fool here and there and everywhere, lady.

SHE: Yet have I heard Duke Jocelyn was a mighty man-at-arms and, though youthful, sober-minded, full of cares of state and kept no Fool at court.

HE: Lady, his court is filled o' fools as is the way of other courts and amongst these many fools first cometh the Duke himself—

SHE: How, and darest thou call this mighty Duke a fool?

HE: Often, lady!

SHE: And what like is he?

HE: Very like a man, being endowed of arms, legs, eyes, ears—of each two, no more and no less, as is the vulgar custom.

SHE: But is he not of beauty high and noble, of god-like perfection far beyond poor, common flesh and blood? 'Tis so the painter has limned his face, 'tis so I dream him to my fancy.

HE: Lady, I am but a Fool, let the picture answer thee.

SHE: And he, this mighty Duke of god-like beauty doth woo me to his wife—

HE (*bitterly*): With my tongue.

SHE: Why came he not in his own glorious person?

HE: Lady, though a Duke, he hath his moments of wisdom and argueth thus: "I, though a Duke, am yet a man. Thus, should I as Duke woo her, she may wed the Duke, loving not the man—"

SHE: And so he sent a Fool as his ambassador! And so do I scorn this god-like Duke—

HE: Ha! Scorn him! My lady—O Yolande, what of me?

She: Thou, false to him and faithless to thy trust, didst woo me for thyself which was ill in thee. But thou didst throw the terrible Red Gui into my lily-pool which was brave in thee. Thou didst endure

199

chains and a prison undaunted which was noble in thee. Thou didst this night at peril of thy life save me from shame, but thou didst bear me urgently here into the wild, and in the wild here lie I beside thee, lost, yet warm and sleepy and safe beneath thy cloak—and so—'tis very well—

HE: Safe, Yolande? Hath thy heart told thee this at last? But thou didst fear me—

SHE: Because to-night thou didst clasp me in cruel arms and spake me words of love passionate and fierce and—and—

HE: Kissed thee, Yolande!

SHE: Many times—O cruel! And bore me hither and lost me in these dark solitudes! Here was good cause for any maid to fear thee methinks.

Yet thou didst basely mock my fears with thy hateful song of "Derry down. "

HE: Because thy fears, being unjust, hurt me, for ah, Yolande, my love for thee is deep and true, and True-love is ever gentle and very humble.

SHE: Thus do I fear thee no more, Joconde!

HE: Because I am but lowly—a Fool beneath thy proud disdain?

SHE: Nay, Joconde. Because thou art indeed a very man. So now shall I sleep secure since nought of evil may come nigh me whiles I lie in thy care.

Thus spake she softly 'mid the gloom, and turning upon her rustling couch sighed and presently fell to slumber.

Now, sitting thus beside her as she slept, Jocelyn heard the stream ripple in the shadows like one that laughed soft but very joyously and, as he gazed up at the solitary star with eyes enraptured, this elfin laughter found its echo in his heart.

* * * * *

A bird chirped drowsily from mazy thicket where sullen shadow thinned, little by little, until behind leaf and twig was a glimmer of light that waxed ever brighter. And presently amid this growing brightness was soft stir and twitter, sleepy chirpings changed to notes of wistful sweetness, a plaintive calling that was answered from afar.

Thus the birds awaking sounded pretty warnings summoning each to each for that the day-spring was at hand, while ever the brightness changed to radiance and radiance to an orient glory and up flamed the sun in majesty and it was day. And now, from brake and thicket, from dewy mysteries of green boskage burst forth the sweet, glad chorus of bird-song, full throated, passionate of joy.

And Jocelyn, sitting broad back against a tree, felt his soul uplifted thereby what time his eyes missed nothing of the beauties about him: the rugged boles of mighty trees bedappled with sunny splendour, the glittering dew that gemmed leaf and twig and fronded bracken, and the shapely loveliness of her who slumbered couched beneath his worn cloak, the gentle rise and fall of rounded bosom and the tress of hair that a fugitive sunbeam kissed to ruddy gold. Thus sat Jocelyn regardful, gladness in the heart of him, and a song of gladness bubbling to his lips.

Suddenly he saw her lashes quiver, her rosy lips parted to a smile and, stirring in her slumber, she sighed and stretched shapely arms; so waked she to a glory of sun and, starting to an elbow, gazed round, great-eyed, until espying him, she smiled again.

"Good morrow, Joconde! Ne'er have I slept sweeter. But thou hast out-watched dark night and art a-weary, so shalt sleep awhile—"

"Nay, " he answered, "a plunge in the stream yonder and I shall be blithe for the road—an we find one. And I do fear me thou'rt hungry, Yolande, and I have nought to give thee—"

"And what of thyself, man? Verily, I read hunger in thy look and weariness also, so, an thou may'st not eat, sleep thou shalt awhile here—in my place. "

"Nay, Yolande, indeed—"

"Yea, but thou must indeed whiles I watch over thee. 'Tis a sweet bed—come thy ways. "

"And what wilt thou do? " he questioned.

"Much! " she answered, viewing her rumpled, gown with rueful eyes. "As thou sayest, there is the pool yonder! So come, get thee to bed and—sleep! Come, let me cover thee with thy cloak and gainsay me not; sleep thou must and shalt. "

So Duke Jocelyn stretched himself obediently upon the bed of fern and suffered her to cover him with the cloak; but as she stooped above him thus, he lifted the hem of her dress to reverent lips.

"My lady! " he murmured. "My dear lady! "

"Now close me thine eyes, wearied child! " she commanded. And, like a child, in this also he obeyed her, albeit unwillingly by reason of her radiant beauty, but hearing her beside him, was content, and thus presently fell to happy sleeping.

When he awoke the sun was high and he lay awhile basking in this grateful radiance and joying in the pervading quiet; but little by little, growing uneasy by reason of this stillness, he started up to glance about him and knew sudden dread—for the little glade was empty—Yolande had vanished; moreover the horse was gone also.

Cold with an awful fear he got him to his feet and looked hither and yon, but nowhere found any sign of violence or struggle. But like one distraught he turned to seek her, her name upon his lips, then, checking voice and movement, stood rigid, smitten by hateful doubt. For now it seemed to him that her gentle looks and words had been but sweet deceits to blind him to her purpose and now, so soon as she had lulled him to sleep, she had stolen away, leaving him for the poor, piteous fool he was. And now his despair was 'whelmed in sudden anger, and anger, little by little, changed to grief. She was fled away and he a sorry fool and very desolate.

Full of these bitter thoughts he cast himself upon his face and, lying as in a pit of gloom, knew a great bitterness.

Slowly, slowly, borne upon the gentle wind came a fragrance strange and unexpected, a savour delectable of cooking meat that made him know himself a man vastly hungry despite his grievous woe. But, lying within the black gulf of bitterness, he stirred not until, of a sudden, he heard a voice, rich and full and very sweet, upraised in joyous singing; and these the words:

"Rise, O laggard! See the sun,
To climb in glory hath begun:
The flowers have oped their pretty eyes,
The happy lark doth songful rise,
And merry birds in flowery brake,
Full-throated, joyous clamours make;
And I, indeed, that love it not,
Do sit alone and keel the pot,
Whiles thus I sing thee to entreat,
O sleepy laggard — come and eat! "

"Forsooth and art sleeping yet, Joconde? " the voice questioned. Duke Jocelyn lifted woeful head and saw her standing tall and shapely amid the leaves, fresh and sweet as the morn itself, with laughter within her dream-soft eyes and laughter on her vivid lips and the sun bright in the braided tresses of her hair wherein she had set wild flowers like jewels.

"Yolande! " he murmured, coming to his knees "Yolande — how glorious thou art! "

"Nay, " she laughed, yet flushing to the worship of his eyes, "and my habit woefully torn of wicked bramble-thorns, and my hair ill-braided and all uncombed and —"

"Ah, Yolande, I thought thee fled and I left to loneliness, and my pain was very sore. "

"Then am I avenged thy mockery, Joconde, and thy song of 'Derry down. ' 'Twas for this I stole away! But now, if thou 'rt hungry man, come this ways. " And she reached him her hand. So she brought him to a little dell where burned a fire of sticks beneath a pot whence stole right savoury odour.

"O most wonderful! " quoth he. "Whence came these goodly viands? "

"Where but from the wallet behind thy horse's saddle, Joconde? " Then down sat they forthwith side by side and ate heartily and were very blithe together; and oft-times their looks would meet and they would fall silent awhile. At last, the meal ended, Jocelyn, turning from Yolande's beauty to the beauty of the world around, spake soft-voiced:

"Yolande, were mine a selfish love, here, lost within these green solitudes, would I keep thee for mine own—to serve and worship thee unto my life's end. But, since I count thy happiness above my dearest desires, now will I go saddle the horse and bear thee hence. "

"Whither, Joconde, whither wilt thou bear me? "

"Back to the world, " said he ruefully, "thy world of prideful luxury, to thy kindred. "

"But I have no kindred, alas! " sighed she, stooping to caress a daisy-flower that grew adjacent.

"Why, then, thy friends—"

"My friends be very few, Joconde, and Benedicta hath her husband. "

"Yolande, " said he, leaning nearer, "whither should I bear thee? "

"Nay, " saith she, patting the daisy with gentle finger-tip, "go thou and saddle thy horse, mayhap I shall know this anon. Go thou and saddle the horse. " So Jocelyn arose and having saddled and bridled the horse, back he cometh to find Yolande on her knees beside the stream, and she, hearing his step, bowed her head, hiding her face from him; now on the sward beside her lay the picture shattered beyond repair.

"How, " said Jocelyn, "hast broken the Duke's picture, lady! "

"Thou seest! " she answered.

"And must thou weep therefore? " said he a little bitterly. "Oh, be comforted; 't was but a toy—soon will I get thee another. "

"An thou bring me another, Joconde, that will I break also. "

"Ha—thou didst break it—wilfully, then? "

"With this stone, Joconde. "

"Wherefore, O wherefore? " he questioned eagerly.

"For that it was but painted toy, even as thou sayest! " she answered. "Moreover, I—love not Duke Jocelyn. "

"And't was for this thou didst break the picture? "

"Nay, 'twas because these painted features may never compare with the face of him I love. "

"And whom—whom dost thou love? " quoth he, in voice low and unsteady. Speaking not, she pointed with slender finger down into the placid, stream. Wondering, he bent to look and thus from the stilly water his mirrored image looked back at him; now as he stooped so stooped she, and in this watery mirror their glances met.

"Yolande? " he whispered. "O my lady, shall a Fool's fond dream come true, or am I mad indeed? Thou in thy beauty and I—"

"Thou, Joconde, " said she, fronting him with head proudly uplift, "to my thought thou art man greater, nobler than any proud lord or mighty duke soever. And thou hast loved and wooed as never man wooed, methinks. And thou art so brave and strong and so very gentle and—thus it is—I do love thee. "

"But my—my motley habit, my—"

"Thy cap of Folly, Joconde, these garments pied thou hast dignified by thy very manhood, so are they dearer to me than lordly tire or knightly armour. And thy jingling bells—ah, Joconde, the jingle of thy bells hath waked within my heart that which shall never die— long time my heart hath cried for thee, and I, to my shame, heeded not the cry, wherefore here and now, thus upon my knees, I do most humbly confess my love. "

"Thy love, Yolande—for me? Then dost truly love me? Oh, here is marvel beyond my understanding and belief. "

"Why, Joconde, ah, why? "

"See! " he cried, flinging back his head. "Look now upon this blemished face—here where the cruel sun may shew thee all my ugliness, every scar—behold! How may one so beautiful as thou learn love for one so lowly and with face thus hatefully marred? I have watched thee shrink from me ere now! I mind how, beside the lily-pool within thy garden, thou didst view me with eyes of horror! I do mind thy very words—the first that e'er I heard thee utter:

'What thing art thou that 'neath thy hood doth show A visage that might shame the gladsome day? '

Yolande, Yolande, this poor blemished face is nothing changed since then; such as I was, such I am! "

"Alas, Joconde! " she cried, reaching out her hands in passionate appeal. "My words were base, cruel—and hurt me now more, ah, much more, than e'er they wounded thee. For I do love thee with love as deep, as true as is thine own! Wilt not believe me? "

"Oh, that I might indeed! " he groaned. "But—thou'rt alone, far from thy home and friends, thy wonted pride and state forgotten all—mayhap thou dost pity me or mayhap 'tis thy gratitude in guise of love doth speak me thus? But as thou art still thine own lovely self, so am I that same poor, motley Fool whose hateful face—"

"Joconde, " she cried, "hush thee—Oh, hush thee! Thy words are whips to lash me! " and catching his hand she kissed it and cherished it 'gainst tear-wet cheek. "Ah, Joconde, " she sighed, "so wise and yet so foolish, know'st thou not thy dear, scarred face is the face of him I love, for love hath touched my eyes and I do see thee at last as thou truly art, a man great of soul, tender and strong-hearted. So art thou a man, the only man, my man. Oh, that I might but prove my love for thee, prove it to thee and before all men, no matter how, so I might but banish thy cruel doubts for ever. But now, for thy dear, scarred face—"

Her soft, round arms were about his neck; and drawing him to her lips she kissed him, his scarred brow and cheek, his eyes, his lips grown dumb with wondering joy. Thus, lip to lip and with arms entwined, knelt they beside that slow-moving stream that whispered softly beneath the bank and gurgled roguish laughter in the shallows.

A dog barked faintly in the distance, a frog croaked hoarsely from the neighbouring sedge, but lost in the wonder of their love, they heeded only the beating of their hearts.

"A-billing and a-cooing! A-cooing and a-billing, as I'm a tanner true! " exclaimed a hoarse voice. Up started Jocelyn, fierce-eyed and with hand on dagger-hilt, to behold a man with shock of red hair, a man squat and burly who, leaning on bow-stave, peered at them across the stream.

"And is it Will the Tanner? " quoth Jocelyn, loosing his dagger.

"None else, friend Motley. "

"Why then, God keep thee! And now go about thy business. "

"Marry, Fool, I am about my business, the which is to find thee. By Saint Nick, there's mighty hue and cry for thee up and down within the greenwood, aye—marry is there, as I'm a tanner tried and true. So needs must thou along wi' me. "

"With thee, Tanner? And wherefore? "

"Why, I know not wherefore, Fool, but must along. Here's me and Lob and the potent hag that is Mopsa the Witch, lain a-watching and a-watching ye a-billing—nay, scowl not, friend Fool, on tanner trusty, tried and true. For hark now, here's great stir, clamour and to-do within this forest-country for thee, Fool, the which is strange, seeing thou art but a motley fool. Howbeit there be many great lords and knights from beyond the Southern March a-seeking of thee, Fool. "

"Ha! " quoth Jocelyn, frowning. "Envoys from Brocelaunde! "

"Alas, Joconde, and seeking thee! " saith Yolande in troubled voice.

"Moreover, " continued Will, "here's our Duke Pertinax and his lady Duchess yearning for thee, here's Robin that is Sir Robert a-clamouring for thee and all his goodly foresters, as myself, a-seeking thee. "

"But't is I found thee, Sir Long-legged Fool, I—I! " croaked a voice, and old Mopsa the Witch peered at them from a bush hard by.

The Geste of Duke Jocelyn

"Verily, thou hast found us! " quoth Jocelyn ruefully. "And what now? "

"Oho! " cried the Witch, cracking her finger-bones. "Now go I hot-foot to weave spells and enchantments, aha—oho! Spells that shall prove the false from the true, the gold from the dross. Thou, Sir Fool, art doubting lover, so art thou blind lover! I will resolve thee thy doubts, open thy eyes and show thee great joy or bitter sorrow—oho! Thou, proud lady, hast stooped to love a motley mountebank—nay, flash not thy bright eyes nor toss haughty head at an old woman—but here is solitude with none to mock thy lowly choice or cry thee shame to love a motley Fool, aha! And thou would'st fain prove thy love True-love, says thou? Why, so thou shalt—beyond all doubting now and for ever, aha—oho! Truest of true or falsest of false. Beware. Farewell, and remember:

"Follow Folly and be wise,
In such folly wisdom lies,
Love's blind, they say; but Love hath eyes,
So follow Folly, follow.

Hither-ho, Lob-Lobkyn! Lend thine old granddam thine arm. Come, my pretty bantling, sweet poppet—come and—away! " o spake old Mopsa the Witch, and vanished into the green with Lobkyn, who turned to flourish his club in cheery salutation ere he plunged into the underbrush. Then Jocelyn smiled down on Yolande to find her pale and trembling, so would he have clasped her to his heart, but a hand grasped him and, turning, he beheld the Tanner at his elbow.

"Friend Fool, " quoth he, "needs must I take thee to Robin that Sir Robert is, e'en as he did command, so come now thy ways with trusty tanner tried. "

"Off, Red-head! " saith Jocelyn, frowning a little. "Away now, lest this my dagger bite thee. " Back leapt Will into the stream whence he had come, and there standing, clapped bugle to lip and winded it lustily, whereupon came divers fellows running, bow in hand, who beset Jocelyn on every side.

"Now yield thee to Tanner, friend, " quoth Will, knee-deep in the stream, "for no mind have I to hurt thee. So away with thy dagger like gentle, kindly Fool, and away with thee to Sir Robin. "

Now hereupon, as Jocelyn frowned upon them, Yolande, standing a-tiptoe, kissed his scarred cheek and clasped his dagger-hand in soft fingers.

"Come, " she pleaded, "they be a-many, so yield me thy dagger and let us go with them, beloved! " At the whispered word Jocelyn loosed the dagger and, clasping her instead, kissed her full-lipped. Then turned he to his captors.

"I'm with thee, Will, thou—tanner! " quoth he. "And now bring hither the horse for my lady's going. "

"Nay, " answered Will, scratching red head, "Rob—Sir Robert spake nothing of horse for thee, or lady. "

"Nor will I ride, Joconde, " she murmured happily, "rather will I trudge beside thee, my hand in thine—thus! "

So, hand in hand, they went close-guarded by their captors yet heeding them not at all, having eyes but for each other. And oft her cheek flushed rosy beneath his look, and oft he thrilled to the warm, close pressure of her fingers; and thus tramped they happy in their captivity.

The sun rose high and higher, but since for them their captors were not, neither was fatigue; and, if the way was rough there was Jocelyn's ready hand, while for him swamps and brooks were a joy since he might bear her in his arms. Thus tramped they by shady dingle and sunny glade, through marshy hollows and over laughing rills, until the men began to mutter their discontent, in especial a swart, hairy wight, and Will, glancing up at the sun, spake:

"Two hours, lads, judge I. "

"Nigher three, Tanner, nigher three! " growled the chief mutterer.

"Why so much the better, Rafe, though two was the word. Howbeit we be come far enow, I judge, and 'tis hot I judge, so hey for Robin— and a draught o' perry! "

"Art thou weary, my Yolande? "

"Nay, is not thy dear arm about me! "

"And—thou dost love me indeed? "

"Indeed, Joconde! Mine is a love that ever groweth—"

A horn's shrill challenge; a sound of voices, and below them opened a great, green hollow, shady with trees beneath whose shade were huts of wattle cunningly wrought, a brook that flowed sparkling, and beyond caves hollowed in the steepy bank.

"How now, Tanner Will, " questioned Jocelyn, "hast brought us to the outlaw's refuge? "

"Not so, good friend-Fool, not outlaws, foresters we of Duke Pertinax, and yonder, look 'ee, cometh Rob—Sir Robert to greet ye! " And the Tanner pointed where one came running, a man long of leg, long of arm and very bright of eye, a goodly man clad in hood and jerkin of neat's leather as aforetime, only now his bugle swung from baldrick of gold and silver and in his hood was brooched a long scarlet feather.

"What brother! " cried he joyously. "By saint Nicholas, 'tis sweet to see thee again, thou lovely Fool! " And he clasped Jocelyn in brotherly embrace, which done, he stood off and shook doleful head. "Alas, brother! " quoth he. "Alas! my prisoner art thou this day, wherefor I grieve, and wherefor I know not save that it is by my lady Benedicta's strict command and her I must obey. " And now, turning to Yolande, he bared his head, louting full low. "Lady, " quoth he, "by thy rare and so great beauty I do know thee for Yolande the Fair, so do we of the wild give thee humble greeting. Here may'st thou rest awhile ere we bring thee to Canalise. "

"But, messire, " answered Yolande, clasping Jocelyn's hand, "no mind have I to go to Canalise. "

"Then alack for me, fair lady, for needs must I carry thee there within the hour along of my motley brother. Meanwhile here within yon bower thou shalt find cushions to thy repose, and all things to thy comfort and refreshment. "

"O Sir Robert! O for a comb! " she sighed.

"Expectant it waiteth thee, lady, together with water cool, sweet-perfumed essences, unguents and other nice, lady-like toys.

Moreover, there be mirrors two of Venice and in pretty coffer—" But Yolande had vanished.

Hereupon Robin led the way into a cool, arras-hung cave where was table set out with divers comfortable things both eatable and drinkable.

Quoth Jocelyn, hunger and thirst appeased: "And now good Robin, what do these envoys from Brocelaunde? Why am I thy prisoner and wherefore must I to Canalise? "

"Ha! " saith Robin, cocking merry eye, "and thy name is Joconde, the which is an excellent name, brother, and suiteth thee well, and yet— hum! Howbeit, friend, remember Robin loved thee for the Fool he found thee, that same Fool foolish enow to spare a rogue his life. Dost mind my Song o' Rogues? A good song, methinks, tripping merrily o' the tongue:

> "'I'll sing a song
> Not over long,
> A song o' roguery,
> For I'm a rogue,
> And thou'rt a rogue,
> And so, in faith is he. '

I mind thy fierce, hawk-nosed gossip in rusty jack and ragged cloak, his curses! Troth brother, 'tis a world of change methinks, this same fierce, cursing, hook-nose rogue a noble knight and to-day my lord Duke! I, that was poor outlaw, knight-at-arms and lord warden, and thou—a motley Fool still—and my prisoner. How say'st thou, brother? "

"Why I say, Robin, that my three questions wait thy answers! "

"Verily, brother, and for this reason. I am a knight and noble, and so being have learned me policy, and my policy is, when unable to give answer direct to question direct, to question myself direct thus directing question to questions other or to talk of matters of interest universal, so do I of thyself and myself speak. And talking of myself I have on myself, of myself, of myself made a song, and these the words, hark 'ee:

"Now Rob that was Robin Sir Robert is hight
Though Rob oft did rob when outlaw,
Since outlaw now in law is dubbed a good knight,
Robin's robbing is done, Rob robbeth no more.

Fair words brother, I think, and yet a little sad. 'But, ' says you in
vasty amaze, 'my very noble and right potent Sir Robert, ' says you,
'if thou art indeed noble knight, wherefore go ye devoid of mail,
surcoat, cyclas, crested helm, banderol, lance, shield and the like
pomps and gauds? ' 'Brother, ' says I, 'habit is habit and habit
sticketh habitual, and my habit is to go habited as suiteth my habit,
suiting habit o' body to habit o' mind. ' Thus I, though Sir Robert, am
Robin still, and go in soft leather 'stead of chafing steel, and my
rogues, loving Robin, love Sir Robert the better therefor, as sayeth
my song in fashion apt and pertinent:

"Since habit is habit, my habit hath been
To wear habit habitually comely —

Ha, there soundeth the mustering note, so must we away and I sing
no further, which is well, for 'comely' is an ill word to rhyme with.
Howbeit here must I, beginning my song o' Robin, of beginning
must Rob make an end, for duty calleth Sir Robert, so must Robin
away. "

Hereupon he clapped horn to lip at which shrill summons came
archers and pikemen ranked very orderly about a fair horse-litter.
But Yolande coming radiant from the bower and espying the litter,
shook her head. Quoth she:

"An thou go afoot, Joconde, so will I. "

The sun was low when they came before the walls of Canalise, and
passing beneath grim portcullis and through frowning gateway,
with ring and tramp, crossed the wide market square a-throng with
jostling townsfolk, who laughed and pointed, cheered and hooted,
staring amain at Jocelyn in his threadbare motley; but Yolande,
fronting all eyes with proud head aloft, drew nearer and held his
hand in firmer clasp.

Thus they came at last to the great courtyard before the palace,
bright with the glitter of steel, where men-at-arms stood mustered.
Here Robin halted his company, whereon rose the silvery note of a

clarion, and forth paced the dignified Chief Herald, who spake him full-toned and sonorous:

"In the name of our potent Duke Pertinax and his gracious lady Benedicta, I greet thee well, Sir Robert-a-Forest. Now whom bring ye here? Pronounce! "

"Dan Merriment, Sir Gravity, " answered Robin, "a Fool valiant and wise, a maker of songs, of quips and quiddities many and jocund, Joconde hight. Sir Wisdom, Folly behold, himself here *in propriâ personâ.* "

The Chief Herald gestured haughtily with his wand whereupon forth stepped a file of soldiers and surrounded Jocelyn.

"Ah, Joconde! What meaneth this? " said Yolande, in troubled voice.

"Indeed, my lady, I know not! " he answered. "But let not thy brave heart fail thee. "

"Ah, Joconde, I fear for thee—whither would they lead thee? Nay, sweet heaven, they shall not take thee from me! "

"Fear not, beloved, though they part us awhile. "

"Away with the Motley! " thundered the Chief Herald, flourishing his wand.

"Yolande—O my beloved, fear not—" But even as he spake, the pikemen closed in, and Jocelyn was hustled away; so stood she trembling, hands clasped and eyes wide and fearful, until tall motley figure and flaunting cock's-comb were lost to her sight and the jingle of his bells had died away; then, finding herself alone and all men's eyes upon her, she lifted bowed head and stood white-cheeked and proudly patient, waiting for what might betide.

And presently was distant stir that, growing nearer, swelled to the ring and clash of armour and the trampling of many hoofs; and presently through the great gateway rode many knights sumptuously caparisoned, their shields brave with gilded 'scutcheons, pennon and bannerole a-flutter above nodding plumes, and over all the Red Raven banner of Brocelaunde. So rode they two-and-two until the great courtyard blazed with flashing steel and broidered surcoats. And now a trumpet blared, and forth before this glorious array a pursuivant rode and halted to behold Pertinax, who stepped forth of the great banqueting-hall leading his fair Duchess by the hand, and behind them courtiers and ladies attendant.

Once again the trumpets rang, and lifting his hand, the pursuivant spake:

"My Lord Duke Pertinax, most gracious Duchess, Jocelyn the high and mighty Lord Duke of Brocelaunde greeteth you in all love and amity, and hither rideth to claim a fair lady to wife. Behold our Lord Duke Jocelyn! "

Loud and long the trumpets blew as into the courtyard rode a single horseman; tall was he and bedight in plain black armour and white surcoat whereon the Red Raven glowed; but his face was hid in vizored helm. So rode he through his glorious array of knights, checking his fiery steed to gentle gait with practised hand, while thus spake the pursuivant:

"Behold here Jocelyn, Duke of Brocelaunde, to claim this day in marriage the Lady Yolande according to her word. "

"Stay, my lords! " cried a sweet, clear voice, and forth before them all stood Yolande herself, pale-cheeked but stately of bearing and very bright of eye.

"Be it known to all here that I, Yolande, have given neither pledge nor troth unto Duke Jocelyn—"

Now here was silence sudden and profound that none dared break saving only the haughty Chief Herald.

"How lady, how, " quoth he, "no pledge, no troth, quotha—"

"Neither one nor other, messire, nor shall there ever be—"

"Here is madness, lady, madness—"

"Here is truth, messire, truth; I may not pledge my troth with Duke Jocelyn since I have this day pledged myself unto Duke Jocelyn's jester—"

"Jester, lady, jester? Venus aid us—Cupid shield us! A jester, a Fool, a motley mountebank, a—"

"Aye! " cried Yolande. "All this is he, my lords. Very humble and lowly—yet do I love him! Oh, 'tis joy—'tis joy to thus confess my love—his cap and bells and motley livery are fairer to me than velvet mantle or knightly armour; he is but humble jester, a Fool for men's scorn or laughter, yet is he a man, so do I love him and so am I his— unto the end. My lords, I have no more to say save this—give me my jester—this man I love—and suffer us to go forth hand in hand together, even as we came. "

The Duchess Benedicta uttered a soft, glad cry, and seizing her husband's arm, shook it for very joy. But now, as Yolande fronted them all, pale and proudly defiant, was the ring of a mailed foot, and turning, she shrank trembling to see Duke Jocelyn hasting toward her, his black armour glinting, his embroidered surcoat fluttering, his long arms outstretched to her; thus quick-striding he came but, even as she put out shaking hands to stay him, he fell upon his knee before her.

"Most brave and noble lady—beloved Yolande, " he cried, and lifted his vizor. Now beholding the scarred face of him, the tender, smiling lips, the adoration in his grey eyes, she trembled amain and, swaying to him, rested her hands on his mailed shoulders.

"Joconde, " she whispered, "ah, Joconde—what dream is this? "

"Nay, beloved, the dream is ended and findeth me here at thy feet. The dream is past and we do wake at last, for thy motley Fool, thy Duke and lover am I, yet lover most of all. And thou who in thy divine mercy stooped to love the Fool, by that same love shalt thou lift Duke Jocelyn up to thee and heaven at last. And Oh, methinks the memory of thy so great and noble love shall be a memory fragrant everlastingly. "

So speaking, Duke Jocelyn rose, and with her hand fast in his, looked from her loveliness round about him, blithe of eye.

"My lords, " cried he, "behold my well-beloved, brave-hearted lady. Nobles of Brocelaunde, salute your Duchess Yolande. "

Hereupon was shout on shout of joyous acclaim, lost all at once in the sweet, glad clamour of bells pealing near and far; so, hand in hand, while the air thrilled with this merry riot, they crossed the wide courtyard, and she flushed 'neath the worship of his look and he thrilled to the close, warm pressure of her fingers—thus walked they betwixt the ranks of men-at-arms and glittering chivalry, yet saw them not.

But now Yolande was aware of Benedicta's arms about her and Benedicta's voice in her ear.

"Dear my Yolande, so True-love hath found thee at last since thou wert brave indeed and worthy. Come now and let me deck thee to thy bridal. "

"Lord Duke, " quoth Pertinax, "here methinks was notable, worthy wooing. "

"Aha! " quoth Mopsa the Witch, crackling her knuckle-bones. "Here, my children, is wooing that some fool shall strive to tell tale of some day, mayhap; but such love is beyond words and not to be told. Thus by cunning contrivement hath Mopsa the old Witch proved the true from the false, the gold from the dross; thou, my lady, hast proved thy love indeed, and thou, Lord Duke, may nevermore doubt such love. And now away and wed each other to love's fulfilment—hark where the bells do summon ye. "

And thus, as evening fell, they were wed within the great Minster of Canalise, and thereafter came they to the banqueting-hall with retinue of knights and nobles. Last of all strode Robin with his foresters, and as they marched he sang a song he had learned of Jocelyn, and these the words:

"What is love? 'Tis this, I say,
Flower that springeth in a day,
Ne'er to die or fade away,
Since True-love dieth never.

"Though youth alas! too soon shall wane,
Though friend prove false and effort vain,
True-love all changeless shall remain
The same to-day and ever. "

THE END

Printed in the United Kingdom
by Lightning Source UK Ltd.
120528UK00002B/1